Neon Blue:

= Girl, Unlocked =

20th Anniversary Edition

A Novel of Suspense
by

John Argo

First Published Online 1996
Bestseller on the early Internet

Clocktower Books
San Diego

First Published Online in 1996

This claim, made in good faith to the best of our knowledge at Clocktower Books, means these criteria:

1. Proprietary (Not Public Domain; rules out Gutenberg etc);
2. Complete—not sample chapters or teasers;
3. Published in HTML for reading online, not portable formats (e.g., CD-ROM, floppies, etc); on the website Neon Blue Fiction (http://www.neonbluefiction.com/);
4. Simultaneously available online at Neon Blue Fiction in TXT format for download if readers could not wait to read the end because:
5. We published this and our other pioneering novels 1996-1997 using an innovative format of weekly serial chapters never before done in this online setting;
6. Our novels Neon Blue (Suspense), Heartbreaker (SF, retitled This Shoal of Space in 1998), Pioneers (SF), and CON2: The Generals of October (political thriller) were standard format (not hypertext or short forms).

First True Online E-Book In History

More info at the back of this volume.

Neon Blue:
= Girl, Unlocked =

by John Argo

1 · Manhattan

Laurel "Blue" Humboldt finished cleaning her 9 mm automatic, pulling one last cleaning pad through the barrel. She laid the heavy black gun aside, and sighed as she thought about the mess in her so-called love life. A mug of decaf lemon tea steamed by her bed, and she rubbed it absently sorting through jagged impressions of recent dates. Did one ever meet another nice person? Blue kept her emotional life on an even keel by locking her feelings into separate boxes in a dark room at the back of her thoughts, each with an impregnable padlock on it—and no key. That gets me through the day, she told herself absently at rare moments when she even let the thought bubble up through dim, vague, smoky, sometimes scary feelings and desires.

She was 23. A ledge of dark hair floated over her forehead, and her pale skin had a creamy luster in the drowsy half-light of late afternoon. She had a square, fresh face. Alert, dark eyes and skeptical eyebrows under rich dark hair. A pale nose whose narrow verticality had a straight, porcelain look. Thin lips in a wide gentle mouth; a firm jaw and even white teeth. She lay on her single bed lined with stuffed animals and wriggled her toes, clad in pink wool knee-socks. Her jeans skirt fit the tooled curves of her well-exercised body. Her short fingernails had chipped red nail polish.

Wind shoved oppressive gusts of icy rain against her window. It was late afternoon in Manhattan. It had been her day off, but now she had to go in. DEA had a major informant about to drop dimes right and left, and she was to escort him to prison, take a deposition, and waste half the night sitting around.

She stepped into the shower, leaving her tea mug on the tile window sill. Hot water caressed her, pummeled her, warmed her bones. Her nipples hardened with pleasure. She soaped herself. With closed eyes, she turned and let the water gurgle against her face while she cupped her breasts. After the shower, she toweled briskly, put on bikini underwear from a scented drawer, waterproof boots, faded dungarees, a T-shirt with a black kung fu dragon on the front, a bulky white sweater, and her knee-length ski parka. Scarf. Hat. No gloves. 9 mm in shoulder holster. A dab of *Opium* behind each ear. Mascara, faint eye shadow. Ready to do battle.

A viscous mass of Arctic cold hogged the air currents from Canada. Manhattan temperatures dove as darkness set in early. Smoky clouds bumped among high buildings whose computer-card lights winked out one by one. Blue ascended from the subway tunnel. There was a sweet crackle of mystery about the wet brick walls, the smells of steaks and beer and smoke from restaurants, the bluish light of street lamps, the exhaust fumes of taxis, pedestrians with hurried secrets.

Blue pushed through the lobby door of Mercy Midtown Hospital and looked for her colleague Vito in the Emergency Room. She found Antonio Guzman before she found Vito. According to the armed guard keeping a watchful eye, Guzman was in no shape to run away, and Vito had gone outside for a smoke. Guzman, key government witness, had been beaten up at the court house and taken to Mercy. Blue found him puffy-eyed in one of the treatment rooms, with bloodstains on his prison overalls and a shiner to beat the band. His ankles were chained. His hands had been freed and he gingerly, grimacing, leaned on his gurney to sip water through a straw.

A green prison van pulled with noisy brakes and gasoline fumes to the loading dock. The driver was a tall Latino, 25, with sunglasses he made a show of removing. He carried a .357 Magnum Police Special on a wide belt with cuffs and extra rounds. He wore a BOP windbreaker, green trousers, and heavy black boots that offset the slimness of his legs. She introduced herself and asked, "Are you here to pick up Guzman?"

He fiddled with his sunglasses and showed his orders. "George Olvera. I sure am." A ladies' man, she thought, pleased at his visible interest, but noting the wedding band. Why was it always married men or jerks, or both, making passes at her? He said, "It's just a fifteen minute drive."

Ambulances came and went with wailing sirens. The hospital loomed around them, a concrete world. She spotted Vito on the loading ramp and waved. Vito saw George Olvera and looked jealous. Vito used Blue's coat belt to pull her against the icicled wall sheltered from the stabbing wind. He produced a pack of Camels. They lit one and took turns puffing, flapping their arms and stomping up and down to keep warm. Vito, as always, was dressed impeccably and expensively. Under a dark belted loden overcoat he wore a gray suit and pointy black shoes. He wore a gold watch with diamond chip numerals and a gold bracelet on the other wrist. Vito had sharp black eyes, a large nose, and small rosy lips. "What's the matter? You look sad."

She looked at him sharply. Could he know about Maggie?

Vito poked the icy air with his scarred little chin. "Got a bum in your life?" Vito's eyes looked greedy.

"Yes and no." There was nobody in her life, but anything to keep Vito at bay. Blue had a habit of keeping her sanity by dividing her mind into boxes and keeping things separate. Her love life had been a sealed box for quite a while, and now Vito was fumbling with the lock.

"Blue," he said.

"Vito," she mimicked. "What's with this guy's shoes?"

He chewed and inhaled and talked, eyes darting around. "Guzman and some dude got into it back at the court house this morning, something about his shoes then it was the other guy's mother and so on. He got the shit beat out of him, the fool." They hopped, smoking. "This guy's worth a lot. Watch him."

"You get to go home. Lucky Vito."

He jangled a set of keys. "You got yourself this Number One shitbox federal vehicle to drive." He handed her the keys. "Compliments, Chief Tomasi. Take a good deposition." She accepted two grimy keys on a large paper clip. Vito started to turn away, then changed his mind. He flicked the butt away and stomped desperately. "Blue."

"What?"

"Does he beat you?"

"Who?"

"The animal. The guy. The love of your life."

She grinned. "Thanks. Actually, I beat him."

"I can help you," Vito said.

"Oh?"

"Buy you dinner for a start, you know? Treat you right."

"Dinner. Oh. And then what."

"Blue."

"Vito, you've got a wife and three kids, or is it four?"

"Four," he said glumly. "That's marriage. This is love."

"Vito, go blow it out your ear."

"You're the girl next door."

"Vito, I love you too. Get snaked, will you?'

Vito turned and made long annoyed pointy strides away.

Antonio Guzman, face pitted by childhood acne, smoked a cigarette as the E.R. attendant rolled him out in a wheel chair. Guzman insisted on entering the prison van under his own power, despite the leg chains.

George Olvera parked his sunglasses on his forehead, though the gray scudding clouds were turning black and it was getting darker. The government car was like a stale refrigerator. She got it stoked and they drove through the city. She nearly lost George and had to speed through an amber light. Several other cars made the same leap, just as the light turned red, including a dented brown Trans-Am with a loose license plate.

George drove along Central Park. By now two cars were between them and Blue cursed loudly. No opportunity to pass. Out of habit, she scanned for city patrol units. None in sight. The van slowly pulled into a tree-lined parking strip.

"Gawd," Blue said and maneuvered her derby box after him. Ice and snow crunched under the tires. The suspension creaked. A small, dirty white car crawled before her, driven by a girl looking for a parking space. A hundred yards ahead, the prison van pulled to a stop. George stepped over crumbling ice. The girl hadn't found a parking space, so she simply stopped.

Way back the Trans-Am pulled over. Blue heard a noise. Had its door opened and closed?

"Come on, girl!" Why did people stop before parking?

George lifted the hood of the prison van and waved.

A jogger ran past, big blond man with a scar on one cheek.

With glacial slowness, the girl in the white car probed forward. Blue pulled up alongside the van. No George in sight. The windows were dark. "Hey Olvera!" Blue walked around to the front of the van expecting to find him bent over the engine.

George lay on the snow, eyes wide open. There was a bullet hole in his face and blood issued from his lips. His shattered sunglasses lay several yards away. "No," Blue whispered. Scrabbling around the van, fumbling for her gun, she found the side window shattered, Guzman slumped on the seat, still in chains. He had been shot several times; had to be a silencer. Blood and brains were splattered on the window. Like George, his face had a vapid, surprised expression.

Hearing a car door, she whirled. The brown Trans-Am. She was just in time to see the jogger jump in. He glanced at Blue, and she got chills up and down her spine. His cold gray eyes bored into her, memorized her face. The car spewed burnt rubber smoke and skidded away.

"Stop!" Blue yelled, running after them. Her boots felt soggy and fell behind stuck in the snow. Her wet socks stayed in the boots. She ran barefoot, slipping, ignoring the pain in her feet. "Stop!" She was within fifty feet of them. She knelt and aimed. Carefully, she squeezed off a round at the right rear tire. Her balance on the ice slipped. The shot missed and punctured the license plate. The Trans-Am rammed the white car out of its way and tore away catching the lights just right so that they escaped up Fifth Avenue.

Blue rose. The 9 mm pistol dangled from her joined hands between her knees as she stood bent over, gasping for breath. Her feet hurt like hell. Poor George Olvera. "She has a gun," someone said. People were still scattering in all directions.

Wiping her nose with her sleeve, giving a massive sniff, she waved her badge. "Police!" she yelled hoarsely. As she retrieved her shoes, easing her cold feet into them, she kept seeing the jogger's deadly heavy eyes gazing at her from the rear window, memorizing her face.

2 . San Diego

John Connor, 30, had retired four years ago with two million dollars in the bank, well-deserved after his hectic years in New York City. He did not need to work, but a limited partnership at exclusive Ajanian's filled his need to be with people.

Ajanian's In The Mall: A subdued elegance under bluish light, a potpourri of glittering jewels among mirrors, oriental rugs, paintings, watches, statuary, everything highly priced.

John was tall and slim, a shade over six feet. He looked damn good in his dark business suit. He had a small sculpted nose, witty mouth, strong jaw and dimpled chin. He had dark thoughtful eyes, well-shaped, and strong arched eyebrows under a broad intelligent forehead. Wherever he went, women's eyes followed him. He was divorced, and had a number of girl friends, but nobody special in his life.

One February evening, in walked long-legged Jana Andrews. John was standing behind the watch counter when he saw her. He loved the watches. Especially the diving watches. There were Seikos and Bulovas and Rolexes and every brand imaginable. Every watch emitted its glitter and precise perfection. Ajanian did not fool around. No baubles, no trinkets here. He traveled to New York, to Amsterdam, to Rome, to London, to you name it, and he left the loud stuff behind. What came to San Diego on his signature were the silently demanding objects.

Jana Andrews (or whoever) was one of those rare women who leave a propeller wash of stares. She brought a whiff of crisp air, a glitter of night skyline under her long and genuine lashes. Her eyes were a striking color, like a dark blue Porsche freshly waxed. Ouch. Smoldering.

John approached the tall woman, who was eyeing a tasteful s colored luggage. "May I help you?" This was not normal Ajanian etiquette. Ajanian said: Let the customer talk to you first, always. It's a matter of seduction.

S he looked up with an amused look. You've taken your time, her look said. Those skyline eyes, couched in exclusive cheekbones like alabaster, gave him their slitty wounded look. She had wide, expressive lips that would have looked vulgar on a shorter woman. Her skin looked fine and pampered, but this body had to be worked hard somewhere with weights. Her lips slyly wrinkled like a moving caterpillar when she spoke, and her voice had that nasal huskiness that tall stretchy women have. She pointed into the glass case beside the luggage. "The yellow diamond on that man's gold ring is nice. How much is it?"

John stepped around and, with the key on his wrist on a spiral band, opened the back of the case. He placed the ring on the counter on a black velvet pillow. "Two thousand dollars. The stone has exceptional qualities."

She lifted it, touched it with a red lacquered fingernail. "The little diamonds on either side, are they real?"

"Everything here is real," John replied.

"Including you," she countered dryly. There was intelligence about her, but also a hardness. Her gorgeous hair dangled as she opened her purse. "I'll take the ring."

"Would you like these gift-wrapped?" he asked, glancing at her credit card, "Miss, er, Andrews?" She pursed her lips to one side, looked indecisive for an instant, then said "All right."

He engraved Ajanian inside the band and placed the ring on its cushion in its plastic box. He wrapped the box, first in tissue paper, then in foil-backed paper with Ajanian's watermark. A red bow with a dangling miniature card in embossed eggshell stock finished the job. She took the packet. "I keep thinking I've seen you somewhere before."

He thought hard, could not place her. There had been many such women in his life.

She squinched one eye. "Hmm. Long ago, I think New York."

"Really." He felt conflicting emotions, old residuals both exciting and frightening. "I worked in New York a few years."

"Let me guess." There it was again, that edge. "Modeling."

He felt exposed. "Yes. For a number of years. And you?"

She nodded like an old comrade. "Yep. For several years. Dolly Agency, Feltman, Shine, & Shine, you name it."

"Small world. I did TV commercials for Ford, Shulton, IBM, Rolex..."

"Rolex. That was it. You married whatserface."

John was taken back. "Amy."

A reflective nod. "You were a haul, we figured." He felt embarrassed. Her grin flashed like sword steel. "One time, I was draped over your shoulder while you showed off your Oyster."

"I'm sure I noticed at the time."

She softened a bit. "And Amy?"

"History."

"I'm sorry."

"I am too. But it's history. Years."

"You seemed like a nice guy. You still do. I remember that about you."

He was embarrassed that his own memory was so short.

"Well," she said, "I'll be toddling along."

"We should get together and compare old ads," he said.

"No thanks. I'm out of it." She touched his cheek. He felt the faint scraping edge of her red fingernails. Her touch lingered with a hint of, what, nostalgia? wistfulness? She walked rapidly out of the store and did not stop to look at anything more.

3 . Manhattan

Laurel "Blue" Humboldt opened her eyes and uttered a strangled cry.

"Hey," Vito said.

Half off the cot, tangled in old army blankets that smelled of mothballs, her hair matted into strings and her clothes smelling of somebody's old cigar smoke, she gasped for breath and gripped Vito Caparelli's lapels with both fists.

He disengaged himself gently. "I brought you some coffee. Want a cigarette?" He smelled of Lilac Vegetal and stale Camel smoke. Every inch of him was starched, pressed, and manicured. He pried her grubby fingers from his gray suit.

"Jesus. What is this and where am I?" She sat up dry-mouthed and remembered yesterday. "I was dreaming it was just a nightmare. Did you ever do that, dream about something awful that really happened?" She licked her lips, massaged her hair with her finger tips. The memory of dead faces and oozing wounds made her skin crawl. Poor George Olvera.

Her DEA unit shared a precinct house with NYPD. A harsh bar of sunlight stabbed through a high window and gleamed coldly. The white prison tiles in the unused lockup were dirty. She held the styro cup in both hands and slurped. It warmed her, but tasted awful. "What is this, crankcase oil?"

Vito's nose was huge and his mouth tinier than ever. His eyes were like shiny buttons. "From the coffee machine. Best I could do. Sorry, Blue."

She leaned back against the wall. Blankets wrapped around, and the hot cup in her hands warmed her somewhat. The tile room echoed with music and typing and yelling and crying from the precinct office downstairs. She remembered the dreadful night of debriefing and was glad it was over. "Thanks, Vito."

"Think nothing of it. Say, about that lunch."

"Vito, you're a womanizer. I told you. No. En, Oh."

"You're a tough cookie, Blue."

"No. This job really sucks sometimes. Don't you think?"

He nodded and she saw in his eyes that he was thinking of a thousand times that he had thought it sucked. She rested her head against his dry-cleaned arm. "Nothing personal, Vito. I like you well enough. I know how you guys are. I'm not having lunch with you. You have that macho leer. Why don't you just grow up and go back to being a family man?"

Vito rose. He took a deep drag on his Camel. "Honey, you just don't understand. You're the virginal huntress. Catholic school, right?" Smoke billowed around his nose.

She gripped her coffee cup with both hands and blew on it. "I went to Catholic school. So what."

"You remember, don't you? Artemis. From the Greek. I've got a wife, sixty pounds overweight, who couldn't tell Artemis from artichokes. You turn me on."

"Vito, no."

"Okay, okay," he said backing away, "I'm looking at a grubby urchin with hair that sticks straight out. I'm in love and I can't have you. What am I to do?"

She laughed.

He laughed. Their laughter echoed among the tiles. Trying to cheer her up, bless him. She shook her head. "Vito, I saw those two guys wasted." She started to cry.

Vito nodded. "I heard."

She wiped her sleeve across her nose. "It was pretty bad."

"Okay?" He inclined a listening ear.

She rolled her cup between her hands. "I want to do something."

He nodded. "The Chief wants to see you." He meant Chief Special Agent Tomasi, their boss. He rose, adjusting his tie, cigarette dangling. "Go for it. If I can help, glad to."

After Vito left, Blue washed her face at the cracked corner basin. She finished the coffee and had a Chesterfield. There was a box of last night's stale donuts on the chair by the cot and she ate one just out of perversity. Then she went to Tomasi's office.

"Sit down, Special Agent Humboldt." Tomasi was a slight man in his late forties who looked young except for the baldness atop his head, ringed with short pepper hair. He looked even smaller because of the high ceiling. In his office was a jumble of mismatched office furniture. Tomasi's suit coat hung neatly on a hanger. His white shirt was rolled up to the elbows. A gold pen and pencil pair showed in his gray vest pocket.

Blue plopped tiredly in a wood armchair opposite his desk and waited. As always, she felt slightly on edge near her supervisor. The male mystique, or was it mistake, she supposed. She wondered if he knew. A heater blew dryly into her face.

He put her folder down. "Your record is excellent."

"Thank you, Sir," she said squirming.

"This thing yesterday, Humboldt..." he sighed and rubbed the back of his neck.

"Hm, a real mess, sir."

He folded his hands over the file and leaned forward. "Yes. BOP is in a real jam with the Mayor's office and the DA. They're looking at us too, but I don't think DEA will have much of a flap." He rubbed his temples, looking tired. "We're up against professionals. NYPD towed the car to impound and found there was a bomb attached underneath, but apparently it didn't go off. They had a hell of a time disarming it. But our Friends also had a remote cut-off on the fuel line, and that's what they fell back on when the bomb didn't work. They cut the fuel and when the van rolled to a stop they wasted Guzman. Pretty determined bunch."

"I'll say."

"It was a real bad break for us. Guzman could have helped us immensely."

"Yes, Sir."

He held up a composite sketch of the jogger, done by a police artist during debriefing. "This a fair picture?"

"Yes." She felt a shudder of remembrance.

"Think he'd recognize you?"

"Probably."

"How strongly do you feel about getting after these people? I mean, would you be willing to lay it on the line to bust them?"

"Yes."

"We're talking dangerous. We'd have backup available, but not in town. You'd be in the open. A liaison with the locals. See if you can warm up the trail again for us."

"When do I start?"

He stared. "You'd be dangling bait."

"I was the last decent person George Olvera ever spoke to."

He sat back with his feet on a desk drawer; on a newspaper, of course. For the first time, she noticed just how many framed certificates hung on his office walls. Combat citations from the Army and the Republic of Vietnam, awards from the Chicago Police Department, and a master's degree in something, she could not make out the Gothic from her angle of vision. "Go on home, Humboldt. Take some time off. I need to think about this. I'll call you in a day or two."

"A day or two?"

"I'm giving you some administrative time. You can see the shrink if you want to, about this shooting."

She took the subway home, dozing half the way. At 91st Street she got out, bought bagels and milk. She staggered up the creaking wooden stairs to her third-floor apartment. Too long to wait for the single cranky elevator servicing twenty floors. As she approached the door, she heard classical music. She kept her stereo playing when she was out; maybe it fooled at least your dumber burglar into thinking someone was home. In her apartment, she undressed. Sunlight made dusty filtering swirls behind her lace curtains. The apartment was warm and cozy after the cold outside. She threw herself face down on the bed and fell asleep.

A pounding at the door woke her. Muzzy, she jerked up. A trail of saliva trailed from her open mouth to her wrist. More pounding. She was on her feet, naked except for panties and bra. Wrapped herself in the bed coverlet. Picked up her automatic and released the safety. Peered through the eyelet in the door and lowered the pistol. She leaned exhaustedly against the wall and opened the door. The chain bolt allowed it to open about six inches. "Laurel," the woman in the hall said sadly. A pretty hand with chewed fingernails clamped onto the door. "Please, let me in. Let's talk about us."

"Maggie," Blue said. "No. It's over. Go away."

4 . Los Angeles

Hugh Stone stood on the hill one morning while it was still dark, and surveyed what he and Marga had spent their lives building. Stone Electronics sprawled in starlight: dark buildings, winking red air traffic warning lights, empty parking lots with white herringbone lines. A month from bankruptcy.

Money and power were Hugh Stone's aphrodisiacs. Now, for the first time in his adult life, those two intoxicants were being torn from him, and the result was a revelation even to him. He did not feel old or beaten. Angry, yes. He felt alert, combative, and strangely young again. Contracts had stopped coming in, and he needed—quickly—about six million dollars or that parking lot would soon remain empty. He was leveraged to the hilt, and could obtain no new credit. He had not felt—no, the word was tasted—this kind of delicious danger since his youth. He remembered what it had been like: desperate, on the run across Europe from police agencies of a half-dozen countries, in love with his blonde baby goddess Margaret; wanted for everything from drug dealing to murder.

A silver moon drifted in the bluish morning sky like a ship without sails. He smelled juice in stems of grass. His senses were sharpened as they had not been in decades. He thought of his wife: Darling, we did it your way for thirty years, and it was good. Now you are nearly gone, and

Hugo must do it his way. The old lion has not finished with this lovely jungle.

His footsteps rang hollow in the empty factory building. Hugh walked with a sure, steady rhythm. Sunlight stabbed laser-like from high window panes. Motes of dust whirled in these dreamy pillars of light. Shipping crates stood abandoned in hazy stacks. Here and there, a tow motor sat idle, its fork half-raised and abandoned.

Hugh opened a room filled with printed circuits, wire reels, manuals for obsolete equipment. From a sagging cardboard box filled with old personal papers, and clothes he hadn't worn in twenty years, he pulled a black velveteen case with cheap brass corners. Dusting it off, he rose and contemplated it. A shaving kit from long ago, a gift from Pierre LeSable, dotted with primordial bleach stains. He remembered young, lovely Marga reclining on the bed watching him proudly shave forty years ago in Marseilles. Now what was there? A cheap looking case; inside, a cracked, dirty cake of soap that had lost all its fragrance; a shaving brush whose bristles fell out as he touched them; a rusty scissor; and a straight razor. The razor's mother of pearl handle looked dull now. He took the razor out and opened it with an unpracticed hand. Its blade had a ruddy sheen, little red speckles of rust, not from the stainless steel blade but from inside the handle. Hugh tried the blade on a piece of paper. It still cut, silently and stealthily. Nothing that polishing and oiling would not cure.

The mirror embedded in the lid was splotched with water marks from long ago. Mediterranean water. He wiped the mirror, and as he did so, light hit it and it shone. As he looked into the mirror, it was like looking into the past. The light transfigured his face.

Hugo, age 22, feels the Mediterranean sunshine on his shoulders as he sits on the window sill bare-chested and facing the simple one-room apartment with its sagging grayish walls and battered dark-brown furniture (bed, vanity with wash basin, table, chairs, propane stove). He can smell the sour docks, with their fish and rats. The smell of burnt gasoline quickens his blood, for he loves the sound of fast cars on the winding coastal highway. Margarethe, blonde, 17, lies on the bed paring her fingernails with an Emory board. There is, as always, a glass of wine by her side. She drinks more than would please him. "Where are you going, Hugo?" Her pale soft legs are crossed at the ankles. They are not the muscular legs of a woman, but the dimpled knees and plump thighs of a girl. Her skin is so fine that veins and capillaries give off a healthy interior glow. Round soft face, but strong: Direct, big eyes with summer under their lids, full mouth, firm chin. "You always have that look when you are up to no good. You and that *Schwein* LeSable." She is smart for her age.

He cannot bring himself to be angry with her. "Darling, we have six francs, fifty five *sous*."

"Six francs, seventy," she snaps swatting at her nails with the Emory board. No malice, just firmness. "I counted."

"All right so what. Five francs, six francs, what does it matter. We need to eat. I will provide for you. For the baby."

She thinks for a moment, probably about the baby, puts the file down and holds her arms out. "All right then. Be careful. Come here first." As he takes her in his arms, he remembers that each time he goes like this, she sits on a chair by the window without lights on, by day or night, vigilant until her man is back. Often she holds the baby like that for hours.

Then there is LeSable. "Hugo, all you have to do is step in close like this, see, use your left shoulder, and the guy will push against you with both hands, it's a normal human reaction, and you let him, but as he pushes you open the razor behind your back, you reach out—like this, see, one motion—and cut his throat wide open. He never knows what hits him. Just make sure the blood doesn't splash on you because it's going to pump out all over the place. It's effective, quick, and quiet—they never cry out, they just look surprised, and then they drop, suddenly, they're dead before they hit the ground."

Hugh Stone, 59, snapped the lid shut. It was back to that. He put the case under his arm, stepped out of the conference room, locked the door, and strode away through the echoing, ghostly factory with its stabbing beams of sunlight.

Hugh spent a quiet evening at home. Marga had moved back. She brought their daughter Astrid, who did not work for a living. Hugh was used to these turnarounds and took them without flinching. Marga, drinking, had bouts of egomania in which she moved out and had grand pretensions. This usually lasted six months or until her money ran out. Hugh paid his on-again, off- again wife the proper courtesies and listened to his daughter play piano. As he listened, he smoked a cigar and sipped brandy.

The Palm Springs estate reposed in shadowed sleep, guarded by armed men with dogs who hovered unobtrusively on the grounds. In the family room, candlelight converged into a quiet blaze among the mirrors, glass surfaces, and lavishly framed wall mirrors. Ten years earlier, Marga had

had the room "done." It was still as her emotional little homosexual designer had created it: Lavish, overblown, rankling like too much perfume.

Astrid played a workmanlike "*Für Elise*." Marga, looking frail, and very drunk, went to bed. It was nine o'clock. Hugh sat on the couch enduring a social necessity.

Astrid, blonde and slender, in a white pants suit, earlobes crawling with cruel-looking little gold rings, ended the concert by running the back of her hand from the low to the high keys and then slamming the lid down. As she whirled on her stool, the room echoed with bundled discordant notes. "Daddy, you looked at your watch at least three times!"

Hugh set his drink down. "I was listening, darling."

She jumped up. "Listening!" She made claws at the ceiling. "Listening! Ahh!" She confronted him with arched back and knotted fists. "You, listen? Don't make me laugh. You were cruel to Mother."

Hugh sighed. "Darling, I love your mother very much."

"You treat her like ... like a drunk."

"She is a drunk, darling."

Astrid stood up straight. "What a cold, arrogant man you are. She is a drunk, darling. She is your wife, and she drinks because ..." Words seemed to be failing.

"Your mother is an alcoholic, Astrid. I let her go when she leaves me, I pay all of her credit cards and bills, and I take her back in when she returns. All of this has been going on for years. And it will go on." He felt like adding, *as with you.*

"All her life, she stood by you while you looked at your watch."

"This is a very old discussion," Hugh said. "Your mother has suffered, I admit. She has been through several programs, and cannot stop drinking. The doctors have told me to stop blaming myself, and I have. I have spent my life building a fortune that you are going to inherit. If I look at my watch a lot, it's from old and good habit."

Astrid stormed past him. "I hate you."

After the door had slammed, Hugh rose and finished his drink. He left the family room, closing the door behind him. It was a room he never went to unless Marga and Astrid were home.

Later that evening, Pierre LeSable welcomed Hugh into Pierre's big car. "I have it all set up with Alvaro," he told Hugh. "We will make a lot of money together. We will save your company."

Hugh was shocked at Pierre's age, his weight, his wheeze.

LeSable said: "You are still so trim. Your hair has turned white, but there are lines in your face—you were such a baby face back then."

Hugh and LeSable rode in a Cadillac that smelled of upholstery cleaner and chocolate. The neon rainbow of Los Angeles sailed past. Fishing a liquor-filled bittersweet from a lacy box, LeSable remarked: "I have in recent years developed a taste for these things. They put a few pounds on one."

"You just like the brandy inside," Hugh countered.

LeSable drove slowly, deliberately. "Hugh, it is a serious matter. My *padrone* in Colombia has given me thirty days or else I will be in serious difficulties. Already this is the third day. You won't let me down? Can you come up with the money? It would otherwise go very badly for both of us."

"I'll have it in a few days," Hugh said curtly. LeSable knew nothing about Hugh's source of money, and Hugh intended to keep it that way. "About tonight," Hugh changed the subject.

LeSable pulled out into a deserted street. "This young college student has been asking for more of our product than he has been paying for. I think either he has developed a heavy habit, or else he has been carefree at parties. We are to meet him here this evening. I want to send a message to his friends. It will take him a few minutes to get here from the college."

"I understand," Hugh said.

The two men sat quietly. A lacework of steel was overhead, a railway overpass. The street was hidden between concrete revetments. One street light on shone the opposite side. LeSable had parked facing the cross street for a quick getaway.

"These people get involved for fun or quick money," LeSable said. "I tell them it is serious business, but they rarely listen. Oops, here he comes." Quickly he stepped out. Hugh followed suit. "This is your show, Hugh. Let's see if you still have the old touch, eh?"

A moped wavered into sight in the intersection several hundred feet away. The young black seemed ludicrously too big for the small vehicle. He wore a white tank top, gray sweat pants, and ankle-high red sneakers. The moped's headlight focused on the two men. The moped weaved a little, getting underway. It sped toward them.

Hugh felt the casing of the razor in his hand. He had rubbed violin wax on the handle in case he got sweaty palms. A giant. His bare shoulders and arms shone like the skin of a plum. Here and there, a rivulet of sweat meandered crazily among his steel-cable muscles. A basketball player, Hugh guessed; a real challenge.

The boy gave his moped one last rev and then shut the engine off. His lips looked pink and tight, pulled back in fear over his white teeth. The boy did not have to climb down. He rose and stepped back from the moped. He had huge, powerful looking hands hidden inside black leather gloves. He approached with raised hands, and Hugh could feel the tremor in his voice behind the false bravado. "Now look here, man, I came here like you said I should. I got a thousand bucks on me, and you can have it all, and then I'm through." His hands waved agitatedly.

"Quiet down, sonny," LeSable said. "We are still friends, are we not?"

The boy tore his gloves off and threw them on the ground. Tears streamed and his voice rose to a shrill squeak. "Aw man, I tole you time and again I got a girl and I just wanna get out. Cain't you understand when I say No?"

LeSable laughed. "Relax, sonny. Let's count the money."

Quickly, wiping his wrist against his nose, the boy fished a wallet from his back pocket. "Man, I took up a collection in a hurry." LeSable had him count the bills onto the hood of the car. They boy's hands shook, and wind rattled the money. Hugh maneuvered to the boy's right.

"Four hundred...five hundred..." the boy sobbed.

"Keep counting."

"I have a basketball scholarship."

"I understand. We understand, don't we, Monsieur?"

Hugh cleared his throat. "Yes, of course."

The boy looked at LeSable, at his left, and Hugh, at his right. "We have a message for your friends," LeSable said.

Hugh tapped the boy on the right shoulder. The boy looked at him, and Hugh crooked his left index finger as though he wanted to whisper something into his ear. The boy bent close, and it was over in a moment. LeSable stepped out of the way. The boy wheezed and touched his throat where, one supposed, there might have been a brief stinging sensation. Then he gasped. His eyes widened, in a last instant of horrified understanding. Blood spurted through the air with an audible hiss and spattering. The boy keeled over backwards, dead before his head shattered on the hard pavement.

Driving back along the neon-jazzy streets, LeSable told him: "I haven't seen anything like that since the old days."

Hugh held up the bag containing the bloody razor. "This goes into the bleach, like you taught me, remember?"

LeSable looked pale. "You enjoyed that, didn't you?"

"It has to be done."

LeSable looked troubled. "You haven't lost your touch. But I want you as a manager, not street killer. We have Garth to do that for us. People are more sophisticated now."

Hugh shrugged. "The Guzman hit was really sophisticated. Your bomb didn't go off, and Garth had to stiff him by hand."

After a while of silence, LeSable said: "And what about your lovely wife and daughter—"

"Don't ask," Hugh said sharply.

5 • West Haven

Blue spent two days with her parents in Connecticut, thirty miles west along the coast from the town of Hamilton, and about a million miles from her former lover.

She packed a single suitcase with only the most dire necessities, including several stuffed animals. She took the helicopter shuttle from the old Pan Am skyscraper in Manhattan to JFK, and a Pilgrim Airlines puddle jumper from Long Island to New Haven.

At home she was a kid again, after a fashion. Slept in her old room. Watched late movies with Dad. Made sandwiches at midnight, like the old days, only Dad tended now to be asleep by the time she brightly reappeared in the living room with a sandwich tray.

Things got a little heated only once, at dinner on her first evening at home. Her mother, a small fussy woman of Italian extraction, had made kielbasa, sauerkraut, and potatoes. Her father, a big quiet man of German extraction, had drunk several beers and looked a bit glassy when he came to the table. Blue shook her head and looked down in embarrassment, fiddling with her food. Her mother began scolding Dad.

"Things haven't changed," Blue said. She rose, picked up her father's beer, and poured it down the kitchen sink. Then she hugged him.

"He would never allow me to do something like that," her mother said loudly while serving up the potatoes.

Blue laughed. "You just don't know how to handle men."

"Tomorrow," Dad said, "we'll take a look at that car of yours." He was referring to the MGA in the garage.

"That thing goes in the paper," Mom said, meaning not the car but the ad to sell it. "And he does not lift the battery with his bad back."

"I'll lift the battery, Mom. Please, sit and eat will you?"

"Whatcha figure you'll get for it? And are you sure you want to sell it," Dad asked chewing a piece of kielbasa dipped in horseradish mustard.

She put her elbows on the table and leaned her chin on her hands. "I dunno. Two grand? It's in pretty good shape, except a little rust around the wheel wells."

"We could get Artie to patch her up for you." Artie was his boyhood friend who owned a service station on Ocean Avenue.

"Yes, I want to sell it," she said. It was the quintessential family conversation, everybody talking at once, each with a conversation of their own.

"I could put in a sewing room in the back of the garage," Mom said. "You could help me sew things. I always wanted you to learn how to sew."

"She can sew buttons on, what more does she need."

"Mom, I'm living in New York." Blue laughed. "You want me to commute here every evening after work to sew?"

"You could spend more weekends like a good girl."

"Girl? Anna, this is a woman. A grown woman. She has a college degree and works for the government." That impressed Dad. He'd never finished high school, and he'd worked forty years at the rubber factory in Allingtown.

Mom stepped behind Blue. Massaging Blue's shoulders, she declared: "This is my little girl. What's happened to you, Laurel? What happened to my little girl who used to play piano in the living room for all the family?"

"I grew up, Mom. Went into the world and became worldly."

Dad said: "They do the damndest things in college. Always did, Anna. Used to swallow goldfish."

"But she's done with college," Mom wailed. "Married, divorced, gone and joined the DEA. Shoots a gun for all I know. Where's the husb—"

"MOM! Don't start that, will you?"

"Now, now," Daddy said, "let her be herself. I never did like that Latin creep. She knows what she's doing. I always tell you that, Anna. She's a modern woman, and you've got to give them their head of steam."

After dinner they watched TV. Dad got a couple of beers from the garage. Mother and daughter exchanged glances but said nothing.

Mother said: "I'm always so glad when you're here. You have my eyes, you know, dark and flashing like your Uncle Pasquale. And my build, not big like Daddy. And my nose, thin like. But you have Daddy's square face. German." She made muscles and fists. "Strong."

"Anna, watch the show," Dad said.

"But those clothes."

"M-o-o-m!"

"Still rebelling. Always rebelling."

And so it went. By ten, Mom kissed them goodnight, put the cat outside, and went to bed. The news update came on. "I'm going to fix us some sandwiches," Blue said to Dad. "You want liverwurst? Summer sausage?" He grunted, and she took it for a yes. She went to the fridge. "And a pickle. Yep. One for me, one for you. Horseradish, even though it makes you fart all night. Wow, here's a few deviled eggs. We're going to live it up, Daddy."

When she came into the living room with a laden tray, however, he was fast asleep, snoring with his face tilted up, his socks at the ankles, his gnarled wrists curled over the arm rests.

"Jesus Christ, I might as well go out and feed the alley cats with all this stuff." She ate a sandwich, a deviled egg, drank a beer, and then did the remaining dishes. Put the left-overs away. And stepped outside into the cold winter air for a cigarette under the eternal blanket of stars stretched over the barren trees.

Next day, Dad took her down to Artie's and got the battery for the MGA recharged. She labored lovingly over the ancient sports car most of the day, washing and polishing it then rolling it out into the driveway. She lifted the battery in. She took off the oil pan, lying in the heated garage under the car into the evening with a beer at her side and the radio playing rock music. She sprawled under the car, small breasts floating under her olive t-shirt. Cleaned out the oil pan, changed the filter, bolted the oil pan back on, and poured fresh oil in the engine before starting it up. By then it was late night.

Blasting rock music from the car stereo, she went for a ride down along the beach. Felt nostalgic driving past West Haven High, Ocean Avenue, South Street beach. Took Murphy for a ride down to the beach, watched fog roll in with the tide. Heard the mournful basso of ocean freighters at slow intervals.

Blue had a way of separating things into boxes. It was the way she had always been. You had to do it, she figured without thinking about it much, to survive. A box for work. A box for shopping. A box for Mom and Dad. A box for memories. A box for love, and that was the most tightly shut box of all.

The old subjects would surface inevitably, she knew as she tossed a stick and tired old Murphy chased after it. Why the DEA after she'd spent time and money getting a degree in chemistry, why Manhattan, why no new and better marriage. She smoked while she waited for Murphy. Damn things; she'd quit one of these days. Why did people smoke anyway? Frustration?

Why no marriage? Why, indeed? All through high school, Blue had been a shy, quiet girl. Naive. Pianist, giving little family concerts: Beethoven, Satie, Liszt. Unaware that people hurt each other. She gone steady with Ted Monahan who was a year ahead of her and played varsity football. Silly thing, she'd loyally gone to every game. Good old Laurel, skirt folded awkwardly between her legs, cheering touchdowns, yelling herself hoarse. Eating popcorn, letting him pet her at the movies, but unwilling to go all the way. He screwed around left and right.

College, and how dumb could you be. A replay that wouldn't quit. This time it was Donald Sagus, hockey team captain, varsity football, same old shtick. Nice looking guy, enviable Blue, until she'd learned about the others. Donald had given her clap to boot. And run off with an Olympic discus hurler named Tessie O'Brien. Good old Laurel, shouting herself hoarse at the hockey games and football games. Helping Donald with his goddam math, his physics, his chemistry. Today he was probably using some other unsuspecting well-meaning dopey dame to keep his head above water in some corporation. Blue had seen him at one or two ball games with Tessie, a tall blonde with the wide shoulders, frizzy hair, and green eyes. Stunned, Laurel had realized a double pain. First, because she had been dumped and abused again. Secondly, because she realized she had a crush on the woman who was doing this to her.

Blue had gone to work for a consulting firm in Hartford, and helped write proposals for sewage treatment plants. She'd met and married a tall, handsome Ecuadorian-American named Mike Aguilar. Laurel Aguilar. Little more than a shadowy memory now, hard to believe those two years had ever happened.

A radical change: DEA; Manhattan; black belt in karate; jazz and rock gigs around the Apple. And then, Maggie. Solace for a time. Maggie: An older woman, 35, attractive, a nurturer of sorts, when she was not drinking gin out of paint-smeared coffee cups. Wounded, Blue had crawled into her arms. Lost innocence, making up for years spent being the girl next door. Into punk, post-punk, neo-punk. An easy leap into all-woman bands like The Toasters, Five Bad Girls, The Cheries (or The Cherries, as the girls sometimes called themselves). A double life for a while. Straight-arrow DEA by day, rock bitch taking a walk on the wild side by night. Probing.

Trying things. Manhattan, everything possible. What an exploration! A shadowy world, opening up stranger and stranger in the people who frequented it. People who showed up at Bad Girls concerts, men with lipstick, women in tuxedoes, cross-dressers rocking and blaring in a sort of neon wash. Maggie had painted her, too: Girl With Flower, Soft Girl, Love In Clouds, some award winners, a few hanging in the living rooms of Maggie's wealthy admirers. Blue had never allowed Maggie to use 'Laurel' in any of the titles, so Maggie's paramour would forever remain a mystery woman. Always a chimera of sorts, girl with pout, lady with dark sensuous eyes, unreachable. Cat-girl, spitting fire, poised on a tree branch, fight or flight. Flower-girl, Blue's crisp square face drowning in summer sunlight in Maggie's fevered imagination. In her aching woozy love-beyond-love, unrequited love. That, too, was a part of the past now.

Tonight she was here on this familiar beach, with the little family dog, Girl Next Door, Girl With Dog, Girl Confused, Longing Girl, changeless being home again, older but wiser (Hendrix: Are You Experienced?), still looking for that Big Love to fill the void. Alone with mournful fog horns, she wasn't sure whether it was a Donald or a Tessie who would satisfy her. She knew only that there was a longing in her, deep as the ocean, and it ached like a hunger

6 • Los Angeles

Payback.

Joanna McIvory, 35, alias Jana Andrews, had long dark hair, a stunning figure, and dark blue eyes with a sultry skyline glint. As she sat in her silvery BMW beside a desert road in California, she decided to go through with her plan. With the sudden slam of her hand on the gear shift knob, the car roared into life. Kicking up dust that drifted quietly in starry night, she drove the remaining miles into Palm Springs.

She found the Hugh Stone mansion with little trouble. Valet parking attendants hustled her wheels out from under her on the broad horseshoe driveway. She stepped up to the floodlit, pillared entrance with a clear, almost numb mind. The high-ceilinged foyer bustled with guests in evening dress. Carrying a champagne glass, Joanna looked about for the man she wanted to destroy.

Briefly she met Brady's accomplice, Hugh Stone, the estate's owner, who had made his fortune in electronics manufacturing. Stone turned out to be a good-looking man. She had expected somehow a toadier looking individual. Stone's cheeks had pink highlights. His gray eyes were chilly and penetrating, and she shivered slightly. Dangerous eyes. She extricated herself from that conversation with an unholy crawling feel about her spine.

The house smelled of coffee, fresh bread, and roast meat. Guests wandered everywhere, chattering and laughing. Snatches of piano music filtered through the heavy curtains and the ivied trellises. After about twenty minutes, she saw Vincent Brady.

A smile here, a smile there. A pair of eyes, a laugh, a charge up the stairs by a portly man who carried himself lightly, like a successful salesman. He had dark, full hair just sprinkled with gray. Joanna put his age around 45. She trailed Brady for a few minutes. He had charm all right, but then so had the serpent in Eden. He was a loner, too. He moved among people with that dazzling face, that guileless baby face with its pink dimpled cheeks and rosy lips, its boyish dark eyes and roguish eyebrows, and everywhere people smiled and nodded, but he never really stopped to speak with anyone. Collar open, neck tanned and ruddy looking. Cigar in hand. Joanna timed her approach. She blocked his path, cocking her head to one side and smiling meaningfully. Vincent Brady raised an eyebrow. "I'm... charmed." Under the smile was something serious like the darkness on an antique gold coin. He extended a hand. "Vincent Brady."

"Pleased to meet you," Joanna said, "Jana Andrews. Are you enjoying yourself?"

He slipped the cigar into a sand tray. "Dear Lady, an occasional vice, these excellent cigars of Hugh's. Oh, that you should ask such a question. I am now, more than ever."

The steady party chatter in the house, the rattle of glasses and the glossy piano phrases, were punctuated by an occasional plush of a dive into the pool in the house's inner courtyard.

Vincent liked tall woman with poise. Jana's red satin gown left much of her chest and shoulders bare, what was not covered by her black lace shawl. She was leggy, drifting through the gaze of every man she passed, and a few tried to make conversation, but she walked away from each of them. To an observant man, she was genteel, but had something hard about her. Not an abrasive hardness exactly, but a subtle steeliness. She had a rather bony face with hard cheekbones, a gently curved nose, lush lips that rolled with character and humor as the muscles in her face moved. She had a low, almost husky voice and a slow, measured way of talking. Vincent asked: "Do you know about Aphrodite?"

"The Greek Venus? Goddess of Love?"

His eyes glittered over his champagne. He put the glass down and drew a satisfied breath. "The original. Not the Roman imitation. The original, precious and pristine as the creation of the world. Born in foam at the edge of the sea. Botticelli painted her as standing in a huge seashell."

"How charming. I take it you are an art expert?"

"No, not an expert. Just a connoisseur. I have the fortune to have a classical education. Fordham. Jesuits. Life is short and we should reach out and touch the finest things." Vincent lied without a thought; he'd walked across the Fordham campus once. He ached to touch her long limbs, her easy gracefulness, her laughing eyes.

Her hip touched him with a sharp edge. "And what are some of the finest things?"

He looked her directly in the eye, and she did not flinch. "The finest things present themselves and then vanish forever if we don't reach out and take them. Like you. Like now."

She laughed uproariously. Big girl, big vocal chords. "You're going to reach out and grab me? Here?"

He smiled and looked at his feet. "No, Miss Andrews, I'm not a satyr. I'd like to be friends if that's possible. I'm not staying long. That's why I am so forward. I'd like to call you next time I'm in Palm Springs."

Jana brushed his lapel with her champagne glass. With her little finger under the lapel, she pulled him closer. "But I don't live in Palm Springs and I don't visit here often."

"Well darn it," he said, "I get around quite a bit. I'm in the computer business. I sell big industrial accounts around the country. Maybe I'll be in your neck of the woods one day." He reached out with his index finger to touch the spot on her red gown where her belly button ought to be. He felt an outie. His fingertip ran lightly down the midline of her belly.

Suddenly she put her glass aside. The way she loomed over him, he thought she was going to hit him. She laid her arms over his shoulders and brought her face close to his. Her breath was grapey and musty, like a wine cellar. Her skin was lightly but seductively perfumed. "Why don't we dance?"

He placed his arms around her waist. His fingers dallied about the dimples on either side of her tailbone.

"I'll give you my card," she whispered. "I can't promise anything, but you could give me a call. We could have dinner."

Vincent was confused. She was baiting him and then pushing him away. What was this game? He did not have the experience with women that his schooled, easy manner suggested. He never admitted this to anyone, of course. Probably she sensed money and was playing hard to get while trying to reel him in. Why did women do these things? Well, she was welcome to his ass. She was a beautiful woman. Venus on the half-shell.

Soon they were kissing deeply. They maneuvered into a dark, quiet corner half hidden behind a heavy brocade curtain and some palms. There, his breath came faster, and his hands massaged the soft round places under her gown. Her tongue sucked at his and her hands stroked the back of his neck until it burned. She would be more than passionate, he decided, she would be violent in bed. Gasping, he thrust his hand through a slit in the side of her gown. She was wearing only a finger's width of breath- thin lace. When his finger tips encountered a mons of the purest Venus, she pulled away.

"Not here."

"Please."

"Not now. Not tonight.."

"I must have you..."

"No!" Surprising vehemence, almost anger.

He took a deep breath and rubbed his cheek. "All right."

She laughed. A mean little gurgle. "You're out of breath."

"You aren't?"

She held up a business card and cocked her head to one side, rolling her lips together. He took the card. She dabbed at his mouth with a tissue that smelled of too-sweet birthday cake. He looked at the card. "Jana Andrews. Consultant. Chicago." She pulled his bow tie too tight. He freed his neck, annoyed.

She touched his chin with her finger. "You like your women spirited. No wimps for you. I can tell. I'm right, aren't I? You like to fight your women into bed."

Weakly, he said: "Yes."

She forced a dry, close-lipped kiss on his lips and strode away. She winked over her shoulder. "Don't wait too long."

He stared after her, addicted to her perfume, to her.

Vincent found Hugh near the pool, speaking with a distinguished looking jowly man in a tux with tanned, wrinkled wife who made admiring blinky eyes and whose powdered and rouged face seemed permanently supportive and admiring.

"Jana?" Hugh answered Vincent. "I don't know. Briefly met her for the first time tonight. Why?"

"I got her card," Vincent said patting his breast pocket.

"You bad boy," Hugh said. "Excuse me," he told the man and woman and they nodded. "Vincent," he said putting his arm around his companion's shoulder, "why don't we go into the library. I know you have a flight out."

They passed the pool, where the band was beginning to tune up. They just avoided getting splashed by the people playing in the pool. Vincent saw Hugh's eyes. Ducking to avoid getting splashed, Hugh suddenly had a veiled look of utter irrational anger. It passed in a nanosecond. The two men laughed it off. A trail of hackles burned softly on Vincent's back. Fear.

In a carpeted, quiet room, Stone closed the door. "Drink?"

"Scotch and soda on the rocks."

The books on the walls muffled their voices. The party sounded mute and distant. Ice crackled as alcohol and seltzer attacked it. "I have good news for you, Vincent." Hugh lit a large cigar, working the soapstone lighter around its tip.

"That's what I like to hear."

"I spoke with my friend and we are ready to do business." Cigar smoke filled the room. Hugh sucked on the cigar.

"I seem to be on a roll tonight." Vincent felt giddy.

"Indeed you are." Hugh set his drink aside. He had a way of being pontific that irked Vincent, but what the hell, they were using each other. "There is a time element involved. My friend is very nervous. He has been given a very short time to put this deal together, or else he will be in trouble. So, we must receive your money post-haste, as the deal depends on you."

"How much?" Vincent asked, his stomach fluttering.

"Your entire three million."

"You're kidding." The floor seemed to drop away.

"Nope."

"If something went wrong, I'd... have to start over..."

"Nothing will go wrong."

"How can you be sure?"

"Think, Vincent. I know it's scary. But it's simple and foolproof. I've done it before. You'll be free, just think, isn't that what you want? To be free?"

"God, yes." In some ways, he felt frightened, even angry at himself. He didn't need this. He could be free anyway with the money he'd gotten together. But his greed... "Suppose I don't want to go through with this."

"Oh you will," Hugh said. "You have too much at stake." He puffed happily on his cigar.

"What if you keep my money and just kiss me off?"

Hugh cleared his throat. "Vincent," he said, and Vincent's stomach knotted up, "let me explain something to you. You hold something over me, and I hold something over you. We could burn one another. I don't normally do business like this, but I'm desperate. Do you understand? Desperate. I need three million dollars to finance my business, and I'll need more money on subsequent deals. We'll both do okay, don't worry. But let me tell you one thing. I want this to be clear. If you screw up on me, I will blow the whistle on you, do you understand?"

Vincent slept most of the way to New York City. He ate a light dinner in the airport lounge and had two drinks to fortify himself before finding the limo to Hamilton, Connecticut.

It was drizzling lightly when he walked the long glass corridors at JFK on Long Island. Taxis circled the concourse and rain (ice?) glittered on their yellow bodies. The sky thundered as planes landed or took off. He found the limo station rest room.

Coming out moments later, he avoided two stewardesses passing by. Lovely girls. Rakish caps, sweet dark uniforms, legs, conversation... Having changed his clothing, he felt home again. He felt it going the other way, too, always the excitement of changing worlds, tension between heaven and hell.

"Take your bags?"

"Why certainly, thank you."

Little Italian looking boy, peppy, eager to please, twentyish, maybe a college student. "Where are you headed, Monsignor?"

"Just over there. The limousine stand for Connecticut."

"Ah... well, here we are. Thanks!" The boy hurried off with a two-dollar tip.

Monsignor Vincent Gordon smiled and raised his hand in blessing amid a streaming rain.

7 . Hamilton, Connecticut

Blue found the temptation to drive the MG too great. The rag top rattled pleasurably as the car burred along I-95 going east toward Hamilton. The white church on the town green was within earshot of the ocean's mournful horns. Sere, leafless, millions of trees slept through winter.

Detective Eddie Stosik was a little guy and a smoker. He was freckled, thirty, with a Jimmie Olson boyishness and red hair. They met outside a diner overlooking the Old Boston Post Road on one side and Long Island Sound on the other. He pointed with his overcoat pocket. "That's a nice car, Miss Humboldt."

"Blue."

"Nice car, Blue. I heard the Federal Government was going to furnish you a car, but I had no idea—" He opened the door for her. She read the wry in his tone and laughed. "You know they don't provide sport scars."

Coffee arrived at their table. Eddie's index and middle fingers were orange with cigarette detritus. He had dirty fingernails and slurped his coffee. He had marvelous hazel eyes and was full of jokes. Of course he was married with three kids. He shuttled his Marlboros on the table from one hand to the other. "I'll show you to your apartment later on."

"That'll be nice," she said.

"I checked it out for you. You've got quiet neighbors, mostly, sorta. Coupla college families. They play seem to play hard rock at one in the morning sometimes though."

"I'll manage," Blue said. "My apartment in Manhattan is over a subway and under where the jets fly. Not to mention the trash that sails down from the twentieth floor to the dumpster."

"Manhattan," Eddie said.

"It's pretty lively."

"Yeah, well here, this place will bore you."

"Depends." She leaned forward. "You busted Guzman but he's dead and our leads are gone. Is there a next straw to grasp?"

Eddie shrugged. He had a smug mouth. "I don't know what the next straw is. Let me tell you about my job. I was a patrolman in New Haven. Quit and came here to be a detective. Do you know what I detect? Building code violations. No shit. This is a small department and I do all sorts of stuff. In between building code violations, truancy, welfare complaints, once every decade a murder... This Guzman thing was a fluke. I don't expect to see another one like it in my lifetime. What I'm trying to say is, cool it. We're just small town cops here. That's the way I like it. Quiet. I have a chance here to reach my retirement date in one piece. Do you ever think about that?"

"You have a point there," Blue said. "Well, Eddie, this coffee is real nice and you're real nice. But I just saw two people murdered in cold blood, one of them a pretty nice guy. So you'll pardon me if I don't cool it too much."

Eddie made a face. "Blue, all I'm saying is, get used to the pace here. It's slow. Like a glacier. An inch a year."

She put her hands over his. "Eddie, I read the police reports. You went in there with guns blazing. Now that's not a guy who wants to ride things out."

He shrugged lightly. "Well, something came over me."

"Well, something could come over you again, couldn't it?"

He laughed. "Things are going to be interesting with you around. When we finish our coffees, let's take a ride."

She liked Eddie. There was something warm and straight about him. Playful. He drove her through the snow-dusted streets. To the edge of town. Even here, in this postcard tourist town on the Old Boston Post Road, were poor areas. He pointed to a burned-out house on a dead-end street, enough left to suggest a typical New England house with gray shingles and a wooden porch. "What do you see, Blue?"

"It's depressing." Singed, burned. Broken glass, twisted plumbing, a basement filled with snow. "Maybe some family lived there for generations. And then—"

"The people sold, moved, whatever, the place was on the market, and Our Friends moved in. Look around the neighborhood." She saw broken toy wagons on frosty lawns. Rusty cars on bricks.

"Toy wagons," he mused over a cigarette. "Children. I have three. Somehow, children live here, and there was a crack house in the middle of their neighborhood. The house was up for sale, empty, and those bastards moved in. Like catching a cold. They appear from nowhere. We staked the place out. You could see, night after night, a path worn to the side window. That's where they were taking the money and handing the dope out. And there were children playing on the lawns. Doesn't that make your skin crawl? Could be your own kids someday. Place like that appears. No warning, no nothing, the ghouls start showing up at night. They go in there, buy some, buy quick sex too, a real AIDS factory. I got pissed when I saw the toy wagons." He sucked on his cigarette, then tossed it sizzling into the snow. "Guzman made the mistake of being in the neighborhood same time as me."

She nodded. "Reminds me of the neighborhood I grew up in. Same lawns, same wagons, same everything."

"That why you joined DEA?"

"I just wanted to do something a little different. I wasn't ready for toy wagons." I was, she thought, Mike wasn't. Now?

Eddie made a wry mouth. "With three kids, I've got wagons on my lawn, hey."

"Nothing wrong with wagons if they're on the right lawn."

"You haven't found the right lawn yet, huh?"

"I had a wagon but he rolled away. Come on, take me to the police station. Let me see the files on the case."

"Okay, but you won't like what you'll see."

8 . Hamilton, Connecticut

Vincent Brady's nightmare, the one he'd had since childhood: Here it was again. Another tormented night. The night was black and bitter cold. Flurries of snow (tiny, crabbed flakes tortured into ice) rattled against the windows, dark granite blocks rimed with black ice. In the dark, wood-floored room, a clock ticked loudly. There was always, somewhere in this big building, water sighing and gurgling stealthily in pipes. As he snored, the Monsignor twisted and moaned.

East Texas. The town of Careyville, population 350, all pious Southern Baptists. The way the town wags had it, it waren't the widda's fault. Her old man, the preacher Nesbitt Brady, a good man and a rousing preacher but a mean drunk, had come home and knocked the boy about. Upended the table. Beat the widda. She knocked him on the head in self-defense while the boy cowered in the closet crying. Old Nesbitt done got in his car—folks wonderin' how, maybe the car done drove itself—and went to Ledbetter's Tavern crost the river for another pint or so of that Texas lightnin'. Returned at four in the morning ragin' like a fleabit ox. Hollerin' his fool head off he was gonna kill Edna and the boy cause she'd been foolin' around with some other man, which was pure hokum, cause the widda's pure as Sunday lace. Anyhow he got a pitchfork from the barn and was kickin' the front door in when Edna blew him away with both barrels of his own twelve gauge shotgun. Some say the boy's watchin' the whole thing from the side o' the porch and got slightly tetched ever since.

Snow rattled against the loose window pane near the TV, and Monsignor Gordon cried out in his sleep. He moaned, he cried.

Fearfully, he climbed out the window when he heard his daddy driving in swearing and yelling. From the side of the porch he watched his daddy kicking at the door. Then the door opened. The Angel of Death stepped forth and belched mouthfuls of fire. His daddy flew away in a mangle and tangle of blood and bone. The boy screamed and screamed. His momma came and hugged him. The Angel of Death took flight because of Momma's powerful love. But sometimes Momma's eyes lit up like the Angel of Death's. At such times Vincent Brady would hide behind the sofa or in the closet. In time he came to hate his momma as much as he loved her. He hit the road when she died, a chicken bone stuck in her gullet, a final steely glance as she reached out to him.

Next morning, at breakfast, Vincent Brady, a.k.a. Monsignor Gordon, was stirring his coffee at the kitchen table in the rectory of the Church of the Good Shepherd when his eyes chanced upon an article on page 4 of the Hamilton Daily Watch: FEDERAL WITNESS, PRISON GUARD SLAIN; KEY TO DRUG INVESTIGATION LOST. Vincent shook, and the coffee cup rattled. Father Tiernan, the pastor, looked out from behind the sports section. "Are you all right, Monsignor?" Tiernan was a slight, owlish man with a halo of dark hair around a bald pate. He wore black-rimmed glasses and had a warped nose.

"I just dropped my spoon, Father."

Tiernan fluffed the sports page and buried himself back in the horse racing articles. Vincent glanced aside quickly to see if anyone had noticed. But the three younger priests had already left—one to say Mass, another to visit the sick, and the third to argue at the bank about a bounced check. Vincent read the rest of the article and blanched. Until now he had looked at his involvement as a harmless game; not any more. He left his coffee and rose. "Father, I'll be going."

The sports page rattled. "Okay, Monsignor," Father Tiernan said without flinching from his favorite morning pastime. Vincent went to his small suite of rooms. It was a cozy but austere setup on the second floor of the rectory. He had a television set and books. He loved glossy art books. Every Christmas he would pointedly buy himself a new colorful collection of Titian or Tissot or Rembrandt masterpieces, instead of something godly, just to spite her. He found his black hat and coat and car keys.

Vincent Brady had escaped from the tiny East Texas town of Careyville and worked his way north, first picking cotton and fruit, later doing custodial work at a small Pennsylvania Catholic parish and reading voraciously in his free time. There he'd gotten the idea, slowly, to become a Catholic priest. The exposure to this Mediterranean culture, with its statues and outward symbolisms that he'd heard condemned all his life as idolatry and worse, had fascinated him. There was power in this ancient and primitive ceremonial religion. In his heart of hearts he'd never really taken it completely seriously. But there was one pressing reason why he pursued it all the way to seminary. As a priest, he had the power to ward off devils and evil spirits. One of the ranks you had to attain before becoming a priest was that of exorcist—porter, lector, acolyte, subdeacon, deacon, exorcist, priest. With that power, he should be able to raise his hand in the sign of the cross and drive away the Angel of Death who seemed to haunt him wherever he went. The Church had paid his way through seminary and then graduate school. He was a Monsignor by the age of 38, sort of the Church's MBA, in charge of administrative and financial matters, ranking above the priests and the parish pastor, and able to lead a life of his own. Then, like most men in their forties, he'd begun to be tormented by his mortality. His marriage to this Church was little different from marriage to a wife. The Church demanded his chastity, much as an aging wife (he'd heard all this in confessions, nobody could be more attuned than a confessor) demands that her spouse dry up his balls and forget looking at all the pretty little flitty things. The demands of the flesh were severe, and he'd begun to fold to them. He could consort with whores by night, and by day rant and rail all the more strongly against the vices of the flesh. It was a self-sustaining cycle, and he felt at home in the company both of corrupt popes and fallen evangelists. He was like a drunk. In the morning he'd swear he'd never again, and by nightfall the demon was out of the bottle again. The demon of it grew voracious. The Angel of Death stayed with him, and that made him slightly dotty. If only he could rid himself of that. Every time he turned and said, "Go, the Mass is ended," there she was, Edna, his mother, sour disapproving face, eyes filled with hellfire and condemnation, in the back of the church, and when he gave the blessing, she disappeared, so there truly was something to this Catholic business.

Vincent parked his old Mercedes and found the familiar phone booth by the park. Using the credit card Hugh Stone had provided him (under an assumed name) he called Palm Springs.

"Hugh. I read the paper this morning. Witness slain."

"He was going to key them to a lot of information about us."

"Hugh, I never thought...this is...it's gone too far."

"No, Vincent, it's going along fine. You're safe now, don't you see? Are you nervous?"

"I'm floored. I'm nauseous. Murder!"

"Listen, little man, this is all a little bit over your head. You just keep counting the alms and leave the serious stuff to the big guys. Do you understand?"

"Hugh, I want out."

"No, Vincent. There is no way on God's earth you can get out. Don't be a fool, man. You wanted to play in the big leagues, and you had the chips, so we let you. Now you want to cut and run. Well, that isn't how it goes. You're along for the ride. Any further questions?"

"No, Hugh."

"Good. It's day six and the clock is ticking. Are you about ready to turn the money over so we can get on with it?"

"Yes," Vincent said miserably. After the call, Vincent wiped a tear from his eyes and staggered back to his car. The icy cold weighed on him like old age. Sitting behind the steering wheel, he thought about his options. They were scarce. Sometime soon, he would have to disappear from the Church. That much was clear. At the moment, he had three million dollars salted away in about twenty bank accounts. He wondered how many of those bank accounts Hugh Stone knew about. One consolation: He could not know about the Chicago account.

Vincent appeared at the Church of the Good Shepherd in time for his eleven o'clock Mass. He went through the motions, and as always at this particular Mass, there were two knowledgeable altar boys from the grammar school, and a congregation of mostly elderly women who adored Vincent and preferred to attend a monsignor's Mass. As the church bells rang in appeal for the coming twelve o'clock Mass, the rafters rocked majestically under the motion of the massive bells. Vincent changed the bread into the Body of Christ, imploring his sins be forgiven. As he changed the wine into the Blood of Christ, he begged for mercy. Minutes later, Vincent turned and blessed the congregation: "Go, the Mass is ended."

In the back of the church stood the Angel of Death. No, it was his mother, Edna Brady. Or was it both. As he made the sign of the cross, she looked at him full of sour condemnation, turned away, and disappeared into the solid stone wall.

"We thank the Lord our God," the congregation answered.

Vincent trembled. Once again, he'd driven it away. How many more times could he? He followed the altar boys into the sacristy where they would trade their red cassocks and virgin-white surplices for play clothes and run outside, while a stashed bottle of Johnny Walker Black awaited Vincent.

٩ . Hamilton, Connecticut

Eddie, this can't be for real!" Blue stood in Eddie's cramped, cluttered office in the police station holding a single file folder. Eddie shrugged, picking tobacco from his lip. "I'm afraid so, Blue." The waning light cast a silvery light on his pale face and red hair.

She sat down heavily. The file folder and her long scarf slid down between her knees. "Oh Eddie, there's nothing here."

"There's my police report, lab results, that kind of thing."

"Isn't there something more? What about the FBI? DEA?"

"I already did that." He bristled. "We do get work done, despite the low-key laid-back beach atmosphere."

"I'm sorry," she said quickly. "I guess I should have known. If there were any solid leads, they'd have hot dogs working the case and I wouldn't have been sent here."

"Well, maybe this is your chance to become a hot dog," Eddie said, a twinkle in his eye. "Maybe a chili dog or a corn pup."

"Hah," she exclaimed, but had to laugh. Eddie put one booted foot on his chair and looked out the window. "It's already getting late, Blue. Suppose we grab a bite and then I take you to your place?"

"Sounds okay."

Eddie showed her the rest of the town. The main street, passing through the Green with its church, town hall, and police station, was U. S. Route 1, the Old Boston Post Road, two lanes each way. South of U.S. 1 lay snowy-scraggly beaches opening on Long Island Sound. In summer, the area was a tourist hive for New Yorkers. In winter, it was a gray desolation of the soul.

Blue enjoyed Eddie's company. Despite his outgoing nature, she sensed something closed and mysterious. She couldn't put her finger on what or why, but it was refreshing to have his warm personality in this strange new place.

As the afternoon waned, and passing cars turned headlights on, Eddie stopped nervously at a service station and made a phone call while Blue waited in the unmarked car, listening to jazz music and watching Eddie twist himself in harried conversation in the telephone booth. When he returned to the car, he noted her puzzlement. "My wife," he said. "I told her I'd be late." She said nothing, but thought he made a grand case of it to her.

It was good to get in from the cold, and Eddie told dumb jokes. The windows in Frog's Restaurant were steamed. The darkly paneled walls were covered with knick-knacks like old Pepsi posters, black and white photos of '50's Yale football players, a wagon wheel, old bubblegum dispensers. The place rumbled with conversation, shuffling feet, scraping chairs, clattering dinnerware, laughter. Beer flowed freely, and waitresses hustled with hoisted trays. When they were seated in a nook, Eddie regarded her over his menu. "This is the first time I've really seen you laugh, Blue." His eyes glowed.

She patted her scarf, coat, mittens, and wool cap into a pile. "Must be the thought of eating, Eddie. I'm famished."

"I thought you were strictly the serious type."

"I must have given the wrong impression."

"So what do you do in New York City besides work?"

She patted her napkin in place. Beers arrived. "Well, I have some friends. I play keyboard sometimes when I get calls."

"Keyboard? You mean typing?"

"You're teasing. No, I mean like jazz groups. Rock groups sometimes."

"You're kidding. A musician?" They toasted and then sipped draft beers. He was probing, and she let him. If probing was like biting, he had milk teeth. She was accustomed to dodging personal questions. "Sure. I was the girl next door. Grew up playing little Beethoven pieces. Then I got to college and went nuts. Made up for all that lost time."

"I'll bet you've always had a lot of boyfriends." He leaned forward with boyish sincerity. "You're very pretty."

She rolled her eyes up. "Eddie, you're embarrassing me."

He leered. "I have this awful urge to tease you."

"Eddie, STOP it!" Inwardly, she felt a bubbling crazy kind of happiness. Maybe it was just that she had been feeling sad about the shootings and about being alone in a strange town, and now she was beginning to warm up to... Stop it, she told herself.

The waitress took their orders.

"So you play keyboard. Maybe that's why you have that sort of hard rock edge about you. Leather jacket maybe."

She glanced at her ski parka, puzzled. "I have one, but it's in my closet in Manhattan. How did you guess?"

He shrugged, smugly. "Just the air about you." He tapped his fingers on the table. "And what else?"

"Well, I have a black belt in karate."

"You're kidding."

"No, honest."

"I know a little judo, but jeez, Blue, a black belt? Wow." He looked serious. Daunted.

"So who are you, Eddie?"

His boyish glow lost some of its spin. "I'm trying to raise a family. Three little kids." He made a wry, almost sad face. "Love them, I really do. It's a full time job. Not so glamorous." What about this Wife, Blue wondered. The food came. Hamburgers, juicy, with onions. Fries, lots of ketchup. A pitcher of beer. They ate in silence. Afterward, they settled back and stared at the people around them. Young married couples at splattered tables, managing little kids who crawled among the chair legs. Young single men with intense smiles, working the single women with wrap-around eyes. What hard work, Blue thought, being single. Why weren't young men like that working their balls off trying to talk to her? She'd listen to their nonsense. She'd be glad to, if only they would. She sort of envied the tight jean blondes who flirted with those tall thin bearded home-grown types. Yet, she did not see any man who particularly appealed to her. They had the bodies, sure, but their intense, phony flirting left her cold. Eddie now, he was a little older, had some maturity, too bad he was married. There was definite interest in his eyes, and what surprised her was that it did not turn her off.

"Oh hey," Eddie said. A good looking dark haired man, about 28, walked up. "Meet my friend Father Joe."

"How do you do?" she said. Father?

"Joe Travignan," Eddie said, "meet Blue Humboldt."

"A bolt out of the blue?" said Travignan, who wore a preppy sweat jacket, red flannel shirt, jeans, and work boots. He offered a hand, and Blue shook it. She noticed, on the expensive looking cream sweat jacket breast, an emblem that looked like an Epsilon with a wide W through it, inside a ring of laurels. He had sad eyes, she noticed also.

"He's assistant pastor at Sacred Heart Parish. Coaches basketball, teaches Sunday school, plays guitar—hey, you two should get together. She plays keyboard, Joe."

Father Joe beamed. "That's great."

Eddie stammered: "She's here on business." Blue wondered.

"Really." Joe looked around. Blue followed his gaze and saw a portly, smiling man coming out of the john. Joe waved to him. "Well, the Monsignor and I are here for burgers. Nice to meet you, Miss Humboldt. Keyboard, huh?"

"Your church organist died," she guessed, "and you need a replacement."

"Maybe a backup. Our organist is 82. See you soon, Eddie. Nice meeting you, Miss Humboldt. See you in church?" He threaded through the crowd.

"It's a small town," Eddie said as if apologizing.

"I like it. You need to get home, don't you?" Jealous wife, she guessed. Poor Eddie.

"Yeah, I'm afraid so."

Her apartment was in an old house with high ceilings and creaky walls. Hot air from a basement boiler sighed in the walls and blew into the rooms through ornate grates. Blue had a bedroom, kitchen and bath. Two Yale families lived in the main apartments, entered by the stately front porch where greenish light glimmered through the leaded glass in a massive front door. Nesting, Blue puttered about putting things here and there. She had put posters on the wall: a nude girl draped over a mossy, green-glowing MGA (me, Blue liked to think, if I were longer and had darker nipples); a dark handsome man with thin unshaven cheeks, mussy hair, and riveting eyes, standing by yellow diesel locomotive in a brick railway station (him, Blue liked to think, whoever, wherever he might be); a sunny Alpine scene, snow and flowers mixed at just that spring moment three or four thousand feet high and not quite in heaven; and a seductive girl in red miniskirt, strapless black high heels, and white lace gloves, glancing over her shoulder (the photo was slightly blurred, one white glove brushing heavy gorgeous black hair out of her eyes) as she stepped into a black limousine (her, Blue thought sometimes when that mood struck).

She warmed up for her kata exercises by stretching well. She turned on rock music and donned athletic bra and shorts. As in her Manhattan apartment, the old heating system made it like ninety in the shade. She stretched fully, breathing deeply, and felt her body relax. She rose and did bends. At first sweat, she began her katas. Her movements were a mixture of the hard angular Japanese blocks, punches, and kicks, and the more circular Chinese parries. At first she moved slowly at a tai ch'i pace, each movement slowly and deliberately executed and flowing into the next. As she warmed, she sped the pace. Soon she was performing at a steady aerobic tempo, dispatching dozens of imaginary opponents who were running and jumping at her from all sides. Twelve katas and a half hour later, she jogged in place and started to wind down. Sweat sprayed from her head and body, soaking the rug. The bedroom mirror was steamed up, and the thermometer on the wall had risen several degrees from her body heat. For another ten minutes, she wound down. She rolled up the rug and stripped naked. She put rug and shorts and bra in the laundry hamper, then showered.

The shower had warmed her, and she fell asleep in the first pages of a historical novel. If Stosik did not help her, how could she hope to make a dent in this town?

Something woke her. Someone stood before her door. A glance at the LED clock in the dark room told her it was midnight. Shivers crept up and down her back. She heard creaking sounds. Someone heavy, a man probably, was tiptoeing in the carpeted wood-floored hallway. One of the Yale people? Not likely. Why the stealth? The wan hall light under her door dimmed as he, whoever he was, stopped. The door crackled faintly as a weight pressed against it. Her breath came in short gasps, while her hand fumbled over the edge of the bed. She stretched, trying not to make the bed creak, while her fingers grasped empty air, seeking the 9 mm in its holster on the carpet by the bed.

The door knob murmured lightly, turning. The knob rattled ever so softly.

She sat up, holding the automatic in both hands by her cheek. Waiting. A car door slammed outside. Whoever was at her door abruptly turned and hurried off. The house door was unlocked noisily by someone who sounded like he or she belonged there, a young couple with a sleepy, mewling baby, who let themselves into their apartment and then were quiet.

Blue made sure the door was double-bolted before she slipped back to sleep.

10 · Los Angeles

Hugh Stone was disconcerted. Bill Garth showed up unexpectedly at Stone Electronics instead of arranging a discreet meeting. Things were out of control, and Hugh didn't like it. Because he needed the money so badly, he decided not to berate Garth. No sense making more waves in an already shaky situation. The clock was ticking, and LeSable needed his money. Hugh sensed that Vincent was getting cold feet, and that scared Hugh.

Garth was a big blond man. Sitting on the couch opposite Hugh's desk, he shifted his martial arts-honed frame forward and looked at the check for $5000 Hugh had written him, over and above the $75,000 LeSable had already paid him for the Guzman hit. Garth's rugged features brightened. He had a full, low voice that growled like a big engine. "Money talks, Mr. Stone. This says it all. Thanks for the bonus."

Stone smiled coldly. "I thought it would serve as a nice introduction. I think you see exactly where I am coming from."

Garth looked up, honestly flattered. "I've never seen this kind of shall we say friendliness before."

Hugh dropped a pencil he had been holding. "Garth, I admire your skill and your strength. You are a very intelligent man." Garth was eating it up. "Did anybody see you waste Guzman?"

Garth was momentarily troubled. "A young woman cop. Why?"

Hugh sighed. "It's the matter of control. We like to know all of our factors. Do you think she would recognize you again?"

"Maybe. I could finish her off fast enough. Little dark-haired butch type, cute as a button though. Her name is Laurel Humboldt."

"Did you learn that from our source in Manhattan?"

"Sure. Why call attention to ourselves. Wasting a DEA type would only draw more heat. I can kill her any time we want."

"Smart thinking," Hugh said. He briefed Garth about Vincent Brady, without revealing his own desperation. "Somewhere in San Diego, Brady has a house. When he's not playing priest in Hamilton, he goes to San Diego and lives a life of sin."

"And fun," Garth said grinning.

"And fun. I want you to go to San Diego, find Brady's place, and stake it out. If he tries to run out on me, that's the first place he'll go. I'll send someone else to Hamilton." He added: "If we lose him, Garth, our whole show is gone."

Next morning at nine, Roger Filmore was ushered into Hugh's office. Filmore accepted coffee and a donut. He was a trim man of fifty, with short gray hair and a nice face. He looked as though he had just stepped out of a golf course shower after an easy four or five holes.

Preppy. That was Roger Filmore. Wingtips, dark slacks, red sweater, white shirt open at the collar. Filmore had been a high school principal in Oregon until fired and convicted for fondling a student. He had sold real estate later, made and lost a fortune. After his wife's death (from unhappiness?) he had moved to Del Mar, California, where he'd gotten involved in LeSable's organization and found the easy money of crime worth the risks.

Filmore raised his eyebrows and smiled. "I'm so happy to see you come aboard and take charge. We're creating a businesslike organization, and I like that."

"Thanks, Roger. I want you to head East. Little town called Hamilton, Connecticut. One of my sources of funds called me up and started to sound wishy-washy. I wonder if you could visit him and just introduce yourself. Remind him that our organization can get to him, no matter where he is."

"Fine," Filmore smiled. "I like that. The other type of organization would have sent Garth."

Hugh said: "The guy's name is Vincent Brady, but he goes by Gordon. Be subtle with this bird. Don't be rough. Just let him know he promised us money, and he won't get away from us."

11. Hamilton, Conn.

Blue met Eddie for breakfast the next morning at a coffee shop on the Boston Post Road. He slurped his coffee, hunched across from her in a cozy booth. The waitress brought a menu. Blue wrapped her hands around the coffee cup and ordered a ham and cheese omelet. "Blue, you're on your own today. Like I told you, I've got code violations, truants, you name it."

"I can keep busy," she said. And she did. The town looked gray, cold, shuttered, somehow menacing. She crunched across the snow after saying goodbye to Eddie. In the cold sunlight of a winter's day she regarded the golden gleam of a church dome. Not a clue; but what could they do to her, send her back to Manhattan? She began by wandering through the town shopping center, just talking to shop people. The store keepers were friendly. She felt guilty, as though playing hookey; must get to know the town though. She talked, she shopped, lightly for her budget was limited. A poster, a scented bar of soap.

Near a small Episcopal church in the central walking mall, she spied a sign: An E with a W, laurel wreath. She remembered. What's his face, Joe Travelgram, had worn a sweat jacket with that logo. She peered in a store window. Looked like a travel agency inside. A bell tinkled as she entered. "Yes?" asked the woman behind the counter.

"I was wondering what this is," Blue said.

"We are a drug rehab agency."

Blue reeled. "What?"

The woman had large, sympathetic eyes that had seen much suffering. "Are you in trouble?"

Blue stammered: "What, you mean like, drugs, cocaine...?"

"Heroin, you name it."

"I saw the sign. I wondered what it means."

"E for Episcopal. W for winners. It's okay if you're some other religion."

"Is there a counselor named Father Joe Travelgland here?"

"You mean Travignan. Joe. Yes. But he's not a counselor."

She was again startled. "Oh."

"Want to come to a meeting?" The woman offered a signup sheet full of names. Blue spotted the priest's name. "I'll think about it."

She raced to her apartment. Burdened with parcels, she unlocked the door and called Vito. "Vito, can you make a guy named Joe Travignan? He's a priest here in Hamilton."

"Look in the phone book."

"Vito, humor me? Stop giving me gas." She put up her posters and hung a new shower curtain, one with lavish summer flowers against a pale pink background; something to reach out and grab the cold neutral air, dissolving it with Blueness. As

she put the soap by the tub, the phone rang. Vito: "Hey, Blue, that guy you asked me to run a check on? Father Joe Travignan? You may have hit something, I don't know what. National Agency Check came back on the guy. He's a priest all right, legit and all, but he does have a sheet."

"Veeeto!" she squealed.

"Couple of years back in San Francisco, got picked up for possession, also for a small street deal. Heroin, cocaine, marijuana. Probation. It gets interesting. The archdiocese in Frisco cut a deal with the Probation Department. Father Joe was assistant pastor in a parish, was doing good work, the Church wanted to get him back in the fold, can't afford to lose priests. So they agreed to send him to a parish far away, and guess where that turned out to be."

"Sacred Heart, Hamilton, Connecticut."

"Bingo. Tomasi says give you a gold star. Musician, poet, real beatnik from the looks of it. Comes from Akron, Ohio. No juvenile arrests, nice middle-class family. College at Canisius, seminary at Mt. Holyoke, assigned to Frisco, then screwed up. You follow up on this, Blue, let's see where it leads."

12 · San Diego

Joe Travignan, 29, stepped off the plane feeling muzzy. He'd shot up in the plane's bathroom, slept a while, and now it was wearing off. He took a taxi from the airport to Vincent's hideaway in La Mesa. Under sighing eucalyptus trees, he found the place shuttered and empty. Disappointed, he broke in and made himself comfortable. What had happened? Why had Vincent not showed up as he'd promised. Vincent knew about Joe's problem, had promised to help find a solution. He depended on Vincent now, dammit, where was he? It was getting out of hand again. He craved the stuff. He tried calling Hamilton, but Vincent was not taking calls. Shit.

Oh Lord, he thought doubled on the floor, you have sent this scourge to tax me and test me. How can a guy break your bread and drink your wine and be so whacked out and all alone? Jesus, help me. Vincent did not show up.

Joe took a taxi downtown, past palm-swept streets. In the Mission District, where bums kissed the sidewalk and bag ladies pushed carts, he shambled into a cheap hotel. Before he entered, he took off the ring Joanna had given him and stuck it in his sock. Jesus, he thought, help me carry this cross. A scroungy blond man was waiting in the lobby for deals. Joe said: "I need."

The man rolled his eyes upward, along the stairwell. "Room 301. A guy's got."

Joe hurried up the stairwell, thinking about his money. On the third floor, wall paper sagged. There was a musty smell. The doors looked constricted, dark, and foreboding. Joe felt his way along, touching the crumbling numbers on doors. He was so intent, he didn't notice a door open, a body move out, a blow struck against his head. Vomiting, he lolled about, groggy, until he woke dry-mouthed and felt his pants. His wallet was gone. He spat blood, sitting up. He'd been rolled. God, where was Vincent now? Vincent always had money. Vincent, who wanted the names of elderly ladies. Vincent, who promised to fix things. Who could get money.

Joe staggered down the hallway. Room 301. The door swung on its hinges. He entered. Burst in upon a deal going down. A black man and a white man looked up with bruised faces, murderous eyes. There was a pile of bags on the naked floor. Heroin. At the same moment, a door opened and a spray of gunfire spewed out. Joe had just enough time to see a Tek-10 assault pistol methodically chew up the two men. Then the bullets tore into him, and he started to tumble down a long corridor, toward a bright light, where his sister Joanna stood waiting.

13 · San Diego

The telephone chime woke John Connor. Early sunlight beamed through the venetian blinds in his bedroom. He had been dreaming incoherently but pleasantly about pink pigs rolling down a ramp. He had been jostled by happy pigs which, he recently read, made great pets. As he groped for the telephone, he remembered he had recently seen a Porky Pig cartoon at a pizza place. The bedroom smelled of socks and wood. A rustling palm tree nuzzled the sliding glass door. Birds trilled. "M'ello?"

"John, are you awake?"

"M'no."

"This is Lollie. How are you?"

He yawned. "Aren't you going to work?"

"Work? What's that? It's a beautiful sunny day and I thought I would go shopping instead. Then I thought of you. What are you up to?"

He scrunched the pillow up behind his head. The clock's display read 7:35. "Well, I've got to work this evening." He felt good about that. These two working days gave his entire week structure. Because he worked Thursday and Saturday evenings, he always had to be aware of what day it was. When you were retired, that made a big difference. "And I have six star pines, two giant bird of paradise plants, eight Canary Island date palms, and a flat of ivy to plant."

"I could use some exercise."

"I'll fix us an omelet."

"What a guy." She added a kiss and hung up.

John stretched and sat up. Stepping into the hot, steamy shower, he remembered his dream with faded affection. Lots of round, pink pigs rolling down a chute, and he with them, jostled, nuzzled, snorted on. His dominant feeling from the dream was one of feeling the pigs' affection. So he wanted affection, that was it. Didn't everyone? Wasn't everyone starved for affection?

He tied a towel around his waist and went barefoot into the kitchen. His wet dark hair was plastered around his forehead and neck. At 29, he had everything, really, but something was seriously missing. A family, perhaps. He'd tried that once. He had plenty of women to draw from, and they were all his friends, respected, admired, accomplished, attractive—but none could offer a relationship for one reason or another.

"Waahh." Fontainebleau, the Siamese tomcat, was sitting on the blond chopping block. The cat's creamy fur was fluffed out and his tail stood straight up in a "hello." Fontainebleau owed his name to a wine label. John and a young woman—name since forgotten—were partaking of Fontainebleau wine when, shivering and hungry, this beautiful kitten had come crying at the sliding glass door. For a retainer of milk and cat food, Fontainebleau provided companionship and an occasional slain mouse or lizard left at the sliding glass door for inspection and approval.

"Oh yes," John said rubbing the cat's back. Fontainebleau rolled over onto his back and John rubbed his belly. "You want your milk. Okay." The cat prowled between his legs at risk of being stepped on while John opened the refrigerator and extracted a quart of milk and poured a smidge into Fontainebleau's bowl. The cat discovered the milk and forgot all about his master, though his tail remained hoisted in thanks, or was it self-love. After Fontainebleau had eaten he gave John a long, agate stare and thudded toward the canyon to sun himself.

John prepared eggs, bacon, and toast. Lollie, a tall blonde of forty, arrived with paper sacks. "Picked up a few things."

He embraced her in the doorway. They went through the living room, through the den, through the kitchen, to the little garden he had built on. The garden had a white wrought-iron table and chairs on sugar-fine gravel, shaded by palms and broad-leafed tropical plants on the northern side of the house. They ate a leisurely breakfast.

Lollie had finished the family-raising part of her life. In their honest discussions, she had made it clear she would not marry again to start a new family, not that he had really considered it, but it made her a safe playmate. She would step out of the way if he met a woman he loved.

In the yard below the redwood deck they carted his plants around. The morning fog had burned off and they worked in full sunlight. Sweat dribbled down Lollie's face and neck. Her T-shirt clung to her and was specked with dirt. the T-shirt became transparent and revealed a bikini bathing suit. Laughing, they hoed and spaded and planted.

Connor's garden had a northeastern exposure overlooking the two-mile wide, quarter-mile deep Mission Valley which cut through San Diego. It was slightly more than an acre of land, much of it at a steep angle like an amphitheater overlooking magnificent freeway architectures straddling the sky. The sky was cloudless, with a sort of haze and the yard had the transcendent stillness of being above everything.

John was drenched with sweat when he was done. They packed away empty pots and clodded shovels, showered in the house, and, protected by high walls overgrown with bougainvillea, swam near nude in his pool. The shirt was by now translucent, revealing expansive brown aureoles.

They dried off and entered the living room. There, John put on slow dance music amid mingled aromas of lemon blossoms and jasmine. The house throbbed with music. She stepped expectantly close to him and put her arms around his neck. Declining her face—cheeks flushed, eyes half closed—she sought his mouth with hers. His arms slipped around her. At 6'2", she was taller than he. There was a thing they had discovered together. A naked man dancing with a naked woman taller than he can dance together while sexually joined. Their passion was aroused. Her every movement was graceful. Slowly, she moved one leg slightly apart and grasped his erect penis. She was soaked for him and he slipped in easily. She shuddered, arms on his shoulders and head arched back. They swayed slowly together. As she moved with him, he marveled at her big body's china-lightness, the ease with which he could lead and she followed, just like at a high school dance. She lifted each ankle in turn, in a swaying motion, and moaned. He felt the firm weight of her breasts against his chest. Her aureoles were hard, almost scratchy, and he had only to raise his hand and guide a willing nipple to his lips. It was exquisite torture, a contest to see who could last the longest in this breathless state before pulling the other on the floor.

He felt Lollie grasp his head against her cheek, thought her knees wobbled...He moaned. Gently, without disengaging, he guided her down onto the floor. He grasped her by her buttocks, as her heels rested on his shoulders. He rocked hard while she bit her knuckles. They rose to an explosion of pleasure.

The doorbell rang insistently. John, belting his bathrobe, found a man and woman at his front door. The man, dressed in a well-pressed tan suit, showed a gold badge. "Detective Sergeant Barnes, SDPD. How are you, Mr. Connor?" He was a light-complexioned black man, slim, with short flat-topped hair and the most startling hazel eyes like maple syrup in autumn sunlight. "The young lady with me is Detective Martha Yee."

Martha Yee smiled with chiclet teeth. Her mascara eyes squinched into equal signs. Her oval face had a butterscotch complexion and her cheeks dimpled. "How do you do, Mr. Connor?" She had a custard cup of rich black hair that feathered when she moved her head. Her inflection was multi-generation American. She wore a white blouse, dark pants with knife-sharp creases, and black flats.

Barnes said: "You are Mr. Connor of Ajanian's, right?"

"Yes?"

"I wonder if you would be helpful. It's about a homicide."

"A homicide! Come in."

"Thanks." They stayed near the door, respecting his privacy. "There was a shoot-out over a drug deal yesterday. One of the bodies had no ID, just a gold ring in his sock. The ring had a yellow diamond in it, worth a lot. Ajanian was graved inside. We checked and Mr. Ajanian says according to the records you sold the ring a few days ago. Do you remember?"

Dread panged in John's innards. "Yes. A tall woman named, let's see...Jana...Jana Andrews bought them."

"We got that name. The credit card turned out to be stolen, so that's a dead end. What can you tell us about this woman?"

"She said she was a model in New York City while I was one there also. We were supposedly in a watch ad together."

Lollie leaned into the room and waved a perfunctory goodbye to John. "See you soon." Now why was she sneaking out the back. *Chicken-chips*, he mouthed at her with a mock frown.

"Sorry we intruded," Barnes remarked. Martha Yee's gaze followed Lollie musingly, then her coal eyes, in sliced-nectarine eyelids, turned chilly attention on John.

"No problem," John told Barnes. He told them of his years' background as a male model, his recent encounter with Jana Andrews, her claim of having known him, and his lack of recall.

Barnes said. "What we are after is who ordered this little drug battle. We might catch a drug lord or two. First problem, we don't know who the dead man was. Young guy, maybe thirty. Clean looking, but he had tracks. Heroin addict, but not your shooting gallery stiff. If he had a wallet, it was taken. Without ID, it's real hard. He looked clean-cut but strung out. Second problem, we don't know the woman who bought the ring. A strange case. Suppose you describe this woman as best you can."

14 . Hamilton, Conn.

Blue visited the pastor of Sacred Heart Church, a complex of massive century-old brownstone buildings in a field of snow. There were two Catholic parishes, Sacred Heart and Good Shepherd, at opposite ends of town.

Father Pollack led her into his book-lined office and closed the door. He was in his late fifties, white-haired, with a soft strong hands, a wide-shouldered, flat-stomached physique, and a narrow, severe face. His dark eyes were sensitive and grave. He sat behind a glass-topped desk, Blue in a high-backed wood chair.

He folded his hands near a well-thumbed breviary. No mistaking this guy, Blue thought, he was a priest from the old school, the kind she remembered from her own parochial school days. "What can I do to help you, Miss Humboldt?"

"Just a quiet check," she said, displaying her wallet ID to a wary closing of his eyes. "I'm with DEA, in Hamilton as part of a drug investigation that ended in a murder." Vivid pictures flashed before her eyes. Olvera. Guzman.

"You were asking about one of my assistant pastors, Father Travignan."

"Yes. We ran a national agency check on him. He has a history of drug involvement. He was on probation 'til recently."

"Has he done something?"

"I'm sure he hasn't. I'm sorry, I'm grasping at straws." For a moment she thought he was going to tell her to leave it alone, get out of his study. He was silent for some long moments, during which time the clock in his bookcase ticked loudly. Blue swallowed hard. At last, he looked down at his folded hands. "Well," he said clearing his throat, "I must tell you that I am not surprised."

"You're not?" She was.

He looked sad. "What you say is true. I try to work closely with my priests. We are a very large parish, and it's hard to keep tabs. Joe is a charming man, and he's made friends here. He worked hard, he was clean, he was happy."

"Was?"

"I misspoke. I really can't tell you anything."

"Seal of the Confessional?" Grammar school memories.

"You are Catholic. You understand. I can't give you any information because I'd be damned to hell for all eternity."

She rose. "Thanks, Father. You kind of wanted me to come here so you could question me. That's okay."

He reddened. "I didn't quite see it that way. Yes, I'd appreciate any information you can give me." He extended a hand.

She shook his hand. "I'd like to speak with him. Where is he?"

Pollack phoned someone. "Have Father Joe call me immediately please." His face darkened. "What? Again?" He hung up. "That was the duty secretary. Joe's in Akron again, seeing his parents. Lots of trips lately." He picked up again. "Mario, please get me Father Joe's home in Akron." They waited. The phone rang through, and Pollack picked up. "Hello, Mrs. Travignan, Father Pollack. How are you. That's good. Fine, fine..."

Minutes later, Father Pollack hung up. "They haven't seen him in six months."

Shadows fell long on snowy hills, and winds blew cold between bare black trees. Blue spoke with drivers of the Martin Limousine Service at the town rail terminal.

Cappy was a small Greek-American nuzzling a steaming coffee cup. Blue joined him for coffee as he waited outside the Desiree Diner for his scheduled 5 p.m. drive to JFK on Long Island. Cappy had fiery dark eyes and a heavy beard shadow. "Yeah, as time goes on you see the repeat customers. Same business people, week in week out. Yes, I know Father Joe. Sure. He travels quite a bit lately. Nice guy if you ask me. Takes the limo mostly Friday afternoons for the weekend flight out."

"Goes to Akron?" Blue asked.

"Well I don't know about that," Cappy said. "Sometimes it's Akron, sometimes it's San Diego. I see the tags on his luggage. He went to JFK a couple of days ago. I don't ask no questions, hell, why should I? Why do these religion guys take all that stuff so seriously. Me, I'm an atheist. That's right, I don't believe in no God." Cappy sipped his coffee and regarded her with some intensity. "Honey, we're here and we're gone. But we're here and we gotta play the game. I gotta make a living. I don't say nothing. I watch people come and go. He ain't the only one I wonder about, I'll tell you that."

"What do you mean?"

Cappy took on a try-to-figure-me-out look. "Them priests is traveling all the time."

"So?" His attempted cleverness annoyed her.

"Well now, there's trips and then there's trips, right?" He waggled a finger. "I had a guy change clothes right in the back of my cab."

"Sounds kinky."

"This guy had a lot to drink. I picked him up at JFK one night, oh quite a while ago. He was dressed like some bar stud, you know, shirt open down the front, gold medallion. Next thing I know, he's decked out in black, with a roman collar."

"Got a name?" She waved a fifty dollar bill.

"Monsignor Gordon." The bill blurred into Cappy's pocket.

"Where does Gordon go?" Another fifty, last cash on hand.

"He flies to San Diego a lot. Usually he tears the tags off his suitcases, but once in a while he's too bombed and forgets."

"Do you think he and Father Joe know each other?"

"I've never seen them together."

Then she remembered Frog's on the BPR. But I have.

15 · Hamilton, Conn.

Eddie opened the door and whistled softly. "Blue, is this really you?" She smiled at the compliment. The bluish street lights illumined the snow and her eyes and her teeth. Her mahogany loafers crunched softly on ice by the doorway. She wore dark hose, a gray wool skirt, and a dark wool overcoat with cream scarf. Her dark hair peeked from a cream wool cap. Her lips and eyes sparkled with light make-up. "Do I get to come in?"

"Wh-Yes, I'm sorry, I was just looking at you. My God, Blue, I had no idea. You're the Girl Next Door."

"When I dress up. People have told me that." She stepped in and peeled off her overclothes. She wore a plain white linen blouse with peaches and green leaves on a brown twig embroidered over the heart. Her watch, her ring, her necklace, were gold. "I can be disgustingly middle class, Eddie."

Eddie's wife Innocenta was a heavy girl with a beautiful face. They had three small children and dinner was noodles almondine with glazed chicken breasts. Innee loved to cook. She also had a contract at a local gift shop to produce ceramics.

The huge house, anno 1890, had high ceilings and a central brick fireplace that Eddie liked to keep in elm or oak logs. Snow might pile outside, but Eddie kept the entire house heated.

The Stosik children were blond-haired and dark-eyed, from their Polish-Italian heritage. There were three, ranging from one to four, solid, happy kids that blared constantly for attention.

"Blue. A nickname?" Innee asked, lifting a glass of Chianti. Jealousy dripped from her little rouged lips. Her eyes were dark and poisonous. Eddie seemed not to notice.

"Yes. I play keyboard. Sometimes. You know, rock music. Blues. "Awkward.

Little Arthur bellowed, turning purple, and Innie directed a curved plastic spoon dripping with Gerber's at his mouth.

They all laughed. Blue still detected the jealousy in Innie's eyes. This woman, Blue decided, is capable of Rage. No wonder Eddie seemed so cowed.

16 · Hamilton, Conn.

Vincent Brady, a.k.a. Vincent Gordon, canceled several appointments. He did stop by to see Mrs. Dearborn and then Mrs. O'Flannery, two elderly ladies who had recently lost their husbands and were bed-ridden. He administered Confession and Communion, collected their wills leaving a total of $700,303 to the church in Vincent's name, and drove to the bank. When he left the bank, he had nearly four million in there.

He stopped at a phone booth by the town green. Using Hugh Stone's credit card, he called the number Jana Andrews had given. In Chicago, an answering service took his number. Shortly, the phone in the park rang. Vincent lifted the receiver. "Hello?"

"Mr. Brady, Jana Andrews. How are you?"

"Miss Andrews. you are a very charming person. I'm going to be on a sales trip, and I thought we could touch base."

"You are a charmer, aren't you? I'm pretty tied up but I'd love to make some time for us. What did you have in mind?"

"I was going to leave that up to you. I'm all over the country in my computer business. Where can we meet?"

"How about my neck of the woods?"

Next day, as he trudged through the miserable slush in Chicago, he briefly thought about turning Hugh Stone in to the police before disappearing forever from the Catholic Church. He dismissed the thought; such a radical move scared him. But could he continue to suffer silently while Hugh tightened the screws? A moment of reckoning had to be near at hand.

Jana Andrews ran toward him with a mischievous smile of recognition. She seemed, somehow, more distant, less lurid than in Palm Springs. She deflected his passionate kiss with a brief, hard hug around the shoulders and a peck on the lips.

"Were you waiting long?" she asked breathlessly, pulling off her gloves and pushing back the wool cap holding her thick hair. Her cheeks were flushed from the cold, her lips chapped.

"I just got here. Hungry?"

"I could eat a horse."

He took her to Faw Ming in the Loop. She let him take her coat and scarf. The maitre d'hotel escorted them to a table. He recalled her rough manner in Palm Springs. She was brusque, bright like a sunny but freezing Chicago winter's day.

"Let's look at this menu," she said. "Aren't you hungry?"

"I'm starving," he said, staring at her. For you. She was exquisite. He picked up the burgundy leather- bound menu with its gold tassel. The menu was predictable. He put his hand over hers—it was cold—and after a minute she pulled her hand away. A young Chinese woman took their order for aperitifs. Vincent ordered a martini. Jana surprised him by ordering the same.

"So what have you been up to?" she asked. Her eyes were rarely on him. They looked down as she fussed with her table setting. They looked away at people at other tables. When they met his, they seemed cold and impatient. He remembered she had insinuated she would play hard to get. "I've sold a contract recently, but I'm thinking of backing out."

"What kind of contract?"

"Three million dollars of software. To a foreign company."

"Sounds very impressive, Vincent."

"The deal might compromise our national interest." He had been reading a lot of business magazines lately. A couple million dollars in the bank made one. The waiter arrived. Vincent ordered Mu Shu Pork. "Is that good?" she asked Vincent, who nodded (why, he thought, would I order it if it weren't?). "I'll have the same," she said. The waiter filled their little tea cups, bowed, and left.

The martinis arrived. Vincent and Jana clinked glasses in a toast. She downed hers. He finished his in slow gulps. She waved for another. She opened a few buttons on her vest. Her face was flushed, and she wriggled on her seat. She smiled and gave him a look. He was dazzled to his toes. He took her hand and kissed her fingers one by one. She let him hold her hand on the table until the food and more martinis arrived.

"I'm starved," she said. "I've been dieting."

"You broke your diet for me? I'm touched."

She laughed out loud. "You bad man." When the Chinese girl passed, Jana ordered a third pair of martinis.

"Very good food," Vincent commented. Her knee brushed against his. They ate in silence. Drank the second martinis. "I should eat more Chinese food," she pronounced. "I think I'll come here more often. Do you think you'll come by more often, Vincent?"

"Of course." Her knee was resting against his now, and her voice was slurry. "Do you mean Chicago, or this restaurant, or to see you?"

She gleamed. "All three, of course."

"I would be pleased." The small talk puzzled him. He wondered if this woman were okay in the head. Was she an air head? So many people were; it was the reason he'd been able to accomplish what he had. He revisited certain thoughts he had had and calculated whether or not she would make a good wife. After all, he was a millionaire, unless Stone could get the money away from him. In any case, he was lonely and she would do at least for a while, if she did not drive him crazy first. "Would you like to visit me sometime? Say for a weekend? I have a lovely home in San Diego."

She pushed her empty plate away and leaned forward, laying her hands over one another. "That sounds very nice. How many places do you live, Vincent? You never did tell me."

"Well, I have houses in New York and San Diego. Or, I did. I'm just thinking of retiring and moving to someplace really warm. Like one of the Mexican resorts. Or Brazil."

She rested her hand on his forearm. "I've had thoughts of settling in Palm Springs, but my business keeps me here."

"Your business...you mentioned that when we met. You didn't want to tell me. You said something about politics."

She placed a finger on his lips. "I'll tell you all about it in due time. Look, why don't we pay and take in a little bit of that art gallery before I have to run."

"I was hoping we could spend the afternoon. Have dinner."

He left fifty dollars and walked her out.

"I'd like to," she said bundling up against the cold, "but I have several commitments. I'm a busy person, like yourself."

He pulled her close in front of the restaurant and their lips met. He smelled her gin and felt the wax on her lips. Her tongue darted out and briefly touched his. He found it hard to believe that she'd had him fly all this distance just to have lunch. Her capriciousness was monumental, but he was ready to excuse it because he longed, no, he was dying, to bed her.

They wandered arm in arm through the art gallery, wondering at huge polychrome canvases that seemed to float under high ceilings. She bent close to read several of the plaques. He had eyes only for her. They came to a gray room in a far wing of the upper floor. Lacquer and pottery items glowed darkly on glass shelves. Through the closed double windows, street noises and wan cheerless light seeped in. They were alone. Vincent stepped close and embraced her. His mouth sought hers passionately while his hands roughly grasped her belly, her breasts. They heard approaching footsteps and she shoved him away so roughly it hurt his collarbones. He felt hurt, in body and soul.

"Not here, darling. Not now." Two well-dressed women entered the room and studied each pottery item minutely. Jana took Vincent's hand and led him briskly downstairs and out onto the sidewalk. "We can't be seen petting in public," she said firmly. For an instant, her hand stole around his head, and she kissed his cheek lovingly. Then her brusqueness returned. "You just turn me on, Vincent. You ought to have more self-control. Be a gentleman."

Restored, healed, penitent, he took her hands. "Jana, come spend a weekend with me? Alone? Just you and me?"

"Soon, darling." She got a faraway look. "Call me, Vincent, I mean it. And thanks for lunch." She blew him a kiss and walked away. He watched her tall figure recede in long strides among the jostling crowds. He felt cheated. But he knew he would fly here a thousand times for this.

17 · Hamilton, Conn.

In the morning, Blue stopped by the limo office. Cappy was on duty. "Hey!" he greeted her like an old friend, offered coffee, but she waved a fifty. "Cappy, have you seen Father Joe recently?"

"I drove Father Joe to JFK day before yesterday."

"Thanks."

She rushed to the apartment for lunch. Spooning hot soup and crackers she called Tomasi. She explained, adding "Can I get some help over here?"

"Not yet, Humboldt. Sorry, you're the whole budget for now. Keep slugging away."

Next she called the Church of the Good Shepherd and asked for Monsignor Gordon. A secretary said: "I'm sorry, the Monsignor is away on travel. Can Father Tiernan help you?"

"No thanks. I'll call again."

She called Vito. "Can you check old passenger manifests for me at JFK?" A while later, he called back. "Fry, what are you doing? Yes, there was a Joe Travignan on the afternoon plane to San Diego two days ago. Keep up the—" She hung up.

Blue met Eddie by the town green at four, when it was already starting to get dark. The white steepled Congregationalist Church's bells were chiming lightly. School children cried out in high voices as they played and slid around on an icy spot. The air smelled of snow. He had a grin as he got out of his car. She could feel something coming. She hoped it wouldn't turn her off too much. But no time now.

"Hello, Eddie." She lit a Chesterfield in the warm, dry car. "Time for a reality check. I want to know about your friend Father Joe."

His grin disappeared. "What about him?"

"He's a junkie, right?"

In the bluish glowering twilight, Eddie looked inscrutable. "He's a sick man, so just leave him alone."

"I'll bet money, Eddie, that he's bingeing. He takes trips to San Diego. You know who else takes trips to San Diego? His buddy the Monsignor. What do you know about Gordon?"

"Blue, you're stirring up a lot of stuff here."

"All I want is a trail to my drug dealers. I wasn't looking for two laurel and hardy priests, but now that I got 'em I'm not letting go until I see bottom."

Eddie banged his fist on the dashboard.

"This may be Smalltown USA but you can't cover forever."

"I know," Eddie said softly. "I know."

"Where is Joe getting his next fix? Are we going to be there to catch the guy who sells to him? Most importantly for me, is he getting his stuff from the same outfit that popped Guzman? That's what I want to know."

"I don't know. He's my friend, he's a good guy, he's an asshole in over his ears, and I feel sorry for him, okay?"

"People die because of drugs. We're cops, remember? We're supposed to save people from drugs. Or have you forgotten?"

Eddie lit a cigarette.

"It's getting cold," Blue said. With the car engine and heater off, the interior was quickly assuming an Arctic climate. "Brrr, Eddie, can't we go have coffee somewhere?"

"Yeah, I'm freezing my bunzos." They went to a fast food place and had burgers, fries, and cokes. They had to ask for ketchup, and were reluctantly handed little plastic squeeze containers. Eddie asked for salt. "That's real great for your blood pressure," Blue said.

"What are you, my mother?"

"Eddie, don't be a boy. Here, here's some extra salt. Put it all over everything."

"I don't know that anyone can help Joe and that hurts."

"So you're not only pissed off, you're hurt. Well that makes sense. I'm sorry."

"Just eat your fries, Blue."

She thought about Vito. She could hear his voice: That's marriage. This is love. Eddie had not mentioned a word about dinner the other night, and she wasn't going to.

She offered to pay, but he said the town would pick up the tab. He touched her hands twice. He was working up to something. It made her uneasy. Partly because she liked him a lot. He was developing a crush on her, she could tell.

She rose. "Come on, let's cruise by Father Joe's place. If he's in maybe we can talk with him."

A light snow was falling when they drove past the Sacred Heart church. Eddie appeared quiet, as though he were deliberating. He seemed reluctant. Finally, resolutely, he pulled over. "All right then, C'mon, let's stop in and say hello. I'm sure he's in there reading his Bible or something."

They trudged through the fluff of fresh snow. Their footsteps were muffled. Breathy steam poured around their ears.

Eddie rapped on the window, the door. "Joe? You in there? It's Eddie." No answer.

Eddie loosened his automatic. "Joe?" The door stood partway open. There was a slight crash inside.

Eddie kicked the door open and presented his weapon. A tall, elderly stranger inside raised his hands. An armful of files slipped and crashed and fanned on the floor. He had a cool, firm voice. "Don't shoot. I'm a priest."

18 · Hamilton, Conn.

Monsignor Vincent Gordon stepped out of the rectory into a cold, clear night. A light scent of snow lay in the air, and a few hard crystalline shreds of white fell here and there, but it was really too cold for a heavy fall. His heavy black shoes crunched on frozen snow as he hastened across the barren grounds of the Church of the Good Shepherd. He was muffled in a scarf and heavy overcoat. A banner of steam trailed from his mouth, lightly scented with scotch.

He drove to the park and with the special credit card returned Hugh's urgent call. Hugh sounded rattled but steely: "Vincent, I'll need your deposit within three days. This is it, man, the clock is ticking. We are to the tenth day, and my friend south of the border is getting frantic."

Vincent bit his lip. Pleading with Hugh Stone would be the wrong move, he knew since the Guzman killing. "I'm getting it together, Hugh. This is going to be the big payoff."

"Vincent, you sound positive. That pleases me very much. Make the deposit as agreed. I'll call you day by day if need be."

Vincent had a heavy feeling in his gut. A thousand times, he kicked himself mentally for getting into this deal. All because of Travignan! Because I am lonely, I sought a friend. Who turns out to have a habit, needs money, gets me involved with drug dealers. Like a fool he had helped Joe, given him money, as a friend. Guzman and the man from out of town, Hugh Stone, had come to visit one day. How had they learned about him? Joe, no doubt. You could twist a weak soul like a sponge. Hugh had threatened, cajoled, finally sold Vincent on this wonderful opportunity to double his money. Then the bust. That fool cop had let Travignan get away. Then Guzman gets murdered in broad daylight and I see what these people really are. Now I am in over my head and Hugh will not let me go. If I rat on him, he rats on me and we are both finished.

And where was Joe anyway? Vincent drove aimlessly, gliding on enigmatic back roads. The car heater kept him warm and dry. From the glove compartment, he nipped at a half-pint hip flask of Canadian Club. He smoked a cigarette, puffing nervously and rapidly. He drove past Travignan's apartment once, twice...no sign of his lamentable friend. It was down to three days then. Time to face destiny, move on.

Stay, Angel.

Parked in the shadows, with the engine running quietly and the window slightly open, he nipped at the whiskey. Father Joe had been his friend, the only person he could confide in because they each shared a secret that threatened to devour them. He pictured Joe: Youthful face, curly hair, alert slightly crazy green eyes. Strumming that guitar. Confessing about his addiction, his hopelessness. Vincent in turn had confessed a little bit about his failings. Had been downhill from there. Money. The root of all evil. Vincent sipped again, coughing at the sting. Travignan. Wasn't really his fault either. Was victim. All victims, dammit. No fault. Like insurance. But Joe, with his boyish enthusiasm. Guitar music. Holy, holy, holy. Ah, such delightful...Swings between depression and elation. Get help...God, Joe, where are you when I need you? We can get out of this together. Good pal, I've got three million buckaroos. Can get you all help y'need. Trust old M'signor Gor'n. Vincent realized he must have dozed off. His head felt woollen and his tongue seemed swollen in an ill-tasting mouth. He slipped the empty bottle out the crack in the window. Opened the window to get air. And saw, in the white snow bowl that was spread before him, the grounds of Sacred Heart Parish, a commotion going on in Joe's apartment.

First he thought it was Joe leading a man and a boy toward the rectory. Then he realized that the man he had thought was Joe was an older man, a priest perhaps. And the boy was a woman, judging from the slightly wider hips and fuller jeans rear end. Vincent coasted along, trying to get a better look without being obvious. They stopped and knocked at the rectory door. It was a bust. He could smell it. Another nail in the coffin of Monsignor Gordon. He accelerated and drove past. He must come up with a plan. And angrily he realized that all the while she had been standing there mocking him, spitting at him, projectile vomiting pints of fire, the Angel of Death.

19. Hamilton, Conn.

Eddie Stosik and Miss Humboldt," Father Pollack said at the rectory door. "What are you doing here at this hour?"

"Found this man in Father Joe's apartment," Eddie said.

Pollack seemed shocked: "Why, it's Father Binder." Binder cleared his throat. "Would you kindly tell this gentleman to put his gun away?"

They trooped into the spacious rectory parlor amid the stale, cold aroma of some evening affair, perhaps a potluck. "Ahem!" said a man.

Eddie jumped. "Chief!" A portly white-haired man in hunting flannels stepped from the kitchen, stirring hot milk and honey. "Blue, meet Chief Francis Murphy, my boss."

Murphy shook her hand. "I know about you, my dear." She wondered if that was good or bad.

Binder said, "I'm an accounting prof at Fairfield U."

"A Jesuit," Pollack muttered under his breath.

"Every little while, I get an unusual auditing job."

"We're onto more than debits tonight," Murphy said.

"We all are concerned," Pollack said, "with about three thousand dollars missing from the roof repair fund, which is one thing, but also with Father Joseph Travignan's eternal soul."

The matter of Jana and the diamond ring troubled John Connor for some reason at a deep level. He called Marcia Jersey at Scripps Institute. Another incomplete relationship, a luscious fruit, an orange with a bite out of it. "Joh-n." She dwelt upon that syllable.

He heard her stop whatever she was doing and settle back in her chair. The starchy sleeve of her lab coat rasped against her phone. "I was just thin-king about you-u."

"Nothing bad, I hope."

"I don't know. You're trouble." She laughed. "What's up?"

"What are you doing for lunch?"

"I was going to feed some hungry porpoises. For me there's half a chicken salad sandwich in the refrigerator. Don't tell me you were going to break the silence and offer to take me to lunch. My heart, you know."

"Your heart is as strong as hearts can be, and I can do better than that half sandwich, if the porpoises let you go."

"Pick me up in an hour."

It was one of the things he liked about her. If she could, she would. If she couldn't, she said so and that was all. They saw each other every two or three weeks. By the time he got there, she was waiting on the sidewalk near the display tidal pool. She had set aside the lab coat and put on make-up. A brunette, thirtyish, straight hair, hazel eyes, and a light tan. Healthy. Your California beach girl. And your Eastern preppy. She wore sandals, jeans, and a crisp white shirt. She had what looked like a gym bag.

"Are we going to the gym?" he asked, easing into traffic. The scents of eucalyptus and sea water tinged the air.

Dr. Marcia Jersey, Ph.D., had a dare-me look. "I'm simply prepared, is all. We have a choice. The quick lunch at Grady's, or the leisurely afternoon at La Jolla Shores. Take your pick."

He laughed. "Marcia, you amaze me. I thought I could squeeze a miserable half hour out of you, away from your fish."

"Mammals."

"To me they're all fish if they're from the ocean."

"Then surfers would be fish."

"Marcia, it never fails. That's why I called you in my hour of need. I don't know anybody more rational than you."

"I brought my swim suit and the badminton gear."

They bought broiled skinless chicken breasts, cole slaw, and beer at a deli. Within a half hour they were sweating on the hot beach sand, chasing the birdie. John felt the welcome pulling in his muscles, the happy strain on his inwardness, the productive outpouring, as he worked to keep up. She was competitive and a head shorter than he, but a dervish in her skimpy white bikini. Hard solid leg muscles pumping, tight butt, she flashed back and forth on her side of the net. Her wiry arms and flat abs rippled. She kept batting the damn thing back down his throat. She had her hair tied back in a pony tail.

"This is what you need," she mocked.

"You," he, "are," said, "going," puffing, "to kill me."

"You're right," she exulted, smashing the birdie over the net with a steel-spring leap that attracted onlookers. Falling down, John told them: "She plays with the Western USA Champions." Marcia sat on his stomach facing him. "Are you going to develop a paunch as you head for middle age? Huh?"

Horrified, he touched his stomach under the V of her bikini between brown thighs. All his life, he had been favored with a metabolism that burned calories like a furnace. Never had there been jelly to be kneaded there. She swatted him. "Silly. You have a washboard stomach. Come on, let's eat."

There was a wind. Small bits of sand flew up, stinging their cheeks, as they ate. He felt good with her, and whole. But it was not the big wrap-around, love forever. Marcia had her career. She was wonderful at moments like this. Had she been large-breasted, he might (subconsciously, in male mammo-mythology) have understood it as some sort of maternal nurturing. But she had the small swellings of the fat-free athlete, and plain nipples, just afterthoughts really.

It was her personality. She was sure. She was secure. You could lie on the sand and absorb her sureness. That was the real wrap-around about Marcia Jersey. She had a fundamental kindness and decency, an answer for every woe. A word from her, matter of fact, and you forgot your problem, your question. Had Marcia been God, it would have been a kinder universe. What a mother she would make, but she had her career. They had talked about these things. With Marcia you could talk. Nothing was too obscure or unreasonable. You could bare your soul. Whatever unmentionable ground you had trodden in your darkest thoughts, Marcia had been there and could shed light on your every sodden footstep. He told her about Jana and the police.

"Honey," she said as they lay side by side on their backs, "it's not the woman. She's two- dimensional. Why, you have no idea who she even is. It's the past she has stirred up, the things you left behind."

He folded his hands on his belly and looked into the clear sky past her flat stomach and freckled neck. "Why do I keep thinking it's all settled, when it keeps stirring up?"

She brushed her hand lightly and repeatedly over his forehead. "It never goes away. Just unclench, let it go. Let the mountains go back to being mole hills."

"I forgot. I should be telling myself that."

"You started a new life when you left New York. You have a right to your new life. You can make the old stuff go away. Just remember the mountains are really mole hills."

That afternoon, they went to his house and made love. Making love with Marcia was a flat, unimaginative matter. Her orgasm was mechanical and predictable. She was very satisfied and showered him with kisses. He lay in bed, watching the palm fronds brush against the door while she made iced tea. Remembering the touch of her skin and her soul, he felt very satisfied also.

They dove into the pool and batted a beach ball around. Even at that, Marcia was competitive. One time, he slammed the ball home. Thought he'd hurt her. It smashed against her lean body. She squealed.

"Did I hurt you?"

She slammed it into his face. "Don't be a sap, Johnno!" Marcia wore a bathing cap. Naked and wet, with her hair back, her face looked almost masculine. Naturally, she dove off the board more times and farther than he. With her, there were only answers. He wondered if she had questions. In the end, he relaxed and let her answers fill him and drive off his questions.

Detective Sergeant Lloyd Barnes and Detective Martha Yee called toward evening. John and Marcia were taking a bubble bath in his large circular tub. They sprawled backwards in the steamy water, legs tangled, hands twined while a Mozart symphony made its little darting advances and coy retreats around them.

"Oh, hello again," he said at the door.

Barnes and Yee gaped. Marcia, in John's terrycloth robe, hair turbaned in a towel, set the table and John checked the roast in the oven, adding a little water and a dash of Maggi.

Barnes had a sympathetic face, appropriately grave, and clear hazel eyes. "Sorry to disturb you." He looked puzzled seeing Marcia, probably remembering Lollie.

Miss Yee's dimpled citron smile (eyes like the slits in walnut shells, lips like red ink squiggles) grew baffled at the sight of Marcia Jersey.

"I'll make coffee and you talk," Marcia offered. Miss Yee's eyes, opaque like dark forest honey, followed Marcia's narrow, rotating gluteal muscles.

"Well, Mr. Connor," Barnes said as they all sat in the living room, "we haven't located Jana Andrews yet. Detective Yee is principal investigator so—carry the ball."

Detective Yee was precise and professional. "Mr. Connor, about those old ads. We brought a stack and we'd like you to look through them. How about after dinner? I'll call you tomorrow." She opened a folder. Old oyster ads spilled out, cut from yellowing magazines. Cars, blondes, beaches, rings, watches, all the temptations luring with youth and skin. "These are from seven or eight years ago," Detective Yee said.

She held one up for John to examine. For a moment all five women draped around him looked alike. Then he pointed. "This one." Same wiggly lips, mysterious eyes, steely sultry look, years younger.

Detective Yee said: "We checked with the watch company. Got the run-around. They say they use models from a dozen agencies or more. They gave us some agency names. We checked with NYPD and they came up with zilch."

"I think she mentioned the Dolly Agency."

"We checked them out. No record of ever having contracted a Jana Andrews."

"Dead end?"

"For now."

After the detectives had left, John and Marcia listened to the evening news. Then they had a beer apiece and watched rock videos. Marcia wrapped a wiry arm around his head. "Come on, Johnno, wild man, oppressor, mad gorilla. Ball me."

The full moon shed delicate light on the fantastic garden, like water from a sprinkling can.

Marcia giggled, and he hunted her down with his nose and hands, pinning her steely wrists (she let him) and forcing her lips against his. "Now what?" he asked, seeing her expression.

She wrapped her arms around him. "That Yee girl." She flicked the tip of her tongue in his ear.

"You were mad about something. You didn't say a word. I saw your face." He touched a hard nipple, a small breast.

"No, silly. I wasn't mad, just avoiding. She got the hots for me." John sat back stunned. Marcia laughed and wrapped herself around his head. "You won't get anywhere with her."

Trust Marcia to know something like that.

21 · Hamilton, Conn.

The atmosphere in the rectory had grown still. "A half million dollars?" Father Pollack echoed. "Travignan's soul?"

"I wanted to settle this without police help," Binder said.

"I am appalled," Chief Murphy said.

Binder said: "There is someone else in with Joe Travignan."

"Who?" they all asked at once.

"I have a suspicion and I am checking it out."

"You'd better tell me," Chief Murphy said.

"I can't. A beautiful woman came to me under the Confessional Seal, told about a shocking series of scams. I am still checking things out. I'll need a few more days. I can't say anything until I'm certain. But there may be hell to pay with older parishioners who give their life's earnings."

Blue took Binder out of earshot. "Is it Monsignor Gordon?"

"Lady, you could pull out my fingernails by the roots and I would not venture any more information until I am absolutely sure who, what, and how much." He waggled a finger. "And you keep your lip zipped for now, young lady!"

Eddie Stosik made his move that evening, and caught Blue off guard. If the slight flirtation could be called a move. They were sitting in the living room of Blue's apartment having hot chocolate. A light rain had fallen, leaving the snow covered with a thin sheet of ice. Temperatures were dropping again.

"This place is really starting to feel like You," Eddie commented, looking around at the apartment.

"Stop it," she protested feeling embarrassed. Her father's old Army duffel bag lay half-emptied on the carpet, a cornucopia spilling forth black and red panties, heavy wool socks, a stuffed bear, paperbacks, a carton of Chesterfields, and more. Cardboard boxes sat scattered. Paper bags stood half-folded in the corner by the fridge waiting one by one to be garbage bags. "I'm working on it in my spare time," Blue said.

Eddie sat on the floor and fiddled with her portable stereo. They chattered for a while. Then he said: "My wife is jealous no matter what I do. She thinks you and I are having a fling." He reached for her leg as she passed. She ignored his hand and went to the couch. Eddie followed, sitting at the other end of the couch. "I might as well have a hot fling."

"You don't have a mistress?"

"No. It occurs to me once in a while, but I keep saying naw, not worth the trouble."

"I don't think you're the type, Eddie. You have character." She thought of Vito. "You don't have the balls." She said this kindly, in a complimentary tone.

"Blue, you might be the exception."

She touched his arm. "Eddie, I like you as a friend. Don't you dare ever make a pass at me or I'll never speak with you again as long as I live."

He swallowed. "Blue..."

She rose. "You're a red-blooded American male. You're normal. The answer is NO." She locked herself into the bathroom with Vanity Fair. When she opened the door, he was gone. Wanting to say goodnight, she followed a chastened Eddie, leaving, in the car with motor running and windows defrosted. "Mmm," she said sticking her head in, "it's nice and toasty."

"Yes, it was kind of frosty there a little while ago."

It was cold and she got in. "You're a nice guy, Eddie. We'll be friends. You'll find yourself a mistress one of these days and find out how much trouble it will cause and then you'll have it out of your system." They talked for a few more minutes. Then he walked her to the outer hall. There, in the dusky chill, suddenly they embraced. With their heavy jackets, it was difficult to take hold of one another. Her hands slipped along his jacket, barely feeling the lean strength of his long back. Eddie's powerful arms pressed her toward him, but she could feel his fingers slipping in the nylon surface of her parka. His lips hungrily sought her lips, and she light-headedly leaned her head back as his tongue found hers. Her cap fell off and her hair stuck out. She welcomed the powerful thrust of his body against hers, but desperately pushed him away. She turned her head away, feeling flushed and breathless. The feel of his body was intoxicating. She longed to take him inside and share her bed with him. But she remembered his Innocenta's vicious little red mouth and felt afraid for him. "Eddie, no."

"Dammit," he said softly.

"Eddie, this is a mistake." She was angry at herself as she pushed him away. She opened the outer door. "Go on, get out. Go home to your wife."

He had a stunned, darkened complexion. His eyes were very big and his breathing was massive. "Dammit."

"Eddie, I don't want you to feel hurt but I'm single and I need to be with a single man. Go on. Don't wreck your home over me. Beat it, Eddie. Go on."

He looked genuinely distressed. Surprised at himself. "I don't know what came over me."

"Hormones." She took his hands. "Before I throw you out of here," she said kissing his fingers, "I want you to know you're a nice guy. You may not be a hundred per cent happy with Innie, but think of all the good things you have. Kids, a house, a decent life, a halfway regular sort of job." She touched his nose. "You're a cute guy. Good night, Eddie."

She slammed the door in his face.

Then she stood behind the stale lace curtain, shivering, and watched him stumble in shock across the piled snow to his car. After he had driven away with a radiant look on his face, she wandered upstairs. She drew a hot bubble bath to soak, aroused, with a sensual red candle by the tub.

22 • San Diego

Detective Martha Yee called at nine in the morning. "Mr. Connor, can I see you right away? I think I have some important new information."

They met an hour later on John's brick patio at a table under an umbrella. John had provided a large pitcher of iced tea with fresh cut lemons. Martha Yee was pleasant. She wore a gray skirt that showed off smoothly muscular legs. Black high heeled shoes added height, and carried herself well. She wore a yellow silk blouse that let a hazy daylight through whenever she sat at a certain angle. "Mr. Connor, I have some more clippings here." She showed him one.

John started. It was the old Rolex ad again. Eight years younger, dressed only in swimming trunks and a Rolex Oyster, he was smiling mysteriously, had a glow in his eyes. Like lions climbing an armorial field, three bikini-clad beauties swarmed up his body while eyeing the camera with a squinty, sultry fury. The backdrop was a seashore wreathed in fog and foggy sunlight. There was beaded water on the watch dial, and the picture was so real that you could still, despite the yellowed page borders, almost hear the surf's rocky shuddering.

"I told you, that woman is definitely Jana Andrews."

"Correction," Miss Yee said, "Jane Willoughby. Someone at Rolex sent us this copy from a storeroom collection. The woman you call Jana Andrews is, or was, Jane Willoughby. That information made the Dolly modeling agency's memory come alive. There was a Jane Willoughby, aged twenty at the time, who modeled for Dolly Agency clients. She gave an Ohio address of origin, and the FBI tried to trace that address and found it was bogus. An empty lot that nobody in recorded history has ever built on. Of course the modeling agencies aren't the federal government. They don't do background investigations. Whatever lies this girl told when she was hired, they accepted as gospel."

"Jane Willoughby was using an assumed name?"

"Well, it's a possibility. People who use pseudonyms frequently, even unconsciously, make up a name that somehow sounds like an echo of their real name."

"Jane/Jana," John mused.

"Yes," Martha said. "Let's try another picture."

She laid a glossy blow-up on the table.

"Holy Smoke! That's her again," he exclaimed. "Even with the eyes and all." It was an advertisement for an automobile. Against a velvet-black night sky, filled with sultry clouds illumined by a mysterious full moon, a slender woman stood in a dance-like pose beside an automobile. The automobile door was open and a soft glow emanated. A neon glow, a Gegenschein. The woman wore an expensive coat thrown open at the edges by her movement, arms spread, legs jackknifed as though she were being pulled into the car by an irresistible force. Her lipstick was a red explosive pout. Her cheeks were vermilion, racy, shameless, hollowed by desire. Her eyes glowed deeply from within, a blue neon joined by threads of light to the light coming from the car. An invitation to get in and ride away. A sensual, sexual message. Get in this car and experience sexual satisfaction on some drug-like plane.

"It was never actually used," Martha said. "The archivist says another version was used in which the eyes had not been touched up to look like blue neon. Here is the version that was actually used." Martha placed another glossy on the table. Same picture. Only no neon eyes."

"No mistake," John said. "That's her. That's the woman who bought the ring from me."

23 • Darien, Conn.

Blue and Chief Tomasi met in a diner in Darien, Connecticut, at the New York State border. Amid the clatter of dishes, the aromas of coffee and eggs and bacon and cigarette smoke, Tomasi said: "Miss Humboldt, hindsight is twenty-twenty. I wish we had listened to you about this Father Joe and his trips to San Diego that cabbie told you about." Tomasi had made a special trip to tell her Joe's body had finally been ID'd in San Diego.

"Thank you, Sir."

"Detective Stosik must be taking it hard. I understand they were friends."

"He is."

"Detective Stosik is being sent to coordinate with the San Diego police and to ID the body for the family. Look for clues, tie-ins, whatever. I want you to go with him."

"Wow." Possibilities swirled suddenly: Palm trees, beaches, but, ouch, Eddie, Innie... "Chief, I've been following a hunch. There may be another priest involved with Travignan, a Monsignor Gordon from the other parish in Hamilton." She explained her reasons, adding: "The church and the police know about him, and this Father Binder asked me to cool it while he checks Gordon out."

"Hm," Tomasi said. "He may nail down the paper trail we need. We'll have to make sure the church doesn't squelch it."

"Sure. Boy, California. Sounds exciting."

"It's seventy-two degrees in San Diego today."

"Can I take my swim suit?"

"Why not. Take some vacation days if the situation allows."

"How is old Vito?"

Tomasi laughed. "Same old Vito. He asks about you every day. I remind him he's married."

"Doesn't faze him a bit," they said in unison and laughed.

"By the way, a Maggie called. Wants you to call her."

"Really?" Blue stiffened.

"Vito took the call. Seemed pretty anxious to get a hold of you. Do you owe her some money or something?"

"No."

Tomasi gave Blue a funny look. "Just some crank?"

"Yes, someone who thinks I owe her something."

24 . San Diego

Hettie VanDerVoort, 23, had a small sturdy build, shoulder-length black hair, frecklesome tanned skin, and brown eyes. Johnno had met her months earlier during a party at the beach. Something about her had attracted him, and he had struck up a conversation. That relationship had sort of half-blossomed in the ensuing months. She did not want to be tied down, and he supposed she was just too young for him.

She had called him on a whim this evening, and he met her for a late dinner at a pancake house. There, she shared her dream about winning a surfing championship. John gamely sipped an orange juice and nodded as she spun her fantasies. She sat beside him and played with his leg.

When he pulled up in his driveway, Hettie was right behind him in her convertible yellow VW beetle, top down of course. She looked enthused in her splashy yellow shirt, tight black skirt, and sandals. White earrings shaped like seashells dangled from her earlobes. The VW's radio belted rock music.

John checked the mailbox—empty—and rattled his key ring while locating the house key. Inside, Hettie unbuttoned her shirt. He poured white wine and sat on the couch.

Hettie went to the stereo. She found her station and the house began thumping. She stripped slowly, gyrating in dance. John had dreamed about Hettie recently. In his dream, he had lain asleep under a warm night sky. Two brown eggs had descended from the stars, wide ends downward, and settled on the earth. A night thing had flown over, dropping two pink blossoms that landed on the pointed ends of the eggs. Instantly, the blossoms had turned into nipples and the eggs into breasts, and Hettie had turned onto her side offering an embrace.

"Love me," the real Hettie cried just now. Her tight butt in black skirt rocked to the music. He pulled her close. Her ripe breasts were firm and jutting as the eggs in his dream. Her arms, wrapped around him, were soft and her hunger was strong.

John woke later because Hettie kissed him goodnight and slammed the door on her way out. She had meant for him to sleep sweet dreams (so her husky voice echoed saying) but he was restless and lay half awake on the couch debating whether he should spend the night on the couch or in his bedroom.

Half-awake, he listened to the night sounds after Hettie had left. A car passed, throwing slats of light on the ceiling, cubes and pentangles that mutated and whisked away into the walls. The car stopped.

He heard footsteps. A woman's heels, clicking. They paused on the sidewalk outside. Clicked again, closer. He pricked his ears up. The footsteps were headed closer to his door. They stopped. He sat up on the couch, his heart pounding. Heard a single thumping noise, a rustle of hedges. Then the sound of a car. He jumped to the window as the footsteps clicked rapidly away. Tore open the curtain, looked over dozing bushes at the street. The woman, walking to the waiting car with its thrumming engine, a white Porsche, plate indecipherable in street lighting, looked back and must have noticed movement in his curtains. She stopped a moment, turned toward him.

She was a slim blonde in sunglasses and miniskirt, wearing a leather coat and pillbox hat. As John stood transfixed, a light flashed on the surface of her sunglasses. Was it the alchemy of night lights, maybe a throw-off from some store window? Just for a moment the light on her sunglasses flashed blue neon.

Frozen a second longer, John watched as she walked to the car, her long legs scissoring.

He bolted for the door, running barefoot onto the sidewalk, just in time to watch them roar off. Did not get a look at the license plate.

Rubbing his eyes, he turned to go back into his house. In the wan light seeping from the living room, he saw a thick manila envelope in the hedge by his door. He took it in the house. After drawing a glass of water, he sat and emptied the envelope onto the couch. Out came newspaper clippings, fresh white ones and old yellowed ones. The clippings had ballpoint stars beside pertinent items and were from various newspapers. "Police Raid Call Girl Service," one read. "Drug Raid Nets Six," another read.

John dialed Martha Yee's private phone number.

She answered in a sleepy voice.

"I'm sorry to bother you," he said, "I know it's late, but the weirdest thing has just happened." She said never mind, she'd be right over. "Former Fashion Model Sentenced," a clipping blared as John kept reading. The name Jana Andrews floated up from the newsprint in several places.

Martha Yee, wearing a beige jump suit and deck shoes, arrived within the hour. He offered tea. Martha Yee let the clippings sift through her fingers one by one. "Amazing." The clippings were dated in a broad, scrawling hand, in ballpoint. "And you say a woman with sunglasses left these things?"

"Yes." He described the woman, the Porsche, the sunglasses flashing with blue neon.

Martha held the clippings outspread in her lap. "Somebody has gone to a great deal of trouble to detail Jana Andrews's life from the time she was a model in New York."

"You mean Jane Willoughby."

"Yes. Let's assume for the moment it's the same person. If we arrange these clippings in chronological order, we have a pretty good history of her life. She worked as a model at the Dolly Agency. Here is her picture. And here is the Rolex Oyster shot. There you are, with her hanging on your arm. A year later, here is a gossip column article about her. She is running with a fast set who are into cocaine and designer drugs. She makes a fool of herself at a New Year's Eve party. Next year, another gossip column about her. She is dating Solly Witz, a prominent New York computer genius who is also underwriting her venture in film noir. Next year we have Solly Witz committing suicide in an upstate New York resort hotel after his company goes belly up. A year later again, we have Jana Andrews a.k.a. Jane Willoughby being arrested in Minneapolis, of all places, as part of a porno ring. She is sentenced to a year in a state penitentiary. Next year, we have Jana Andrews a.k.a. Jane Willoughby, again, arrested in Portland, Oregon as a high-priced call girl involved in the downfall of a city councilman... a steady slide down hill. These pictures of her—is that the woman you remember?"

John looked at the fuzzy newsprint pictures. "I could be wrong. Tall woman. Same glamorous look. She would have been ten years younger. Yes and no. It might be her."

Detective Martha Yee ran her fingertips through her glossy black hair. "By the way, the man with the ring? He's a dead priest from Connecticut. He, and your glamor lady here, may be involved with a big drug ring. There are two police officers flying in from Connecticut. One is a police detective, the other a DEA fed. You will probably get to meet them."

25. Connecticut & Vermont

As usual, Father Tiernan was buried in the sports section.

Vincent/Gordon was just buttering a scone.

"Monsignor, what do you think?" Father Tiernan growled. His raw hands thrust the newspaper to one side.

Vincent was startled. "I'm sorry, Father. What did you say?"

"I was saying I think that Maiorano is going to pull Notre Dame out of the hole next season. Lord knows, they need it."

Vincent leaned his head to one side as though considering this valuable information. "I think you've got a point, Father."

Tiernan shook the paper and pulled it back over his face while his coffee got colder and the elderly woman fussed about them in the empty kitchen. "Oh yes, there was a Jesuit in to see me yesterday. He wanted to talk to you too, but you were out."

"A Jesuit?"

"Old fellow from Fairfield. Binder. Professor of Accounting. Sent by the Chancery. Wants to go over our books. I told him I let you handle that stuff."

"Did he say why?"

Tiernan shrugged. "Didn't bother asking. I'm sure you'll talk to him and get it straightened out."

Vincent went to his room. There, he inspected the small suitcase he had packed and hidden under the bed. In it were his keepsakes as well as clothing. There were twenty bank books, for accounts in various cities, under the name Vincent Ulric. There were also a business application with the City of Chicago for a company called CompuGraphiX USA, and his business license. Also, he had a quart of whiskey in the suitcase.

After a day of fruitless planning and worry, toward evening Vincent poured himself a shot and downed it. Then he lit a cigar and sat down in his easy chair. It was dark in the room, even with the reading lamp on. What a miserable little room. He hated this room and the rectory. His thoughts went to Jana Andrews, and he felt a fiery desire. It was more than physical. He felt a lifetime of denial and privation welling up in him. Then he reminded himself—just a little bit longer. He must be patient and careful perhaps another day or two until he had worked out his plan. He thought about reading, and was too agitated. He thought about the Breviary lying on the desk, and laughed nervously to himself. Instead, he turned on CNN and watched without listening. The thought of reading the Breviary stirred him to sickness. He was staying away from that book with a feeling of dread. Actually, not just dread but a feeling of ridiculous irony. He could not contemplate praying at a time like this, and that filled him with an emptiness, a sour, lonely feeling, an anger.

There was a knock on the door, a muffled voice.

Annoyed, he rose to answer. "Yes?"

"Monsignor, forgive me." It was a trim, fiftyish man wearing a ski parka and a wool cap. "My name is Roger Filmore. I'm a new parishioner here in town, and I wanted to introduce myself. They sent me to your apartment. I hope you don't mind."

Vincent put on his fake face. "Come in. Sir, come in. I was just praying, when my stomach growled. It will be dinner time soon." They shook hands. "What line of work are you in, Mr. Filmore?"

Mr. Filmore raised his eyebrows and rolled his eyes in a droll fashion. "Monkey business, Monsignor."

Vincent felt a thrill of unease.

"Mr. Hugh Stone says hi." Filmore's voice was nasty now.

Vincent felt the floor drop away.

"Surprised? Don't worry, Monsignor. Just a friendly visit to remind you that our organization is very efficient. You will receive an excellent return on your dollar, and we look forward to doing return business with you."

Vincent stammered. "Right here...in the rectory... My God...what if...?"

"Naw," Roger Filmore said. He looked like such a preppy, Vincent thought, how could this be? "I'm very low key about everything, just like you are, Here, what are the Detroit Pistons doing?" He stepped close to the TV and leaned over to watch a play-by-play summary of the basketball game.

"Let me help you tune that in," Vincent said picking up a marble book end.

"No, I can see it quite clearly," Roger Filmore said.

"No really," Vincent said, and brought the book end down on top of Filmore's head. Roger Filmore went down with a crash. Vincent turned the TV off and listened. He stood astraddle Filmore's body, with the book end raised in both hands, ready to strike again, and at the same time listening for any sounds of running feet. Nothing. Silence. He saw his image in the blank screen. Bared teeth. He knelt beside Filmore. Vincent had seen lots of dead people. This guy was not breathing. He got a mirror and knelt again. No breath. He wrestled with Filmore's wrist... no pulse. He sat down beside the body and put his chin in his hands. Strange, to have no remorse. Here was a man who would have turned my life inside out for a few bucks. No, it was self-defense.

He lifted the body and dragged it onto the bed. There, he wrapped it in his worn coverlet. Time had run out. The only question now was, should he wait for supper before moving? On the one hand, he needed every moment of time to get away. On the other hand, he could not be seen dragging a body to his car, so he would have to wait until dark. Yes, that was it, quite clearly.

Dressed in old clothes, Vincent locked and double-bolted his room and sauntered to the kitchen. Father Tiernan was cheerful, and the young priests were tired from their hard day's work, but they still had the energy to banter like altar boys. With Monsignor present, they maintained decorum. Dinner was pastrami on rye, sauerkraut, boiled potatoes, and applesauce. For desert they had red wine and apple cobbler. Vincent ate heartily.

"Did you talk to that Jesuit?" Tiernan asked.

"I called but I couldn't get a hold of him," Vincent replied vaguely. "I'll go over there tomorrow."

Tiernan, dense as ever, shrugged.

Shortly, with a look of farewell at the rectory and its foolish occupants, and a good meal under his belt, Vincent burped and drove off. Filmore's body was in the Mercedes' trunk. Improvise as you go. Vincent had two thousand dollars in cash in his pocket, the money dopey Joe had stolen from his parish and then forgotten in Vincent's apartment. That would certainly help any further improvising. At a little town near the Massachusetts border, he filled the tank. Then he continued north on I-95.

The night was cold and clear. The highway had a little drifting snow, but was otherwise quite clear. At a rest stop near the Vermont border, he drank hot chocolate and a snort of whiskey, then continued north. He saw many cars with ski racks, folks headed for the resorts up north. Around ten o'clock, he neared Burlington. At a gas station, he filled up the tank again, purposefully topping it off. In the restroom, he changed into his black priestly suit and Roman collar. He swigged two shots of whiskey and sprinkled some on his lapels.

He went into a convenience store, stood in line humming to himself (noticed by all the customers), and purchased a quart of milk. As he paid for the milk, he asked for a pack of cigarettes. The clerk rang up the new purchase. Then he added a bag of potato chips. The clerk rang up the new purchase. Then he insisted on trading the cigarettes for another brand. Customers behind him were beginning to grumble. Enough. He'd made himself noticed. He paid and left.

In the warm car, he changed into civvies. He stowed his priest's black clothing and Roman collar in the carryall so he'd look like any other skier.

He found a deserted road at the edge of town and parked the Mercedes among some barren trees. He took his suitcase out and walked it about fifty feet away. He took the sleeping bag with Filmore's body out of the trunk and laid it on the back seat. There was Mr. Filmore, well preserved by the cold. Nicely positioned to look like someone who had fallen asleep.

Vincent left the engine running, lights off, and opened the suitcase. He extracted the whiskey bottle and walked back to the car. He opened the potato chips and poured them over Filmore's head. He opened the quart of milk, took a deep sip, and left the carton on the front seat. He opened the pack of cigarettes and laid it on the floor in the rear. He took one of the cigarettes, lit it, and waited. After a few puffs, he propped the cigarette between Filmore's dangling fingers. Then he opened the whiskey bottle and poured its contents over Filmore. He watched the liquor soak into the seat. He had to add a few lit matches, but then the seat was neatly ablaze. He closed the car door and marched off. He was on the horizon with his suitcase when the fire hit the fuel line under the floor. The gas tank went up with a dull report. The fire was visible for miles.

Vincent, carrying his suitcase, ambled along snowy sidewalks. Despite the late hour, people were all around, skiers having a few nightcaps before going back out on the slopes tomorrow morning. A fire engine wailed past as Vincent checked into a Best Rest motel. The clerk handed him his room key. "Have you got an airline schedule?" Vincent asked. The clerk pointed to a rack filled with such materials. Vincent took a long, hot bath. Smoking a cigar and drinking a glass of whiskey, he relaxed in the crackling bubble bath and avidly consulted the flight schedule. There it was: A noon flight to Boston. *No rush.* He decided he would sleep in.

26 · San Diego

On the night flight to San Diego from Hartford, Blue was too excited to sleep. Eddie, fortified with several scotch and sodas, snored in the middle seat on the jet. Blue watched the passage of brightly lit cities below in the black vastness of the United States.

It was nearly dawn when they arrived. They were hustled by skycaps through the airport, and by taxi to their hotels. Blue slept until noon, then opened the heavy curtains in her hotel room. Sunlight filled the room. Her view overlooked San Diego Harbor, sailboats, excursion ships. A row of gray Navy vessels, including an aircraft carrier, lined the opposite harbor shore.

She and Eddie had gone to separate hotels to keep Innie happy, if that was possible. She dialed Eddie's number and drew a glass of water. She opened the sliding glass door and sat on the 15th-floor balcony. "Morning," he chimed.

"Eddie, this is divine." A large gull rested on a wind current not far away, then flapped away over the harbor. "It's just like spring. Did you call your wife?"

"Yes," he said ruefully. "Chief Murphy promised we'd be in different hotels, but she doesn't believe it."

"Maybe you should get some family counseling."

"I might look into it," he said with reluctance born of pride.

"Palm trees," she breathed. "I've never seen one before."

San Diego Homicide Detective Barnes was a tea-skinned black man with stunning caramel-colored eyes. He seemed in his early forties, a big, quiet man with a firm, dry handshake. They met in the lobby of the Hilton.

Police headquarters was not far away. Blue studied the black-and-white patrol cars and motorcycles with a professional eye. In the building, Barnes picked up at the mail bins and hurried along to his office. Like all city police departments, this one had its bedlam of clattering printers, yelling detainees and their families, and chattering desk employees.

Shortly, Barnes took them across town to the morgue. There, in a chilly room, lay the remains of Father Joe. Eddie Stosik sadly confirmed the ID. An official in white lab coat displayed the track marks along both of the priest's arms. The steel drawer rolled shut and they reemerged into sunlight.

"Where is the body going?" Blue asked.

"To Ohio. Home. To his parents."

"Did he have any brothers or sisters?" Blue asked.

"No," Barnes said. "We checked."

Barnes showed her to a cheerless cinderblock room, with a single high slit-window, in the heart of the station. "Your office," he said. "I'm sure you'll warm things up."

She sighed, wrapped her arms around herself. "Well, it's bright anyway." The cinderblock walls had been painted in light, cool institutional pastels. She eyed the single chair, the single desk, the single phone, all covered with dust. An old phone book lay violently thrown against a wall.

Blue and Eddie ate at a seafood restaurant. Afterward, Eddie was tired and decided on a nap at his hotel. Alone at her hotel, stomach slightly upset, Blue went for a walk along the wharf. A tangy sea breeze, faintly damp, mingled with balmy subtropical air. The tall, rustling palm trees fascinated her. Some were shaped like huge pineapples, their fronds scraping roughly in the late afternoon air. Others were tall and slender and graceful. Some had huge gray beards composed of dead fronds.

By five o'clock it was dusk. The sun, descending over the western horizon, left a black-and-yellow-and-orange blaze that lingered like a gentle aftertaste. At the same time, there was something everyday about the swell of traffic on the crowded roads. Homeless men and women limped with sideshow gracelessness along the edges of the parks and roads. Many of them carried their possessions wrapped in blankets. A few pushed rusty shopping carts and stopped at trash barrels to rummage for empty cans and other salvage, while long limousines pulled in and out of the hotel entrances and liveried valets signaled.

Barnes and an attractive young Asian woman picked Blue up at seven in his enormous Buick, neat as a pin inside and smelling of upholstery cleaner. Barnes said: "Would you care for some ice cream and coffee? You'll meet Mr. Connor, for some flavor of our situation." Swinging into traffic to get Eddie at the other hotel, he introduced Blue to his companion.

The young woman with Barnes was a city detective. Blue felt a faint stray tug in her heart as Barnes introduced her with that slightly formal touch of supervisors everywhere. "Detective Martha Yee, meet Special Agent Laurel Humboldt. Detective Yee works for me. She's going to work with you."

Martha Yee was Chinese-American. She was slender, about Blue's height, and had glossy black hair cut into a page boy style. Her eyes squeezed into fine squiggles when she smiled. She had a small nose and a lush mouth in an oval face. Blue shook Martha Yee's hand and knew. Something electric passed between them. "Hello, Laurel," Martha said. City lights made her lower lip glisten, put an interested glow in her dark eyes.

"Call me Blue. It's my nickname."

"Okay, Blue." Martha wore mahogany loafers, jeans, and, under a white nylon windbreaker, a dark plaid shirt. "Chilly tonight," Martha said.

"I don't know," Blue said. "To me it feels warm. It was twenty degrees back in Connecticut and raining ice."

"How we forget. I grew up in Virginia because my Dad worked in D. C.," Martha said with that melon-sweet dimpled smile.

Barnes stopped and Eddie piled in. Eddie sat in the back with Blue as they cruised through rivers of headlights. The freeways out here were astonishing, Blue thought. Some hung in the sky like ribbons. Overpasses soared among the stars.

"This is the shopping mall where Mr. Connor works." Barnes pulled into a well-lit parking garage full of bustle. "He is all we have to tie this case together so far." Barnes showed them Ajanian's, and the two women sucked breath. One of the store windows had Persian carpets. Another window held a jewelry display where light cascaded among diamond necklaces paced with emeralds, or sapphires, or rubies, all tasteful and understated. A third window displayed well-crafted miscellany including gold-plated shaving kits, leather-bound photo albums, clever office golf practice kits, and more. Blue could not get enough.

Then she saw John Connor, and sucked breath.

Inside, standing at a display case looking at once amused, bored, and intelligent, was one of the most beautiful men Blue had ever seen. He was tall, wearing a blazer, gray trousers, a white shirt, and a regimental-style striped tie. He had dark hair and big quick dark eyes. His nose and jaw were as cut from honey-tanned marble. He had a small, lush mouth with fine ivory teeth.

Barnes herded them into a bustling restaurant with dark booths. They ordered coffee and ice cream. Blue liked fresh decaf and vanilla. Barnes smelled bracingly of drugstore aftershave. He seemed a neat family man out of place in the homicide business. "What have we got? A junkie priest from Connecticut winds up murdered in San Diego County. A beautiful woman named Jana Andrews, probably an alias, shows up a few days before the priest's murder, in Ajanian's, and buys an expensive ring later found on the dead priest. The woman disappears. Mr. Connor sold the ring to her. By coincidence, he was briefly acquainted with Jana Andrews years ago, when they were both fashion models working in New York City. A mysterious woman is leaving news clippings on Connor's doorstep indicating that Jana Andrews became a high-priced call girl and a cocaine addict. Finally, the woman who modeled with Mr. Connor in New York used an alias, Jane Willoughby. Or maybe Jana Andrews was the alias; we just don't know right now."

"Is Mr. Connor a suspect?" Blue asked.

"No trace of a motive. I've checked Connor out from top to bottom. He's divorced, childless. Got into the modeling business in his years in New York City and Los Angeles, made a pile of dough, didn't waste it on drugs or anything. Married another fashion model, Amy Crannard, divorced her two years later, quit the modeling business, retired to San Diego on the death of his parents to live in their old house which he has considerably expanded. He's a partner in Ajanian's, where he works part-time. He's also swimming in women. Every time we've seen him, he's been with a different woman. Somebody has been using him to bring this Jana Andrews to our attention."

John Connor joined them shortly after nine. Blue hovered shyly in the background. Barnes made the introductions. "Mr. Connor, it was good of you to come. About those clippings that were left at your door... do you have any idea yet who might have left those materials?"

John Connor shook his head. "I didn't get a good look at the woman. She was wearing sunglasses."

"And at night," Martha commented, having been through the details with Connor before.

"Yes. More of the Blue Neon Eyes," Connor said.

"The Lady with the Blue Neon Eyes?" Blue blurted.

"Pretty good," Eddie said. "How'd you come up with that?"

Blue's cheeks burned. "I have, er, had a friend, a painter, she'd paint something with a name like that."

"A Lady With Blue Neon Eyes," Connor said looking at Blue.

Martha laid a color glossy on the table.

"Pretty," everyone said except Eddie. He said "Weird." Blue noted the woman's artificial stance in the open car door, on a beach maybe on another planet, with the car and her eyes filled with crisp blue neon light.

Within fifteen minutes, Martha managed to explain the San Diego end of the story to Blue and Eddie, including Jana Andrews's visit to John Connor and the purchase of the ring later found on Father Joe Travignan.

Connor shook his head. "I wonder if it isn't my ex-wife, playing some trick on me." Smoke came from another table, and he made waving and choking motions.

"We checked that out," Barnes said. "Your ex-wife has two children, and married to a dentist far away in Mendocino, and has no apparent reason to bother you."

"This priest's death," Connor said. "I hope you catch the killer. I'm sorry. Someone has to care."

Blue liked him a little after that. And she made sure not to light one of her potent Chesterfields. Time to quit? she wondered. She noticed that Martha seemed more interested in the waitress than in Mr. Connor.

Barnes dropped Blue off at her hotel and continued on with Eddie. Martha and Blue decided to go out for drinks. "I'll show you the town," Martha promised. First, they stopped at a seaside restaurant for a nightcap. There were a few people draped around the bar, but it was slow. Martha bought Drambuies. The sweet, potent liquor made Blue's head reel. Martha's glittering eyes and smiley white teeth were wolfish.

For a while, in a different bar overlooking the harbor, they entertained a wrinkled mariner. He was a rouged, cheerful chap, deep into his cups, who regaled them with stories about how he could outfit his seventy foot sloop with female sailors at a moment's notice at any hour of day or night. He fell asleep face down, and the bar closed. Martha led Blue out before the ancient mariner could be wakened.

Next, they were in a little woody place full of women. "We're in our friend Connor's neighborhood," Martha told a liquescent Blue Humboldt. After one glass of white wine, Blue walked to the ladies' room by feeling her way from pillar to post. Back out amid the cigarette smoke, she leaned against Martha's shoulder. "Blue," Martha said, "are you in the bag already? How disappointing."

"Uhrr," Blue managed to say. Two Drambuies and a glass of white wine had bought her the farm. She stayed glued to a pillar while Martha played pool with a guy-looking woman. Cigarette smoke palled the table, making it boring because Blue couldn't see the balls going around. She was glad when Martha led her outside. It was two a.m. The stars were out. Martha held Blue tightly, massaging her back and butt, while Blue puked over Martha's shoulder. After a while, Blue's head cleared somewhat. She was on all fours, puking, while Martha patted her back. Martha had some tissue in her purse. Blue wiped her mouth. Martha gave her some chewing gum. Blue belched. It was three a.m. She took the gum and allowed the peppermint to saturate her numbed taste organs.

"I'd better get you home," Martha said. "Want to come to my place?"

"Gotta to be hotel," Blue said, "case call."

Next thing, they were outside her hotel and the night wind was rustling in the palm trees overhead. Blue felt half-way sober, and was shivering madly.

"You passed out," Martha said.

"You better help me upstairs," Blue asked.

Ten minutes later, the shower was running, and Blue inhaled the wet hot steam. She saw Martha hovering outside the warm fog. She reached out, feeling very steady, and pulled at Martha's sweater. Martha's face was very serious. "Blue," she said, "you've puked on me, you've passed out in my car, and I've had to carry you up here. What more do you want?" But she peeled off her clothes and stepped into the shower. She was Blue's height, with a ruddy athletic body and little breasts with walnut nipples. Blue pulled her close. Touched her sweet body. Held her tightly. Kissed those shaky nipples. Inwardly she cried don't leave me.

It was a dark, quiet night. The stars shone. A quarter moon lay like a cut orange slice over the horizon. Sailing ships with illumined masts glided in and out of the harbor.

In bed, Blue and Martha made love. Martha was hungry, her teeth nipping here and there, at Blue's nipples, her tongue immediately behind to savor fruit that had been bitten. Blue arched back, moaning, two flat, athletic stomachs pressing against each other, gathering heat between them. Blue held Martha's jet black hair while Martha's mouth moved down to the sweet place that was like a summer berry garden. Martha began to moan, and Blue felt the rhythmic motion in Martha's shoulder. The motion matched the timing of her tongue in Blue's most intimate spot, while Martha rubbed herself in time. One by one, Blue felt the rippling contractions in her gut, the stiffening in her legs, that signaled several small orgasms in slow succession. When she couldn't stand it any longer, she pushed Martha onto her back and, holding Martha's wrists down, showered her with passion. She rubbed Martha's little point quicker and quicker, until Martha convulsed in a great orgasm that made her small, taut body quiver.

After a long stillness, during which they listened to the sound of one another's heartbeats through smooth skin, occasionally giving the other's small breast a kiss, they curled up together and slipped into satisfied sleep.

27 · San Diego

While it was still dark out, Martha Yee whispered something affectionate into Blue's ear and slid away. Later Blue woke alone. Startled, she sat up. And immediately grabbed her head to protect it from the 900-pound pliers pressing on both temples. First she went to the bathroom and threw up. A half-hour session with hot towels, sodium bicarbonate, and glasses of water, and she felt able to call room service. She ordered a toast and black coffee. Never again, she vowed. She found in her bag a megavitamin to replace any essentials the alcohol had leached out of her. By ten a.m. she felt well enough to call Eddie, whose immediate question was: "Blue, where have you been?"

"I was in bed. Hung over."

"The switchboard said you left orders last night not to be disturbed. Geez, what happened?"

"Eddie, I saw the city and it saw me. What did you do?"

"I called to see if you'd like to go for a drink."

"Don't mention drink to me."

"You and Martha Yee must have tied one on."

"You could say that."

"I'm leaving for Connecticut this afternoon."

"You are?"

"Yes. Another priest. A monsignor this time."

"No!"

"Yes. Your Monsignor Gordon. Found burned to death under suspicious circumstances in Vermont at a ski resort."

"Doing what? Don't tell me. Stupid question. Skiing."

"Actually, he was sleeping in his car. Drunk, they think. I don't know any more. Chief Murphy wants me back there today."

She called Tomasi. There was a funny twist to his voice. She could tell he had something on his mind. "Humboldt, I'm glad you called. How are you doing?"

"Just fine, Chief. I've met Barnes and Yee and Connor. I understand Eddie is being pulled back. Also, this Monsignor Gordon has been found dead?"

"Good work on your part. I wish we'd followed it more quickly. I'm having Vito cover that for us. I want you to stay in San Diego for now. Work with Barnes. I'll keep you posted on what goes down back here. I feel good because I'm covering all the bases, I think, with my budget. But Laurel."

He'd never used her first name before. "Yessir?"

"There's a lady who has been making a nuisance of herself."

She wished she could crawl into a hole.

"This lady is a well-known artist, with a rather weird lifestyle. Apparently you befriended her some time ago."

"I was impressed," Blue said, "that she was an artist and an intellectual. I had no idea she was also a nut."

"You made a mistake. But you're young, you're learning, and I don't want to know. I asked her to stop bothering us at the office, since you obviously gave her the high sign."

Blue felt mortified.

"It won't go any further than this. You're an outgoing, friendly little skate. Watch yourself, okay?"

"Yessir. I could call her, ask her not to—"

"No, don't encourage her."

"I'm sorry."

"We all make mistakes. The matter is closed. I said you're indefinitely assigned out of town, don't call us again."

Blue really resented Maggie now. She picked Eddie up at his hotel. It was different with Martha Yee. Martha could not threaten her without exposing herself. It was sad that matters of love should be reduced to such mercenary calculations. Eddie asked her to drive him to the airport. In the hotel restaurant, over sandwiches and beer, Eddie looked at her closely. "Do you have boyfriends?" It seemed to be a question he'd been dying to ask after all this time.

She realized she must be an enigma to him. "Eddie, I just broke up with —someone —in Manhattan. I'm not ready for another relationship. So I'm sort of being a nun."

She drove him to Lindbergh Field. There she helped him unload his baggage while a jet thundered away in the cloudless sky. His hair blew in the balmy breeze. He extended his hand wistfully. "So long, Blue. Hope to see you again soon."

She squeezed him in a brief hug. "Keep an eye on that cold, drafty apartment in Hamilton for me, will you? See you."

⅛ · Burlington, Vermont

Vincent, relaxing in his hot tub in Burlington, raised a whiskey to honor the late Monsignor Gordon. Gone was the pressure of Hugh hounding him. The matter of Filmore—well, the man might have killed him, and he'd killed Filmore by accident, so that was nothing to fret about. The Angel of Death, now that was another matter, and it roiled deeply in his mind; he must keep evading HER. Then his thoughts turned to the desirable Jana Andrews. He imagined her beside him in nubile magnificence, and dialed her number in Chicago.

"Hi there, lover." Her voice was husky and inviting.

He squirmed in his tub. "Ooh, you make me want to reach out and squeeze your toe."

"Are you into toes, Vincent?"

"I'm into toes, fingers, arms, as long as it's Jana Andrews, I'm into it. How are you, doll?"

"Ahh...lonely...bored."

"Would you like to meet me in sunny Southern California for a nice relaxing weekend? You won't be bored or lonely."

"You're on, hot guy!"

In two hops, Vincent went to Boston, then New York City. The pilot announced that it was a bright, cold, sunny day in Manhattan. Vincent was in a good humor. In The Boston Globe was a blip about a body found in a burning car in Vermont.

Vincent took a commuter helicopter from JFK to a skyscraper, where he ate a light meal. Then, in an office supply store, he rented a computer and a modem. Then he took a hotel room in midtown Manhattan and got to work. One by one, he wrote checks against his various accounts—

Citibank, Bank of America, First Federal, and so on—and prepared them for mailing to Mercantile First Bank of Chicago where he had an account under the name Vincent Ulric. Using the computer, he dollied up twenty different letterheads, with company names like Graphics International, InnoForm, Investments Parsis, and so on. He had them printed on a quality laser printer, then enclosed them in the letters. He would not empty any of his twenty accounts. Instead, he transferred a total of just over $3,000,000 to the CompuGraphiX USA account, leaving over half a million spread around. He mailed the letters by registered mail from Manhattan.

He arrived in Chicago just after nightfall.

He took a hotel room, sent up for dinner—Filet Mignon with mushroom caps, boiled salted new potatoes, carrots in parsley, and a chocolate pudding. He sent out for Charles Martel brandy and a box of fine cigars. Then he watched cable movies until the brandy sent him under.

The following day, he went to Chicago Shoreline Savings and Loan and extracted the contents of a small strong box. There were a few negligible items, such as a gold watch and a gold bracelet, both of which he planned to give to darling Jana. Most importantly, he had Vincent Ulric's social security number. On a previous visit, Vincent had spent an entire morning and part of an afternoon at the Motor Vehicles Department, obtaining a picture driver's license that he'd kept in safety deposit like a treasure. He called First Mercantile Bank of Chicago late that afternoon, introduced himself as the President of CompuGraphiX USA, and requested an interview.

At ten o'clock Thursday morning, dressed in a brand-new dark business suit of conservative cut, he was ushered into the office of a Vice President named Charles Graham, a youngish black man. Graham pumped his hand eagerly. "Mr. Ulric, what a pleasure. Will you have tea or coffee?"

"Tea, if you don't mind."

A silver tea service arrived, complete with steaming teapot, china cups and saucers, china sugar and cream containers, a china pot of sliced lemons, pastries, and finger sandwiches. "I understand your company is expanding to Chicago," Graham said.

Vincent buttered a croissant, laid salami and Edam between its buttery flaky halves. "Yes. We expect to transfer funds from our subsidiaries and from other interested parties soon."

"Computer business, is it?" Graham boomed, buttering a crumpet. "Lucrative. I could move in that direction."

"A good way to go, Mr. Graham. What we need are good managers. Such opportunities will exist in the future. Well, I should toddle on."

"Most assuredly," Mr. Graham said, licking butter from his thumb. "What sort of dollar volume are we talking initially?"

"Well," Vincent hazarded, "we're only getting started, of course, but I am already negotiating an order around five million dollars for our integrated circuits. We'll be introducing a line of preprogrammed chips later, and that gets into tens of millions."

Graham gulped.

"Then there are government contracts. I'd say we're looking at a break-even this year and a profit margin approaching two million next year."

Graham swallowed hard.

Satisfied with himself, Vincent had a steak dinner and took an evening flight to San Diego.

Joanna MacIvory, listed in the passenger manifest as Jana Andrews, boarded the commuter flight to San Diego. Munching orange slices, she idly flipped through the morning newspaper.

And caught.

And nearly choked.

"San Diego Murder Victim Identified as Connecticut Priest," the headline read. She broke into tears, reading the article. "No," she cried, "noooo!"

When she arrived in San Diego, Rae Donovan and Virgie DeSanto picked her up at the airport. She buried her face in Rae's lap, and Rae's rough, callused hands patted her. "My God, Joanna, what's wrong?"

"It's not going to go the way we planned it," Joanna blubbered. "My brother! He's dead! That son of a bitch killed him."

Rae, blonde strongwoman, held Joanna's face in her hands like some mask. "What do you mean?"

She told them about Joe, and dissolved in tears again.

Virgie DeSanto, driving, looked shocked. Her pillbox hat tilted rakish on her forehead. "Jesus, no."

Joanna said calmly: "Forget this charade. I am going to kill him."

"No," both women said. "Please, Joanna, think what you're doing. Think about Doug."

Ah, to spend a delicious weekend with Jana Andrews!

Vincent had readied everything. Drinks, fireplace, clean sliding glass door leading out onto beach sand at $4000 per square foot overlooking La Jolla Shores. Sunken marble tub, jacuzzi, pool, squash court, the works. She would stay with him to share all this. As he fixed himself another drink he heard the doorbell.

In the aperture he spied Jana's upper face. "You're early, darling," he chimed. "Wait, I'll open right up." *The key, where was the key?*

The doorbell rang again.

Vincent searched for the key. "Hold on, darling!"

The doorbell chimed incessantly.

"Jana Darling, I'll be right there!" He opened the door, holding a drink in his hand, and rocking slightly on the balls of his feet. He was in a euphoric haze, but his joy fizzled.

She fixed malevolent eyes on him and showed teeth. "You killed him!" Her voice had a fierce, unearthly quality. "You rotten bastard! You goddamn shit!" She lunged at him with a knife.

He dropped his drink and fell backward.

The knife caught on his sleeve, stung his skin. Jana's breath was in his face, and she was grunting like an animal. Her foot caught him in the gut, and he doubled over. "You murdered my brother!"

Vincent was sure now that Jana was a madwoman. She raised the knife in both hands to strike at him. He saw her twisted mouth, her vicious eyes. Desperately, he clawed her face. The knife came down without force. He punched repeatedly, bringing her to the ground inside the tiled entrance. At last, she was still. Breathing heavily, he took the knife and plunged it into her heart. Then, dulled by drink, panicked, sobbing, he gathered his things from around the house. The Angel of Death stood there smiling. Now you've done it, Vincent, I always said you're bad.

"I didn't mean to," he whined. "I'm just trying to be good. I don't want to hurt anybody. She attacked me, Mother, honest. It was just like you and Daddy. You were just trying to protect yourself, weren't you?" He crawled about, slobbering, getting his things. "It was just like that, Mother, I was just trying to protect myself. She came at me. Oh God, she came at me with a knife. I hate her! I hate you!"

29. San Diego

Blue and Martha worked out an angle of attack. Martha had other duties (shades of Eddie!) which left Blue to her own investigation. But San Diego was a huge city, not a little town you could get to know in a day or two.

Martha stepped into Blue's office and closed the door. "About the other night."

"I'm sorry I barfed and all."

"You were very sweet. I'd like to see you more."

"Thanks, Martha. I just broke up with someone in New York, and I'm trying to lay low. Especially with this investigation."

"How about dinner soon?"

"Sure," Blue said.

After many hours of poring over police and paramedic reports, and fruitless phone calls and visits with other detectives, Blue had made no progress. She was home when Eddie called.

She was in the tub. "How are ya?"

"Okay."

"That's a glum howdoyoudo."

"It's cold enough to freeze your balls off."

"That would never be cold enough for me." She moved mounds of bubble foam over her skin.

"Blue, about that other priest from Hamilton who just bit the big one, Monsignor Gordon? I made another pass through Joe's stuff before Pollack sent it to Joe's parents in Ohio. Joe had this monsignor's phone number written down in about six places in his diaries. They were connected, I'm sure."

"Try Father Binder," she suggested. "Ask him how much money Travignan and Gordon stole together." She wondered if the two-timing priests had a little fun-lair someplace in San Diego.

Barnes called not long after her conversation with Eddie. She was drying out on the little balcony overlooking San Diego Harbor from the 15th floor, working on her tan after a swim. "Miss Humboldt, you ought to know, and I'm about to call Mr. Connor. There's a stabbing victim at UCSD Medical Center. Female, and unconscious. Her name is Jana Andrews. We're checking her prints against the state files."

Blue sat up. "Unconscious? Hasn't talked yet?"

As she drove to the hospital in her rental car, she reviewed what Barnes had told her. Jana Andrews was wheeled out of surgery for the third time in two days, still unconscious. Cocaine worth a million dollars on the street had been found in a suitcase in a car rented by one Jana Andrews, all else unknown. Paramedics had found her bleeding and near death. She had a stab wound to the chest, deflected by her sternum. She had a stab wound to the arm, and several blows to the head. She had banged her head on the concrete and surgeons had drained blood and brain fluid from her inner ear. She was under 24 hour watch, not only for her safety, but to catch anyone coming to finish her off. The connection might never have been made were it not for a persistent records clerk.

At the hospital, she met Barnes, Connor, and Martha. They followed an exasperated ward clerk, a chubby little black woman with rattling jewelry and too much make-up, huffing behind two orderlies and a nurse who were pushing the gurney. "I had to know if her dental work has been checked," the clerk explained as the entourage made their way along semidark halls with glistening floors and a smell of boric acid. "Someone somewhere must be missing a wife or a daughter or mother! If figured, time to call the police back and try one last measure—the state fingerprints databank, to see if perhaps she had a record."

"Wonderful work," Barnes said.

As they wheeled Jana Andrews into a room, the nurse said: "She's stable for now. Lost a lot of blood. She's had several operations to relieve pressure from leaking brain fluid." Martha Yee said: "We'll have a round the clock watch in case she talks. Funny part is, SDPD had a watch on her because they found a million bucks of cocaine in her rental car."

Blue asked: "Where did they find her?"

"On the steps of a ritzy place in La Jolla."

"Could that be Monsignor Gordon's little love nest?"

"Something to check out," Martha agreed.

John Connor stepped forward, looked at the swollen, black and blue face, and turned away. "I can't tell if it's her."

Barnes patted Connor's shoulder. "Easy now. We're double checking the fingerprints against state records if we have any."

Outside, Blue bumped into Connor. "You look upset."

"Yeah." He rubbed his cheek in disbelief. "I'm going for some lunch. Care to join me?"

She saw herself falling right into it. "Sure."

He opened the door of a dark Porsche for her. He wore jeans and a white cotton shirt that offset his light tan. His dark hair looked wet and curly, as though he had carelessly combed it after a shower. Round aviator sunglasses hid his eyes. His strong jaw and smooth face with streamlined nose radiated a sense of tiger strength. His long, lanky limbs moved with casual athletic grace. She slid into the seductive smells of leather, upholstery, and a faint, citric aftershave or cologne. The machine growled and started away from the curb. He was a quick, smooth driver, comfortable with the powerful car.

Oddly, she felt as though she were on a date. Not a bad feeling, despite the circumstances. He took her to a restaurant called Kabuki-san. They walked through a pebble courtyard overhung with ivy growing out of pots hung from wooden beams. The interior was festooned with paper lanterns and cord-wrapped white canvas bundles suggesting bales of tea. Buddhas gleamed in little wall niches. There were odd mingled aromas—tea, fish, salty stew, peanut sauce. At the sushi bar, they each drank a small egg-cup of hot sake, rice wine, potent as a martini. They were served small wooden trays of sashimi: Bits of raw fish and vegetables pressed into truncated rice cylinders wrapped in dark green seaweed. He showed her how to hold chopsticks, dip the sashimi in hot green mustard, and after each bite clean her palate by eating a few shreds of pickled ginger.

He toyed with an after-lunch drink. All the women in the restaurant kept looking at him. He seemed almost shy; now why would that be? To break the ice, she touched his hand. "Tell me, why did you quit modeling?"

John Connor felt her cold fingertips on the back of his hand. She was smiling, but with a calculating curiosity.

"I'm sorry, Miss Humboldt, I can't seem to put a picture together. I'm not used to seeing a woman so battered.'

"This has been an upsetting time for you.' She added: "So modeling was not a very happy career for you."

"It was okay. This woman has somehow touched me. Taken me back. It makes me remember a divorce. Some bad times."

She said kindly: "You are handsome, wealthy, can have anyone or anything you like."

"Maybe it seems that way to you." He wondered if she was being condescending or adoring, and wasn't sure.

"I'm not entirely happy either," she confessed. That floored him. "I have a job I sometimes enjoy, even though it's deadly dull or frustrating by turns. I'm wondering if you have the same problem I have."

"What's that?"

"That inner voice. Deep down. Like a nagging bit of heartburn. The feeling there has to be something more."

"Is there a man in your life?" He apologized with his eyes for being so forward.

"Not right now."

Could you believe it, she blushed! Well, she was honest. And her personality had a kind of crackle to it. Like fresh celery, clean and wholesome. Also humorous and kind. He envied her, and he said so.

She laughed. "What?" Her dark eyes mocked. "I have to work for a living. I'm not glamorous. The work I do is not happy or nice or even safe. You're a card!" Her pale, pretty features with their sincerity stirred him.

In a sudden flash of sympathy, her reserve toward him had evaporated. She felt a wave of understanding as he told her his story, which she found interesting.

His parents had been perfectionists, and he knew he had not entirely pleased them, dropping college plans to take up modeling; he was making up for that now, taking courses at San Diego State University. Then he'd been recruited for modeling. For two years, he'd worked hard before the camera. By night he cruised the clubs. He had women several a day, the way ordinary people get hungry or thirsty. However, he did not have the energy. That was the old story. He could have had a thousand women, a Ph. D., or a track championship, but none of those things appealed to him.

While many other male models were gay and lived a totally different lifestyle, and others abused chemicals, John needed normalcy and regularity. So he married one of the many female models who carouseled through his life. A disaster, for she was childish and selfish and ultimately ran around with other men. John, however, formed solid friendships in the Big Apple. One of them was a lady named Sonya Marcus, a plain gal of 26 with thick glasses, who traded on the New York She had long ceased to look on the outside; what Sonya Marcus looked like—a dumpy young woman—did not matter to him as much as the fact that she was a genuine, strong person with great affection. During the worst of his divorce, he'd slept regularly with Sonya Marcus and found more solace there than in all the hard-working young mares on the fashion world trotting track. Sonya had taught John the stock market. She'd taken his earnings and doubled, tripled, quadrupled them for him. She'd done this in a way that he'd been able to avoid most alimony problems. Sonya had drifted out of his life a few years ago, when he'd quit modeling. He was a millionaire by then. His parents were dead, and he'd returned to San Diego to pursue a new life. If he was not competitive by nature, he also resented being used. Modeling was a matter of being used, and once he'd made his money he'd turned his back on it.

"Why do you want to work for me?" Ajanian the purveyor of luxury had asked during the interview four years ago.

"Well," John had told him, "I miss the working world just a little bit. Mostly the everyday contact with people. So I answered your ad. Part-time help wanted. That sounds like what I need."

Ajanian and he stood ankle deep in Persian carpeting. Ajanian's In The Mall had a quiet elegance. Gregor Ajanian had spent a lifetime creating a lavish mystique that made his store the byword for expensive buying. He was a small tidy-looking man with dark eyes, a cashew-shaped nose, a wide full mouth, and a grayish olive complexion. His store had nothing that anybody needed. Just a quarter acre of useless but beautiful furs, jewels, rugs, gadgets, glossy hundred-dollar books, and matte black James Bond novelties. Lots of foot traffic and few buyers, but those who bought spent big bucks. The interior of Ajanian's gleamed in a bluish light that bounced among mirrors.

Gregor Ajanian studied John Connor while gingerly holding a green and gold designer cigarette in a hand glittering with diamond rings. John Connor carried himself well. He had a tall, slender body that was neither soft nor overly hard, muscular but not muscle-bound. Connor's clothes were expensive and understated. Ajanian had a reedy, abrasive voice modulated by a burr like a drill smothered in lubricant soap. "Have you spent any time in Las Vegas, son?"

John Connor had frowned. "Pardon me? Yes, I've been there."

"Do you know what a shill is?"

"Sounds like a rare coin or something," John laughed.

Ajanian kept a pickle face. "You haven't played Chemin de Fer then."

"I don't gamble," John assured him.

"That's good," Ajanian said, reassured. He looked John up and down. "A shill is a come-on. Chemin de Fer is supposed to be a high-brow game. It's a sucker's game the way it's played in the U. S. The casino hires a couple of gorgeous women in evening gowns and studs in tuxedoes to sit at a ritzy looking table and pretend they're playing Chemin de Fer. Joe Shmoe, you walk by, you're a sucker, you want to feel elegant, you step up and play. For a while you pretend you're James Bond. Then you're broke and the shills charm your ass out of there to make room for the next sucker."

"That doesn't sound like my kind of game," John said.

Ajanian burred: "Chemin de Fer is French for Railroad, though I don't think there's any pun intended."

John: "You're very knowledgeable. I understand you travel all over the world to buy the wonderful things you sell here."

Finally, Ajanian laughed. "You'll do fine in sales. You're charming me, and I see you coming." He paused. "Maybe I can use you, John. Have you ever done any sort of sales work before?"

"Not exactly, but you just said I might have charm."

"What kind of money are you used to?"

"I've never earned less than a thousand dollars a day."

Ajanian blinked; a rare event for this accomplished world-class poker player. "Then perhaps this job would be menial for you. I'm paying seven dollars an hour. I could make it ten for you."

"I don't care."

Ajanian not only blinked; he blinked and swallowed. "Very well. Ten dollars an hour."

"Great," John had told him. "You can simply send my pay to a bank account I'll set up. When do I start?"

"I like for my sales staff to dress to the nines. To be polite. Elegant."

"Shills," John said.

"Yes. Only nobody gets suckered here."

"The customer is always right."

"Very well then, you understand. You'll be part of the atmosphere. When you sell a five thousand dollar Rolex or a ten thousand dollar

Persian rug, you're selling yourself and this store. I want the atmosphere of elegance to stay shining on that sold object for as long as the customer owns it. Capisc'?"

For the next four years, John reported religiously on Thursday and Saturday evenings for work at Ajanian's In The Mall. For a while there were a lot of stories about him. That he was a reformed criminal. That he was a European prince in hiding. In exile. That he had no foreign accent had quashed those last tales. In the end, they became used to him. They forgot the weird stories and malicious gossip and were usually too busy working to whisper about him. They called him John, John, Hey You. He loved it. They didn't really understand, but they were the anchor of his weekly schedule. And by now he had bought himself into a limited partnership with Ajanian, a twenty percent share of the business.

Ajanian spent quality hours on the floor with his people. He was a hard man to work for because he was exacting. He was relentlessly critical, but he was also enormously forgiving. If he had a drawback, it was that he was a miser with praise. Only once, about a year after hiring John, he took him aside and whispered: "You know why I've kept you on? Sure, you're beautiful, a lot of ladies come by at least twice a week just to look at you, but that doesn't sell watches and diamonds. I like you because you don't have a fat head. People like you for that, John. You're a nice guy."

"That is a nice story," Blue told him.

Slowly, the earlier grin, a boyish squiggle of the lips against white teeth and light tan skin, broke through like the sun through clouds. "You warm me."

She caught herself. She did not want to get chummy. She stepped away and looked at her watch. "Well, I think I ought to call Barnes and see what's going on." Keep it professional.

"There is a phone in my car," he enthused. Of course, there would be. So, moments later she was in touch with Barnes who had just returned to his office from the hospital. She asked: "Is she conscious yet?"

"No change."

Connor put his sunglasses on and started the car.

"I'll be back in the office shortly," she told Barnes.

"Fine," he said, "I'll be gone the rest of the day. Get with Martha if you need us."

She hung up. John said: "Can I show you around?"

She felt stiff. "I'd like to keep things on a rather formal level. After all, you're a material witness."

"Okay. Let's keep it formal. Where to start?"

Not your house, please, she thought.

"The zoo, then." John Connor paid for their tickets. There were plenty of tourists about, and lots of babies crying in strollers. Flamingoes padded through their wading pool like pink dancers and on the lawn around their pool were ancient pygmy date palms with delicate fronds.

"What about your parents, Miss Humboldt. What do they think about your career?"

"As a cop? I think they hate it. I think they're afraid for my safety. But they've stopped saying things."

"And you're all alone? In the world, I mean? In New York City?"

He seemed to sense her bottomless fright. "Look," he said, "the giraffes. They are the gentlest creatures, don't you think? One of the lady giraffes just had a baby. They have her in that special corner. The other giraffes keep wandering over to look over the fence at the mother and her new baby."

He showed her the Bengal tiger, a massive padding creature with beautiful markings. She saw the sullen gorillas and was sure they resented their captivity. The orangutans were behind a special plastic enclosure whose surface they had marred with vicious clawing attacks. It was cool and shady in the tropical rain forest. Tropical plants grew amid concrete paths and plashing waterfalls. A woman passed, pushing a carriage containing a severely crippled and retarded boy with a deformed head and oddly twisted fingers. With a sudden surge of heart, she turned and told him: "Mr. Connor, we're very lucky. I mean, we look on the negative side, we all do, we human people. But we have so much."

Connor had seen the boy too. "Yes, we're very lucky, Miss Humboldt. We have to keep remembering that."

The elephant triggered another sadness in Blue. "Look how he has to patiently keep walking around and around that dusty path all day with screaming kids on his back."

"Elephants have been doing hard work in India for thousands of years," Connor stated.

"Don't you think he'd be happier in the wild?"

"He'd have to fight for a living. I don't know—maybe he'd be happier. He looks like a happy elephant to me."

Elephant dust drifted before her field of vision. "Are you a happy elephant, Mr. Connor?"

Night fell over the harbor. John Connor watched a two-masted schooner glide past. Her decorated rigging formed a pyramid of little white lights.

John watched Humboldt's pale, harmoniously featured face, under floating puff of black hair and inset with lustrous dark eyes, grow quietly and subtly lovely. He put his hand over hers. "The happy hour crowd is rolling in. The band is tuning up. Let's stay and dance."

For a moment, he thought she would reject his offer. Instead she nodded, pleasure in her eyes. "I'm going to run upstairs for a moment to freshen up. Will you wait for me here?"

Waiting, he ignored watchful eyes. Of a blonde lighting a cigarette. Of the slender brunette hostess each time she passed by. Of two older women with garish wigs and too much makeup who kept looking his way. The harbor had a quiet beauty of lights and cool wind beyond the noise of the four-piece combo doing Beatles songs.

A pair of shapely legs in a jeans miniskirt, white hose, and black high heels caught his eye. He turned his eyes discreetly in that direction, saw that the owner, in a puffy-sleeved white silk blouse, was coming directly toward him among the stares of men, choked, and realized it was Laurel Humboldt. She smiled, and her teeth made an ivory contrast with the darkness of her eyes. He felt comfortable enough with her to say: "I didn't recognize you, Laurel. My god, you're gorgeous."

She blushed. "You have some original lines."

He sat back a little frustrated. He knew better than to argue with a woman about her self-image. Like many women, this one was self-demeaning to a degree.

She tapped his wrist. "Come on, let's dance."

They gyrated through two fast dances, becoming sweaty in the noisy, dense crowd. Young businessmen had loosened their ties and developed red faces in a never-ending call for beers and drinks. Young businesswomen became brash and giggly over their drinks and cigarettes. Connor's eyes reveled in the lithe twisting motions of Blue Humboldt, whom the second drink had also apparently loosened up. Then came a long slow dance. He led, and she followed securely, tucked against his right shoulder. Her left hand splayed against his right shoulder blade. His left hand and her right hand were clasped, and their fingers twined and intertwined like two lovers in bed together.

They stepped outside with their drinks. The harbor breeze was quiet and refreshing. She said: "I've never heard of a cop dancing with a material witness."

"You're undercover, Blue. You're working your way into my sinister private life to set up the drug bust of the century."

"Oh stop it." She slugged him on the shoulder in a sisterly fashion. For a while, they leaned shoulder to shoulder on the wooden railing, watching ships passing on the night water. "It's a lovely city," she said.

"I like it." And he did.

"It would be nice if they reassigned me here."

"That would be nice," he agreed. Impulsively, he put his arm around her, feeling the lightness of her waist, the curve of her hip. Her arm pressed on his. They were that way for a few minutes. He turned toward her, and she faced him. Their faces were inches apart. He inclined his face toward hers, and her eyes sank shut. Her lips parted as though about to drink. Then she squirmed away. She said: "One more fast dance. Then I've got to go upstairs and you have to go home."

Blue ran to her room and bolted the door. She went to the window and looked after him, but all she could see were the myriad flashes of restaurant lights on the dark harbor water.

This guy was a dream. Surely a million women thought so. No way she was going to latch onto a guy like that. I am not going to set myself up to be hurt again. In the shower, surrounded by soothing hot steam, she thought about her innermost doubt. Society liked neat tags. Either you were straight or lesbian. She thought of Donald and Tessie and Mike Aguilar and Maggie. What am I, she wondered. Fifty-fifty, eighty-twenty, sixty/forty? Would such a relationship work? Connor left you breathless. But she would have to be professional. Which would be hard because, she realized, she suddenly had a crush on him. It was a breathless, anxious, hopeful, happy, desperate thing to have a crush on so handsome a man. Keep control, she told herself. Don't let him know. You'll be back in Connecticut within a week.

30 · San Diego

In the morning, in her office, Blue spread Jana Andrews' clippings on the desk. A shaft of sunlight stole in to keep her company. She turned the radio onto a light rock station with soothing background music. She phoned Barnes. "Lloyd, your Rolex contact said the woman we call Jana Andrews is really Jane Willoughby, another unknown. Well, the clippings from our mysterious woman suggest there was a Jana Andrews who was a model in New York City, working for the Dolly Agency a few years back, and then got involved in prostitution and other vices afterwards."

Barnes, busy with other things, seemed to have difficulty tuning in. "What's that, Miss Humboldt?"

"I'm suggesting that Jane Willoughby and Jana Andrews may be two different people. What it boils down to is both women are probably real people, rather than one using two names."

"You may have a point." Barnes sounded harassed. "Talk to Martha Yee. Jana Andrews still is unconscious. Hasn't talked."

Blue called Tomasi next. "Well, our California bathing beauty." She told him of her hunch. "Remember, Humboldt. Leave the murder mystery stuff to Barnes and his crew. They're going to be annoyed if you upstage them—and so will I, since we're in this to cooperate."

Martha Yee stopped in.

"Hello," Blue said.

Martha shut the door. "Blue, how are ya? We'll be strictly business here at work. How about dinner at my place Saturday evening. Candles. Red wine. Pasta. What do you say?"

"Sure." She wanted to say no.

Martha gave her the phone number of Denton Horowitz at the Dolly Agency in New York City. Blue called. An elderly, creaky man answered. "This is Horowitz. How can I help you?"

"Mr. Horowitz, this is Special Agent Laurel Humboldt of the Drug Enforcement Agency. It's about Jana Andrews."

"Who?"

"Jane Willoughby."

"Oh yes. That business. I told Barnes all I know."

"Please, Mr. Horowitz. Does Jana Andrews ring any bells?"

"No, it didn't the other day and I'm afraid it doesn't now. Although, you know, it's been a long time. I've got a pretty sharp memory for an older gent. I've been thinking a lot about the matter, and you know what I think?"

"No, what, Mr. Horowitz."

"There was a Jane Willoughby with us for about two years. Contract, you know, hardly ever see the girl after the initial interviews. I looked and looked, and I could not find any record of a Jana Andrews. Still, I wonder if we weren't mistaken. Maybe there were two women. What I told Barnes was that I supposed Jane Willoughby was an alias for some poor scared little gal trying out her fledgling wings. I'm beginning to wonder."

"Could Jana Andrews have worked for another agency?"

"Sure."

"Would you know which one?"

"Honey, it could any one of a thousand or more. They open and fold on a daily basis."

"Well, I'm glad you've had second thoughts. Let me know if you find anything out, please." She gave him her phone number. He seemed pleasant enough, and eager to cooperate. His doubts gave her ephemeral courage.

31. San Diego

John Connor bought fresh vegetables and a small rump roast at the excellent corner market. As he stood in line, waiting to pay, listening to the banter between shop owners and their customers, he reflected that he'd noticed Blue and Martha Yee being chummy. Marcia Jersey's words echoed in his mind. It couldn't be, he thought. Not again. Please, not Blue.

As John entered the house, Fontainebleau met him and rubbed against his leg with a baby-like aww-ll, the raspy meow of the Siamese feline. "Yes, how do you do too?" John said. In the kitchen, Fontainebleau continued rubbing against his ankles while John put his paper sacks down on the counter. "Yes, you're going to meet Laurel. I think you'll like her."

Fontainebleau's rubbing increased when he heard the electric can opener. "Yes, and Laurel will probably like you, although you will be jealous if she and I pay too much attention to each other." He spooned fresh tuna into a small china dish, which he placed near the water cooler. "That's a good kitty."

Aww-ll, Fontainebleau reiterated and hunched over his dish.

John turned on the stereo to light jazz. "And if she's lonely, you and I will cheer her up, won't we?" The house filled with cooking aromas. Dusk dripped indigo ink down steamy windows.

∃ᒧ • San Diego

Blue appeared at her office at 7:05 a.m., pushing the door open with her butt while juggling a cup of coffee in one hand, and a bag of donuts, a newspaper, and her purse in the other. Morning light slanted through the last shadows of night. It was quiet, except for distant squad room noise burble. How did one connect the dots, complete the circle, from the disastrous spiral of the clippings, to Jana Andrews's battered and swollen near-death on a doorstep? Munching on a donut, dunking it in her coffee (cream no sugar), she thought about this.

She called LAPD. From the clippings, Jana Andrews had been arrested in LA for passing a phony check just two years ago. Officer Reynolds of the LAPD Records Division was just having his morning coffee and he told her so. He was very playful and friendly, but he understood her urgency and logged into the computer system to help her out. As he did so, he engaged in a monologue: "Andrews...Andrews...hm...come on, system...slow this morning...do we have a Social Security Number?...we do? amazing...there it is...Andrews, Jana, DOB..." His voice caught.

"What is it?" Blue asked.

"This is not a personal friend or anything, is it?"

"No."

"Good. 'Cause this lady's been dead and buried over a year." He paused to let that sink in. "According to our data base, Jana Andrews, same SSAN, same DOB, died in a car accident with a boyfriend last year."

"Died?" Blue froze in mid-munch. Holy Toledo.

"Yup. No next of kin. The county did a Neptune job, ashes at sea. This lady did have a long nuisance sheet."

"Can you FAX it?"

"Of course."

"God!" Her hunch about Jane Willoughby and Jana Andrews being two different people was true.

Denton Horowitz at the Dolly Agency in New York City called. Same dry, little-man voice: "Oh, hello, Miss Humboldt. I have some new information for you."

"Shoot."

"Well, it's not much, but I found out that Jana Andrews and Jane Willoughby had different Social Security Account Numbers."

"Oh, Mr. Horowitz, you are a jewel." Blue sat poised to scribble. "I have an SSAN for Jana Andrews, and I wonder if you can verify it." He read it to her. "Wonderful. A perfect match. And now the number for Jane Willoughby?"

He told her Jane Willoughby's SSAN. "The funny thing is that I really can't find much about Jane Willoughby."

She thought about this. "Mr. Horowitz, Jana Andrews died in a car accident last year. I just thought you ought to know."

"That's too bad," he said with a genuine tinge of sadness.

"You've seen a lot of these young women, haven't you?" Blue asked, hearing herself sounding old.

Horowitz sighed. "Yes. Some go on and live useful lives. Some get rich. A few strike out on drugs, booze, you name it. It's always sad when you get a Jana Andrews. Makes you wonder how abused they were as kids, that sort of thing. Well, I'll get on this right away."

Martha Yee came in about nine. "You seem bubbly," Martha said. Blue hugged her. "Martha, I've got news." She told her about the morning's revelations. "Jana Andrews died a year ago. That means who we have in the hospital is Jane Willoughby."

After Martha left, Blue pored over Jana Andrews clippings. And the ancient picture of John Connor, looking scrumptious while the Whositses hung on his arm. Ah! She got a magnifying glass and peered into the past. There, made up for the camera, was the beautiful young woman. John Connor had tentatively identified her as the woman who'd come to Ajanian's two weeks ago. But he had not remembered her. She'd remembered him, and told him she was Jana Andrews. Was she really Jane Willoughby?

On impulse, Blue called the LA Times. She asked for the morgue, the newspaper's library. She asked the librarian, a young woman, to look up the obit on Jana Andrews. The librarian obliged, but there was no material on Jana Andrews. Dead end. Next, she called the newspaper morgue in Akron, Ohio, Jana Andrews' home town. A middle-aged man with a slow, heavy voice answered. She asked for anything on file about Jana Andrews. The librarian checked and found nothing. His name, he said, was Andreas Gump. Of the Akron Gumps, Blue supposed. Gump said: "Miss Humboldt, the subject and name headings in the morgue only pertain to major people and topics. We don't have a cross- reference for every person who ever lived in Akron."

"That's okay, Mr. Gump, I understand. Please bear with me. This is a homicide investigation."

"My God," the good citizen Gump said.

"Anything you can do would be deeply appreciated."

"What can I do to help?" Mr. Gump demanded.

"Please. We know Jana Andrews's age at death, so we can form a good guess what year she graduated high school. Could you check your microfiche files of Sunday papers during June of that year for articles mentioning her name? In case she made valedictorian or anything. I'd like to know about any mention of her. Also, check the high school yearbook. Use your tremendous intellect, sir."

"I'm proud to help."

"You are a patriot, Mr. Gump."

Late in the afternoon, John Connor called.

"Well, hello there."

"I hope I'm not disturbing you."

You disturb me. "No, not at all."

"How about dinner Saturday night after I get out of work."

She bit her lip. What to say? What to do? She already had a dinner date with Martha Yee, but seeing him appealed to her. Major decision, this. "Yes." She thought about this really hard. Would she choose John Connor or Martha Yee? Did it mean anything? She resolved to listen to the little voice deep in her heart.

She told Martha of the change. Martha seemed nonplused. "How about Friday then?"

They both want me. Argh.

∃∃ · San Diego

On Thursday, Blue continued her research. With a magnifying glass she studied the glossy picture of Jana Andrews. What a beautiful woman. What a shame that she had degenerated and died young. By now Blue had begun to think of the woman in the hospital as Jane Willoughby. Or whatever her real name was. Late in the afternoon, Tomasi called.

"Chief, I'm working this Jane Willoughby angle right now. That's my gut. I hope you'll let me stay with that for a while. I want to be here as soon as she comes to."

∃4 · San Diego

On Friday evening, Blue went out with Martha. They ate pesto pizza, then went to a cold, yawning disco place where mirrors flashed with borrowed neon and rock music pounded. Blue liked Martha but wished Connor were here. Was that dumb?

"It's a cool place," Martha said, ordering daiquiris. She took Blue by the hand and led her onto the dance floor. In one corner, men danced together. In another corner, women. In the middle, men with women. Waiters and waitresses in black and white uniforms raced through the crowd, like shuttling among countries but not needing passports; sort of an economic union.

Blue and Martha danced to slow, throbbing fifties love tunes. Martha held her tightly, and Blue let it flow around her. Under the palm trees, in a California ambiance of understatement, nobody seemed to care. Blue felt Martha's hands roving about her. This was one of the places they'd stopped at the other night when Blue had gotten drunk and barfed over Martha's shoulder. She remembered now. Rocking slowly, feeling Martha's hard slim body in her arms. Martha's cheek nuzzled against hers. A really challenging couple appeared on the dance floor. A tall, rangy blonde, body builder type, small-breasted and muscular, whose hair whipped loosely as she danced with the woman she was with, a slim blonde with a pillbox hat tilted rakishly over her forehead.

Blue remembered "Martha," she whispered. Fascinated, she watched them dance. Martha mmm?ed dreamily. Blue whispered: "Martha! Look!" She turned Martha bodily 180 degrees. "See?"

Martha snapped out of her reverie. "Darling, what is it?"

"Remember Connor's woman who had left the Jana clippings and disappeared? With the flashy blue neon sunglasses?"

Martha groaned. "Honey, let's not be at work. Not now."

Blue squeezed. "That's her!"

Martha's eyes bulged. "You're right."

"Wait here and be cool," Blue said. Martha watched from a window as Blue dug in her purse, found a cigarette, and went out to smoke. The two women were in the parking lot, where they kissed long and hard, stroking each other's limbs. Then the Amazon of the pair went one way, and Miss Neon got into a white Porsche. Connor had mentioned Porsche. Blue memorized the license plate: VIRGIED. She frowned. Virgied? or Virgie D.?

Virgie (and) Ed? She tossed the cigarette, went inside, and told Martha: "You've got to find out who owns that car."

"Like now?" Regretfully, Martha dug out her car keys.

They stopped at Martha's house, overlooking a small canyon, and Martha called Barnes at home. Barnes promised to have Operations make the VIRGIED immediately.

Martha poured a couple of rose coolers. She tried to nuzzle, but Blue gently, firmly pushed her away. "Not now." Seeing Martha's anguish, the pain in those lovely squiggle-eyes, she felt terrible. "I don't seem to be good at saying no. I'm sorry. Why don't I just say it? No."

They went out on a redwood deck overhanging the canyon, easily a hundred foot drop. Hundred twenty foot tall mature eucalyptus trees grew in profusion along the canyon's slopes, affording privacy. "You really confuse me," Martha said without a hint of the bitterness or pain she must be feeling.

"Blue, do you go for men?"

Blue laughed. "I was married to one once."

Martha looked into her wine. "That's not the question. I mean, now in your life. I would really like to know."

Blue took a sip of her own cooler, feeling the fizz and the sweetness in her throat. "Yes. Don't you, at all?"

"No." Martha rubbed her finger along the mouth of her glass. "Have you been leading me on? On purpose?"

"God no, Martha."

"I thought you're lesbian, Blue."

Blue felt confronted. She began to sweat. It was something she had put in one of her boxes. "I never think of it that way. I think percentages. I like women, but I like men too. I just don't know what my percentages are. I don't know if it's fifty-fifty or eighty-twenty. How about you?"

Martha finished her wine and tossed the glass into the canyon. "I get along fine with men except, in sex, to me they are drones. What does that make me, a hundred-ought?"

Blue squirmed. "There really aren't any neat labels, are there? Not when you really look at it."

Martha said, "The reason I asked, Blue, is I've been really thinking about you. You know. I'm glad you're being honest. I have a big crush on you. It's hurts—" her eyes filled, her mouth quavered, her fingers trembled trying to wipe tears, and her gaze fluttered up into the stars, anyplace where she would not have to meet Blue's eyes.

"Martha," Blue said feeling like a total heel.

"I understand," Martha whispered, a quaver. "You're not going to fall in love with me. I'll face that."

Blue went into the kitchen, found the paper towels, brought them. She sat near Martha but resisted the impulse to hug her. Martha took a paper towel and slowly dried her tears away, still sniffling, a hiccup now and then. When she seemed strong, she said: "You bi broads always amaze me."

"I was hoping we could be buddies," Blue said.

"Is that like let's just be friends?"

"Yes."

"No hope?" Martha asked.

"I can't change things."

"All right, I getcha," Martha said.

Blue suggested: "We're supposed to be ace number one cops, remember? Fighting crime and all. We can't very well do that if we're all bummed out about our love lives."

"Are you in love with someone, Blue?"

Blue shook her head.

"The Connor dude," Martha sighed.

Barnes called. "The license on that Porsche."

"Yes?" Blue asked.

"Belongs to a Virgie di Santo. Mean anything to you?"

She thought hard. "No..."

Barnes gave an address that Martha, listening on another phone, wrote down. "The woman has a clean record. Not even a parking ticket. Thirty two, works as a waitress at, oo la la, a lesbian bar on Adams Avenue. It doesn't say lesbian here, I just know the place."

On the way to Martha's car, Blue asked: "You want to check it out? Alone? With me?"

Martha slapped a twenty in Blue's palm. "Take a cab home," she said through swollen crying glands or whatever, "I need to be alone. I'll drive out there tonight and let you know when I've got my soul off the floor and put back together." She walked off, leaving Blue open-mouthed. In the car door, she added: "I'm sorry, I don't want to lay any guilt on you. We are all who we are, the way we are, we didn't ask to be this way, and we're doing the best we can." She drove off in a fishtail of dust, and Blue watched the red lights recede.

35 · San Diego

Saturday, Blue slept late. She woke to a rhythmic sound, like gongs under water, and wasn't sure if she were dreaming. She remembered last night with a pang. Was glad things were settled however painfully; quicker and better that way for everyone. Oh, and today was the big date with Mr. Hunko. She sat up, rubbing her eyes. The gongs were a calypso band playing at the pool many stories below. Tourist stuff.

She took a long hot bath, and while she was immersed in bubbles, John called, that enthusiast. "I spent the morning working in my garden. I'm planting a row of king palms at the edge of my property down in the canyon, and the heat started getting to me, so I took a dip and now I'm flopped on the couch."

"What's a king palm?"

"Opposite of a queen palm."

"Don't tease me.

"I'm not."

"I wish I had a garden. I'd love to work up a sweat."

"Gardening is great fun. You should come over and try it."

An hour later, wearing a burgundy terrycloth dress over her bikini, flip-flops, sunglasses, and a white baseball cap, she rang his doorbell in University Heights. He opened, wearing corduroy shorts. His long body looked slightly sunburned. He put on a cotton shirt. She stepped into a blast of symphony music. Chairs were up on tables. The place reeked of cleaning fluids. A vacuum cleaner sat in the middle of the living room with tangled cord. She put her purse down and flopped onto the couch, glad to be out of the heat and in his company. "Don't you have a cat?" She kicked off her flip-flops.

"He took a hike. Doesn't like the smell of floor wax and cleaning stuff. He's down in the canyon somewhere, pissed off, hunting mice or something. He'll be back tonight." He served a frosty iced tea with lemon wedge.

She laughed. "Sounds like you two are married."

He allowed: "I remember those days. Definitely no bed of roses. You get to know one another; what you're going to say next; what you'll do in an argument; what buttons to push."

"I was married once too." She thought of Mike and shrugged. It all seemed so distant and painless now. She was glad he changed the subject: "Please, come here on vacation. I'll take you to my favorite beach, Coronado. You can see Mexico most days. The surf is nice and there usually aren't any crowds."

She toyed with her lemon. "I've thought of taking some vacation time. Maybe then we could go—?"

"—To Coronado? Sure."

She stirred her tea with one finger. "You live alone."

"Yes. This is a big rambling house, pretty empty at times."

"Barnes blabbed about you. Says you have lots of ladies."

"I don't have them. They're just here." He looked impish. "Sometimes." He shrugged. "Whenever Barnes shows up."

They laughed. She asked: "How does a ladies' man settle down and stay true to one woman? Or does he ever?"

"I'd like to have a family. My problem isn't meeting women. My problem is the same as everybody else's, and that's meeting the right person. I have girlfriends, but they all have some reason why they can't get involved or settle down. I take it you're a free spirit too?"

"We seem to be comparing notes. Do you think I'm weird for not falling all over you?"

He sat closer. Serious. "You are a little different. I don't know why. You're refreshing."

"I do like you."

"I like you too. Is there a but?"

"I'm a little scared." She remembered last night. Poor sweet Martha. Honesty, that was the ticket.

"Blue, I thought you were the big tough detective. The world your oyster. What is this you're saying?"

"At least I have sense enough to be scared." Immediately she regretted her sharpness. He wiped his eye as if she'd spitballed him. "Maybe I'm just cool under fire."

Her cheeks burned. "You're good-looking." Understatement. She confided: "I'm afraid to trust." He gauged his words carefully, which she liked. "I don't want to hurt you."

"Thanks."

"Let's be honest. The thing about let's just be friends?" (She started; did he know Martha intimately? wouldn't put it past him; then again, she—no). "That's bullshit," he said. "I don't care if we ever sleep together. I want romance with you. Something real. How can I explain it? Not just sex, not just friends. Romance. Moonlight. A kiss. A dance."

That sent her. They embraced. She pressed her face against his chest. It was wonderful. She felt a deep shuddering sigh emanate from the depths of her soul. She breathed deeply, sighing at his body heat. She rubbed her face against his skin through the cotton shirt, smelling his body. She pulled him toward her. "Nice man," she said.

"I'll pick you up at 6:30," he promised.

Later, in her car, driving away, she wondered how many women had said 'nice man' to John Connor. It made her mad at herself. The long drive, the lazy afternoon, the many red lights, mellowed her thoughts. If he really knew her, would he trust her? She wished she could put a tag on herself once and for all. She wanted to know. Was she fifty-fifty? or eighty-twenty? Maybe even ninety-ten? She knew she could curl right up with him but for the thought of being used again.

After sightseeing, Blue returned to her hotel room.

Her body seemed to want to pour out katas. First she spent fifteen minutes stretching and relaxing. Then she practiced some tumbles. How quickly one got rusty. When she had worked up a dripping sweat, however, she began to feel strong. An hour later, she showered and lay down to take a brief nap.

It was night out when the phone rang. "Mmmf?"

"Blue? This is John Connor. I'm in the lobby."

"Oh my God. I fell asleep. You'd better come up. I'll just be a few minutes." She quickly put on her long, conservative jeans skirt and a yellow silk blouse before he knocked. He brought white flowers in a pot wrapped with red foil. He wore a dark blazer, white shirt open at the collar, gray slacks, and black loafers. His dark hair was neatly combed and he looked preppy. He had a nice smile, a little wrinkled at the eyes, not enough to make him look old, just a little worn and comfortable. She fussed over the flowers. He settled on the bed. She sat at the vanity and blow-dried her hair, teasing the ledge over her forehead. Warm air caressed her neck, made a soothing melody while he sat on the bed.

She inspected herself in the mirror and decided she did not like the yellow silk blouse. She picked up a men's white cotton shirt and warmed up her travel iron. "Sorry I'm running late. I'm actually a quick dresser for a woman. It's really quite simple, if you have certain set outfits. Of course, I dabble from one blouse to another, or one skirt to another, but I just don't see the sense in trying on dresses for hours."

He had a very serious expression.

She laughed. "I'm chattering. I'm sorry."

He seemed startled. "No, chatter. Do. I don't mind." His eyebrows were arched high.

John Connor drove through town in a sense of wonderment. The whole city looked fresh and new because of Blue. He felt like singing, but could not carry a tune. Her perfume. Her hair. Crisp facial lines. Not model material. But the girl next door. Yes, he really liked starchy white shirts on a woman like that. Her eyes had a different quality than, say, Jana's; not sulky or mysterious, but daring and humorous, dark and mischievous, down to earth. Her hands rested on her pocket book which was in her lap, and the fingers were white and fine. He pushed aside the melancholy thought that she lived so far away and was here for such a short time.

She took to Fontainebleau immediately, and the cat permitted her to adore him. "Oh, it smells so good here." John had an apron he wore for such occasions. It said "Danger—Men at Work." He wore it, and heavy kitchen mittens. He seated Laurel at the dining room table, which was decked out in white linen.

She wowed, admiring every little touch: The flickering candles, oak book cases, perfect fidelity stereo, chrysanthemum- crested silver tableware, Noritake china. It made him feel good. He served up the savory roast, still crackling in its hot sauce; French-style green beans; small round singed potatoes with just that bite to them; and a thick gravy with sliced carrots in it. He poured Napa Cabernet Sauvignon.

"You have a piano," she said, feeling dreamy. She slid onto the seat, opened the cover. Warmed her fingers, touched the keys. "What would you like to hear?"

"You're kidding."

"No, I'm serious." She tapped out an arpeggio. "I get tired of police work and would just like to make music." She banged out a pert little piece of Maple Leaf Rag.

"You are full of surprises," he said, clapping.

She bowed and closed the piano cover. "Get me started, and there is no end. Come on, I want this evening to be about you."

"Or you and me," he said. He started a small fire in the fireplace, using oak and hickory logs he'd been curing on a windy spot out on the hill for several years. He let Fontainebleau out. Smoke tinged the air. He poured more wine and sat on the thick shag before the white-brick fireplace, beside her. The fire crackled behind them, and the flue hissed softly. "That sure is a pretty fireplace," she said, resting her face against his arm.

"Thanks. I built it myself." He settled back with an arm around her. "I've totally redone this house, and I'm still working on it. It was really just a little 1950s box. After my parents died, and I came back from New York City, this house became a hobby, a passion. I'm planning to put up a brick wall with ivy in front, and coach lights. Lots of plans. Want to see the view?" She nodded. He offered his arm and led her out to the redwood deck. She felt hypnotized by the lights spreading for miles in Mission Valley. Black canyon sprawled along the edges of light, a wilderness pinioned by urban expansion. She nuzzled her shoulder blades against his chest as he held her.

Back in the living room, he added another log of hickory to the fire. Fontainebleau had entered the house while they had the door open, and they fussed over him. "I've had a wonderful time," she said (not quite trusting him, yet). "I'd better get back."

He kissed her, and she enjoyed the feel and the taste of him for a minute before pulling away. "Blue," the poor man said, "there is so little time. You'll be going back home soon."

She touched his cheek. "I like you."

He drove her to the hotel. She felt comfortable, tired, anxious to cling to the magic of the moment. Under the Canary Island date palms by the sea, she let him undo some buttons. The flimsy bra slid loosely aside. His tongue darted in her minor cleavage and nuzzled small jutting breasts. If he'll only wait, she thought. She pecked a kiss on his cheek and was out of the car in a second. Ran into the lobby, pausing briefly to see the Porsche's red rear lights receding.

She went up to her room and lay on the bed. With the lights out, and the harbor glow on her pillow, she imagined what it would be like if he were really, truly hers, they two in love.

∃ᖯ · Palm Springs & San Diego

Daddy! Telephone for you!" Astrid's piercing voice rang through the halls.

"All right, thank you," Hugh Stone fairly bellowed in return. He had just put Marga to bed. Drunk, wasted by her self-abuse, with cold hands and feet, and a swollen edemous belly, she weighed next to nothing as he carried her from the sitting room to the bedroom. Repelled by the smells of alcohol and stale cigarette smoke, Hugh hated to touch her anymore. He pulled the coverlet up to her gaunt jaw with a dismal feeling. He sat on the edge of the bed for a few moments, stroking her cold claw. If there was an ounce of sentiment in him, it was through her, for the past. With Marga and Stone Electronics gone, he had no allegiance to this country. His goal had been to return to Switzerland and retire as a wealthy man. For him, the U. S. was no more than a jungle to fight for meat in. And now, his meat threatened by other hunters.

"Daddy! The friggin' phone!"

"I'm coming!" He felt a moment of hatred for Astrid. Spoiled, selfish, self-adoring third-rate pianist. Then again, maybe he should have spent more time with her.

Garth's deep, full voice: "Mr. Stone, bad news. That guy we spoke of, the holy ghost?"

He meant Brady. "Yes?" Hugh fumbled for a cigar.

"He's dead."

"What?"

"No bull. They found him burned to death in his car in Vermont. Seems he went skiing. Got drunk and burned to death."

Hugh slumped down in a chair. He felt the blood drain from his brain as the implications of this latest disaster struck him. "Where the hell is Roger Filmore?"

"I don't know, Mr. Stone."

"You haven't heard from him?"

"No, Mr. Stone."

"Doesn't that strike you as odd?" Hugh fairly shouted.

"No need to get huffy. I'm doing the best I can."

"Of course you are," Hugh said soothingly. He dialed the special number in Mexico City. After interminable delays on staticky lines,

LeSable answered, sounding pissed to begin with. "LeSable, I have problems."

"This better be good, Hugh. My man Alvaro gave me a month to come up with the money, and this is Day 15. Hugh, for God's sake man, don't let me down! I was counting on you!"

"One of our main customers just died. Plop. I'm short three million bucks."

"Hugh," LeSable groaned, "you said you were flush."

"Can you stall them a few days? I don't have cash on hand."

"These people don't want to hear that shit."

"LeSable, be reasonable. We've done business before. You know I'm good for it. Another week. That's what I need."

LeSable seemed near tears: "No, Hugh. The Alvaros have told me they want a meeting. In the next few days. They have their shipment ready to go, and they expect their money. Or else I am in big trouble. And you with me."

Hanging up, Hugh began to consider the necessity for a sudden trip to New England. He called Garth.

"Yes, Mr. Stone?"

"I need some phony DEA ID for myself. Can you help me?"

"Yes, Mr. Stone." Hugh wondered if Garth had sprung from a Frankenstein movie.

After flying into Hartford's Bradley International Airport, Hugh Stone took a Pilgrim Airlines flight to Tweed-New Haven Airport. As the DeHavilland Twin Otter puttered in toward a landing, Hugh smiled into the mirror of the black velveteen case open on his lap. In the case lay the innocuous objects: a bar of soap, a comb, a rubber band, an old straight razor. Gray daylight from a cold, cloudy sky made the mirror shine, illumining his face.

Hugh met Garth in a restaurant in New Haven, a drafty, old-fashioned barn with many rooms paneled in dark wood and with somber stained glass windows depicting the Yale and Harvard football logos. It was located on narrow, snow-choked Wall Street among neo-Gothic buildings. The old tables, heavily carved over generations, filled with lunch time professors and students. Bill Garth looked solid and athletic in a heavy sweater, corduroy trousers, and boots. He slid the phony ID across the table.

Hugh grilled: "Have you seen Roger Filmore?"

Garth's massive forearms folded on the rocking table. Pizza remnants lay under origami napkin debris. "No. He hasn't shown up in days. I checked his hotel room and all."

Hugh glanced at the ID, saw it seemed okay, and pocketed it. "Vincent killed Filmore and left the body. Faked his own death, the slime ball," Hugh said. "It's the only explanation. I never gave him enough credit, the weasel." He finished his beer and wiped his mouth with a paper napkin. "I don't have any time to lose. Garth, get out of town. Let met handle this."

"That's risky, Mr. Stone. You want to expose yourself?"

Hugh pointed a finger in Garth's face. "You are the muscle. I am the brain. You do what you're told."

Garth's face assumed a dark hue.

"I'll get it out of them if I have to hang the police chief by his nuts." He rose and headed for the door. He looked back.

Garth fiddled with his beer glass. His huge hands, with their big blunt fingers, throttled the narrow-necked glass. "Mr. Stone, are you cracking up?"

As he stepped through the snow outside, Hugh kept seeing the look in Garth's eyes, the tone of his voice (expose yourself...) and suddenly he realized that Garth was now working for the Alvaros. Had to be. (very risky...) Garth was too Neanderthal for such thinking. He turned and went back, thinking of slashing Garth, maybe in the men's room. As he swung the door open, Hugh saw that Garth was no longer sitting there. Just as well. It might have been a tough kill. A nuisance.

Hugh drove to Hamilton, smoking a cigar and more comfortable now that Garth was out of the loop, as far as Hugh was concerned. He walked into the town hall and found the police department receptionist's desk. He asked for Special Agent Humboldt.

"I'm sorry," the 50th woman said with a flutter, "Miss Humboldt is unavailable."

"I must speak with her." He flaunted his papers.

The woman warmed a bit. "Oh. In that case, you should speak with Detective Stosik. Eddie Stosik. They were in San Diego together, but he's just flown back. Just a minute, I'll ring him for you." Hugh sat coolly on a wood bench in the hallway. Minutes later, she turned. "You can go in."

"Thank you so much." He entered a dark wood door with POLICE Department bannered on a frosted window. He took the inner offices in with a glance: two fat men in blue uniforms typing one-fingered; a lady with more lipstick than mouth, more glasses than eyes, hunched over some form in a typewriter; not a thing stirring in this pathetic little village. A big red haired man with dirty fingers and glinty eyes stepped out. "Mr.—"

"Silverstone. Special Agent, DEA." They shook hands.

"Eddie Stosik. Detective. Come in." He led Hugh into a cluttered office. Hugh noticed golf clubs, pictures of a fat woman and three grimacing children, a gun in its holster hanging from a hat rack whose crown was a liquor advertisement. All very gauche. "What can I do ya," Stosik asked.

They sat. "I'm on a special investigation, and it looks as though my path has crossed that of a DEA agent named Humboldt. I'm told you have worked with her."

Stosik paused a split second. "Yes."

"In San Diego."

Again that pause. "Yes. Here and in San Diego."

Hugh laid a photo on the desk. "I am after this man."

Stosik looked. "That's Monsignor Gordon. We're looking for him too, and so is Father Binder, only Gordon's dead."

Hugh smiled. "He isn't dead." As Stosik's eyes widened, he laid Filmore's photo before him. "He killed this DEA agent and switched ID's. Your Monsignor Gordon is really a con man named Vincent Brady, and I think he's got several million dollars of local church money."

"Holy Bejayzuz." Stosik rose and held his head. "Wait a minute. Wait. You're DEA, but you didn't know Blue, that's Humboldt, was working with me. I'm a little confused." He took another look at Hugh's ID.

"We all work very independently," Hugh said.

Two minutes later, Stosik slammed through the door carrying two cups of coffee. "Okay, Special Agent Silverstone, I'll buy it. Sorry about the third degree."

Hugh accepted the offering of coffee. "You're just a good cop, doing your duty. Now, can you help me find Brady?"

Stosik shrugged. "There's a suspicion that he's got a little love den in San Diego. That's what Blue calls it."

"Blue?"

"Laurel Humboldt. Your agent." He frowned.

"Oh yes. Her nickname. She's in San Diego?"

Stosik nodded. "San Diego PD. You can call her there if you want." He moved the phone closer.

Hugh said: "Thanks, I'll call her later. In fact, I might fly out there. She'll have the address of this love nest.'

"I imagine so. SDPD has a watch on the place. They found some woman stabbed and half beaten to death there. It's been in the papers." He buckled on his gun. "I'm afraid I've got to run, Silverstone. Got an appointment. Anything else you need?"

Hugh rose. "Not right now. Thanks."

Stosik walked him outside. It was cold. Night was setting in. It was getting inky dark. Their breath came in steamy lungfuls. Their feet crunched on snow glittering with unnatural lamplight. "You sure don't sound like a cop," Stosik said.

"What does a cop sound like?" Hugh asked. He felt the razor in his coat pocket.

"I dunno." Brazenly, he took out a pad and wrote Hugh's license plate number down. "You rented this car in New Haven. That's odd. Aren't you assigned in Manhattan?"

Hugh said *fuck you so very much* in a tiny inaudible voice and leaned forward. Stosik, holding his pencil in one hand and note pad in the other, leaned forward so their foreheads nearly touched. "What did you say?"

Hugh flicked open the razor and, in one motion, thumb on the razor's back for pressure, drew the razor toward himself along Stosik's throat while using his left hand to shove Stosik away, thus adding to the depth of the cut and pushing the explosion of blood away.

Stosik lowered his hands. He stared at Hugh. Blood bubbled out of his mouth and nostrils. Blood spurted in violent pulses from the severed neck artery. Stosik looked shocked. Then his eyes closed and he died as he sagged onto the bright red carpet of snow.

There he lay silently as Hugh lit a cigar and drove off to catch a flight to San Diego. Miss Humboldt, he thought, maybe you know where my dear friend Vincent has run off to.

37 · San Diego

Late Sunday, the phone rang as Blue let herself into her hotel room. She ran to answer. "This is Tomasi. Humboldt, I have bad news."

"Oh?"

"Eddie Stosik is dead."

"No." Her body gave a startled jerk of disbelief.

"I'm sorry, Blue." He'd never called her that before. "I got the news from Chief Murphy this afternoon. It's probably going to be in all the morning newspapers. I wanted you to hear it from me personally." Overwhelmed by grief, she leaned forward and listened as he detailed what he knew. She reached absently for the tissues in her purse and blew her nose. She had a haunting picture of Innocenta and her children looking accusingly at the world, herself included for no rational reason. She listened to Tomasi's story about a mysterious Silverstone who had dropped in and out of Hamilton. "Miss Humboldt, I imagine you want to fly in for the funeral which is on Tuesday?" She did, and he directed: "I'll allocate some money. You take care of the booking."

"I will."

"Humboldt, I want to tell you again how impressed I am with your police work."

"Thanks."

She hardly heard the rest of what he said: "The FBI is running a check on all the Silverstones in the country known to their database for slasher attacks. It was a straight razor, in any case. Humboldt, it was a single firm, slashing cut from a straight razor, drawn toward the killer, who had to be standing directly in front of Eddie. He... he died fast. If he suffered, it was over in seconds."

꒕꒐ · Connecticut

Monday morning, Blue flew home for the funeral.

It was foggy in San Diego. Traffic crawled the two miles along Pacific Highway from her hotel to the airport. She left the car at its rental agency and took the little shuttle bus to the terminal.

At five p.m. she stepped off the plane in New York. Wind wailed on empty runways, and the cold bit fiercely, especially a stray gust right up her back. Passengers hurried out the terminal gates. This can't be real, Blue thought. Wind hurled sheets of powder through angry air. Outdoor lights had a bluish, arctic look. Airport workers moved about in heavy boots and heavy leather mittens with wool gloves on inside the mittens. It was a shock, after sunbathing on her balcony. Blue caught the six p.m. commuter plane to New Haven, a short, choppy ride.

Mom had dinner waiting. Blue hugged her parents. They were scared for her, and she reassured them as best she could. But they never understood half of what she said, so what was the use. Home was warm and dry, and she felt halfway comforted. They sat up until ten, and her parents asked about California. It was like Mars to them. Blue painting a pretty picture to give them joy: The sails on San Diego Harbor by day, the lights of boats passing at night, the sunshine, the gold-like silica in the sand, and the wonderful people she had met.

Her old room seemed like another person's, and she was vaguely grateful. Her mother now used it to iron, so there were stacks of laundry in the room and it smelled of spray starch. Blue made herself drink and fell asleep.

Tuesday morning: She borrowed Dad's car, a clean but unimaginative Dodge sedan ten years old, and drove along the seashore on I-95. Her own car was parked in Hamilton.

Hamilton's town green lay prettily frosted and illumined, a postcard. She drove to Sacred Heart Church.

There, only there, the full impact began to really hit her. Her knees shook slightly, not entirely because of the cold, as she drove up on the scene, and it was very real:

The nineteenth century church, its red bricks and white marble cornices darkened by generations, loomed with back slate roofs and pencil-point bell towers against the icy furnace sky. The small cobblestone square in front of the church was crowded with people, everything from police and fire officers from departments throughout the region, to politicians in black finery, to Catholic school children in uniform, and a lot of parishioners in their Sunday best, the women wearing hats or black lace veils. She bawled and bawled seeing the beautifully detailed black Cadillac hearse with its gray-frosted windows.

There was a row of black limousines. The hearse and the limousines had their lights on and engines running. Before the hearse were a glittering array of police motorcycles, at least forty of them. She lost count of the number of white helmets of the uniformed motorcycle officers. The line stretched out of sight for blocks.

Behind the limousines were the family cars, and behind those were police cars, fire department station wagons, and more official-looking cars.

She had to illegally double-park outside a bar. Then she hurried toward the church. Besides her business skirt suit, she wore a hat whose black lace veil kept fluttering before her eyes. The funeral mass was late getting started. People were still filing into the church as Blue emerged into the square. She spotted Innie and her children among a large family group. Innie looked devastated, and the children had haunted expressions, and Blue's heart went out to them. She saw Chief Murphy and other police officials and hurried that way. She half expected to see Eddie come sauntering up with a twinkle in his eyes and a cigarette hanging out of a crooked grin.

Instead, a hand grabbed her arm and she spun around. "Vito."

"Hi, Blue." He smelled of sour Camel cigarette tobacco. His mouth looked tiny and his nose very large. His dark eyes were sad. "Let's stay in the back of the church."

She held up her veil. "Is Tomasi here?"

He shook his head. "You and me, chum. Come on, it's probably warm inside." He took her hand and towed her along. There must have been two thousand people, too many for the church. Stores on the block had thrown their doors open early to let those who could not get into the church warm themselves.

Blue and Vito managed to squeeze in and stand near the holy water. The crowd surged around them, and Blue's side was pressed painfully against the shell-shaped font jutting out of the wall. Vito stood with his hands folded before him.

Blue bawled some more. Vito gave her a large handkerchief smelling of licorice. "Thanks." She kept blowing, and her nose kept running.

With a thunderous shock that nearly tossed her out of her shoes, the main organ pipes crushed out the opening chords of the Introit. From there it went—Blue could see nothing, save one momentary view of the coffin in the main aisle, draped in the American flag and surrounded by lit candles. Although she had grown up Catholic, she hadn't been to a Mass in ages. From memory, she loosely followed the service. The eulogy was broadcast over a p.a. system. After forty-five minutes it was over, and she was glad to get out.

As Blue and Vito walked to his Chrysler, they looked back and saw the coffin carried heavily down the stairs. Behind it, fatly sprawled, barely able to walk, supported by several relatives, came Innocenta. The children next, walking with confused solemnity. The town's fire horn boomed for miles. Then the sirens began to wail, signaling that the hearse was ready to move. Vito put the Chrysler in drive. They slowly followed a Connecticut State Police car with flashing red lights.

On a cold hillside, the coffin rested under an American flag. What the Vietnamese had once called the Thousand Flowers Flag because of its crisp white stars. Father Pollack read the burial ceremony. His vestments blew in a sharp cold wind. Innie collapsed and had to be carried to an ambulance.

On a promontory nearby, a National Guard Honor Guard loaded, presented, and fired one salute. A bugler blew taps as the flag was folded and the coffin lowered. The flag was given to Eddie's oldest son. "We can go now," Vito said. Blue sniffled, dabbing her eyes as Vito drove his boat onto I-95 and it was *forever goodbye Eddie.*

∃⫞ . Manhattan

Blue met with Tomasi in his Manhattan office Wednesday morning. He poured black home-brewed coffee from his steel thermos. "Must feel like home again."

"Thanks. Yes. I wish it had been for other reasons."

He put his feet up. "I'm sorry, Humboldt. I didn't know the guy but I think he was a good cop and I'm sorry we lost him."

"Do we have any idea where Silverstone is?"

Tomasi held his pencil up with his index fingers like goal posts. "No. The FBI ran a check of all slashers named Silverstone, and while there was one in Colorado ten years ago who used a knife on his mother in law, and another one in Philadelphia two years ago who used a trowel on his construction foreman, there haven't been any Silverstones using straight razors, which is what this weapon seems to have been." He dropped the pencil. "However. Several things. One, the weapon was not left at the scene of the crime, which probably means the guy carries it and may use it again and probably used it before. Second, the FBI computer comes up with a match in Los Angeles about a month ago. What makes the Los Angeles snuff so interesting is that it's the same exact MO, and it's so recent." He pulled out a FAX showing a line diagram of a human body. A dotted line had been drawn along the left side of the neck. "I think the same guy did it. Look at our original drawing that came out of the Coroner's office. Eddie was slashed to the left side of the neck, so was the kid in LA. Both cuts were a single slash from a powerful hand, presumably a man's, and the penetration was enough to induce massive bleeding, an instant drop of blood pressure to the brain, shock, death within seconds. They both literally died before they hit the ground."

"The angles are wrong," Blue said. "The Los Angeles guy's slash was more toward the front, and the angle to the horizontal...oops."

"Exactly," Tomasi said. "You're very sharp, Humboldt. The guy in Los Angeles was a tall man. A basketball player who had gotten himself involved in the drug trade. He was about six inches taller than Eddie. The point is, it gives us the height on our man. I'd say six feet even. Not only that, but the way he slashed both men, he was very close, so he must be respectable, trustworthy looking. He's physically strong, and he packs a razor. A guy wouldn't pack a razor unless he knew how to use it. I mean, a gun would be easier."

"Noisier," she said.

"So get a silencer. Now another thing. The secretary says the guy may have a slight accent. So if nothing turns up in the U.S. we try maybe Canada; Quebec maybe. Or Europe. This guy didn't look Latin. Another thing. Here's a composite sketch."

Blue regarded a chilling face. Total stranger. She turned away. "I'm still waiting for our lady to come out of her coma."

"You've been doing a bang-up job out there. I've got Vito working undercover as a baggage handler at JFK. He says it's a good physical workout and the ladies are nice to look at."

"That sounds like Vito," Blue said smiling.

"There is one other thing." Tomasi leaned forward. "On the personal side, Humboldt. Maggie has called here several times."

"Again?" Blue's stomach sank, and her smile drooped.

Tomasi's eyes dipped in a knowing, ominous nod. "She came in here a week ago confidentially and told me you and she were having an affair and you left her and she didn't know how she could go on without you."

Blue sighed deeply. "It was a mistake, Mr. Tomasi."

He shrugged. "I stay out of personal things, unless other factors affect an agent's work. With you, there isn't anything like that. We get a lot of nuts in here, and she seems pretty nutty. I just thought you ought to know. An embarrassment could really affect your career with law enforcement, especially with the Federal Government. You understand of course."

Blue stopped at her apartment, knees still shaking from the funeral and the conversation with Tomasi. The old red brick high-rise depressed her. Dust on everything upset her, so she did a quick cleaning. It was good to be among her stuffed animals, her books, her favorite chair by the TV. After cleaning, she showered and dressed. She packed her suitcase anew, throwing in more of her nice clothes.

Then she read her piled up mail. Bills; junk mail; and notes from Maggie. Cards, letters, drawings in manila envelopes...sadly, she added them to the O-file. What use, the past? Why did the woman persist, when it was all so long gone and over with?

On impulse, filled with kindness, with a desire to set things straight, to make a nasty break somehow cleaner, she dialed Maggie's number. She remembered it by heart. As the phone rang in the familiar Lower West Side studio, images like old newsreel pictures flipped through Blue's mind. The smell of Maggie's place—paints, acrylics, thinner, always with that overtone of black coffee re-percolated to a tarry state. Maggie, tender. Maggie, jealous. Maggie mothering her through her divorce pains. "Hello?" the familiar voice said, distracted, not happy, busy probably, bitchy. Blue hung up.

40. Chicago

The mishap with Jana Andrews in La Jolla had scared the dickens out of Vincent Brady. What had flipped lovely Jana's switch? He still loved her, in some molecule of his soul, and maybe one day he'd try to approach her. But mostly he was scared.

He fled to Chicago, where he nervously checked his hoard at the First Mercantile Bank. His balance as Vincent Ulric of CompuGraphiX was $3,785,963.47. Wow, not bad at all.

He bought himself a brand-new Mercedes, beautiful job, glossy black with a white interior that smelled of new car smell, loaded with everything from quad stereo to air conditioning.

His apartment was a five room suite with two full baths, kitchen, sunken living room with giant TV screen and full stereo entertainment center, and a jacuzzi built into a sun porch overlooking the Loop. It five thousand dollars a month.

The building was an older brick high-rise, luxurious, with security doorman and video patrolled entrances. The hallways were richly carpeted and smelled of cleaning fluids. The atmosphere was posh and muffled. More than anything, it was very private.

A world-class city beckoned with all of its lusts and temptations. He was of the flesh, and the city was of the flesh, but his soul was with the Lord. He was a spy in the house of the Devil. He stopped into bar after bar and felt himself to be the equal of everyone he met, and then some. He bought drinks here and there, and found himself easily at the center of attention of small groups of people who appreciated his wit and charm. Time and again, women tried to attach themselves to him, but he resisted the temptation because he knew they were only bar flies and he was after the high-class hookers. He would have to build up new connections here. Virgie DeSanto and her outlaw types had been fun to party with in San Diego, but some instinct told Vincent not to try and contact her.

One night, he picked up a young woman with blond hair and a pretty face who could have been a sister of Virgie. Her name was Delilah or something. Vincent took Delilah home, plied her with a fine wine, and bedded her. Delilah fell asleep. Vincent had another two or three drinks which put him under.

In the middle of the night, Vincent woke with a terrible thirst. He staggered toward the kitchen and looked for orange juice. While he did so, shadows followed him along the walls. He screamed.

Delilah sat up in bed. "What is it, dude?"

Vincent saw her outline clearly on the wall. The Angel of Death moved with the breeze, her negligee blowing up. Vincent dropped the orange juice bottle. It shattered on the floor. He ran into the bedroom and threw himself across the bed. "You've got to get out of here," he cried.

"Relax, sweetie," Delilah said.

Vincent smothered her. "Get out while you can. Get out. She's after me."

"Who is after you?" Delilah demanded slipping on her jeans.

"The Angel of Death," Vincent said.

"Right," Delilah said. "I've heard it all before. Your old lady's on the elevator up."

"No," Vincent said. He fumbled in his wallet and found several twenties. He offered them. "Here, darling, take these. Get out of here. Don't let her find you here."

Delilah finished dressing and grasped the bills. "Get yanked, you crazy bastard. I was fast asleep."

"Go on," Vincent said, "quick, and God bless you."

"You're nuts," she said, with a scared expression as she let herself out of Vincent's pad as fast as she could.

Vincent knelt by the bed. The shadow standing there could only be one person. He pretended to be praying, all the while his breath was coming in frightened gasps. When he looked up, the shadow was still there. A mysterious wind was stirring the curtains and the shadow seemed to move closer, old and familiar.

"Mother," he said, "I know it's you. I haven't been bad. Honest, I haven't." The shadow stepped closer, the wind whispered in the curtains, and Vincent curled himself on the floor in a ball.

41 · Palm Springs & San Diego

Hugh Stone found things relatively unchanged at his home in Palm Springs. On the surface, everything seemed calm and orderly. The interweaving sprinklers on his front lawn lent the sprawling estate the effect of a park with fountains. Gardeners were busy about the roses, and landscapers on tractor-mowers rode about trimming the side lawns. On the periphery, his several full-time guards maintained slow but thorough security rounds.

Hugh had just flown in from the East Coast and his head was abuzz with desperate last-minute ideas about how to raise the three million in cash. LeSable was after him, pressing him. Hugh knew the score. LeSable was history unless a miracle happened. And Hugh had no heart for miracles. Now it was every man for himself. The Alvaros were going to waste Pierre; and then they would come for him. Now it was a matter of survival.

The manufacturing plant was totally leveraged. Nothing more to be wrung out of that turnip. His desperation was humiliating. The trip to Connecticut had been wasted. Perhaps he could smoke Vincent out in San Diego. And that young woman—Laurel Humboldt; she might prove to be the key, since the police were undoubtedly hot on Vincent's trail; so if he could get to her... he'd square Pierre away and get the Alvaros off their backs. Then he could sell the drugs, get rid of Vincent, and get himself out of hock.

When he walked through the front door he found his daughter Astrid waiting for him in her night gown holding a cigarette. "Daddy," her sharp voice made piercing echoes in the huge foyer, "Mummy kept calling out for you all night."

Hugh attempted to kiss her as he rushed by. 'Honey, I'm—"

She grasped his sleeve with her free hand and let herself be towed along for several feet before he stopped. "What, Daddy? You're busy? Are you ever not busy?"

"Your hair is a mess, Astrid. Were you out all night?"

"No!" she shrieked, her voice cracking. Her eyes glared at him blackishly, from a mixture of mascara and bags. "Will you wait just once? Mother was in a delirium last night. I had to call Dr. Thompson, and he gave her medicine, but he said she has to go into rehab again right away or her health will fail completely. He needs your signature."

"All right," Hugh said. "Let me put my briefcase in the office and I'll go in to see her." He began to notice again how thin Astrid was. He had a sneaking suspicion, which he dared not voice right now for fear of amusing the staff, that she had been to her diet doctor again. She reached angrily for the briefcase. "Here, I'll take the goddamn thing."

He pulled it away from her. She looked cheap, holding her cigarette up that way. They confronted each other silently, while two Vietnamese women in black maids' uniforms hurried away. He knocked the cigarette out of her hand. She stormed off holding her gown against her thighs.

Leaving the briefcase in his office, he lit a cigar. He locked the office behind him and went to his wife's room. He found her looking wasted and pale, propped among pillows to prevent her falling out of bed. She was sleeping when he opened the door. He regarded her a few minutes, trying to fathom how he felt about this marriage any more. He could get Margaret into a home where she would get excellent care and perhaps dry out enough to be coherent. They'd not spoken coherently in years.

Hugh studied the marble-like skin, the leathery features, and withdrew, closing the door in silent revulsion.

He heard a crash downstairs. He heard the splintering of glass, and then Astrid's shrill screams of fury. Hugh went to his office and called Dr. Thompson to have Marga admitted.

He stopped on an upper landing, looking through a leaded- glass window. He saw Astrid's Ferrari roaring, fish-tailing, away leaving dust drifting over the drive. Poor crazy thing.

A sobbing Vietnamese girl was on her knees, cleaning up a broken crystal vase and spilled chrysanthemums. He stopped, patted her shoulder, and gave her two twenties from his pocket. She wiped her tears and rose, curtseying. She thanked him, but there was dark resentment in her eyes. He didn't blame her.

He got into his car and headed for town. He gave his lawyer limited power of attorney to sign the papers about Marga. By nightfall, he was on a plane bound for San Diego.

That evening, Hugh had dinner at the Radisson, where he had booked a suite. Then he stepped out into the mellow evening and lit a cigar. From a phone booth he called LeSable. "Hugh, what the hell you think you are doing?"

"Keep Garth out of my hair. I don't need him. He's not trustworthy. And you suprise me. Like an old woman."

"You are a fool."

"I get the job done."

"You don't have the money, that's what I got to explain to these people, and they are pissed. I don't think they will let you run the show like we planned. You are too crazy. You killed a cop, and for what? Even Garth has purpose when he kills."

"Just hang in there a while longer, LeSable.'

In the morning, Hugh checked the phone books. There were several Vincent Bradys, and he copied down the addresses and phone numbers. He bought himself breakfast at a fast food restaurant. He ate while driving. One by one he checked them out. And became angrier. The first was a retired Navy commander in a wheelchair in Poway. The second was the fortyish owner of a swimming pool store in La Mesa, no match at all for the Vincent that Hugh would know instantly on sight. The third was a long-haired taxi driver who worked nights and was angry to be disturbed during his daytime sleeping hours. The fourth Vincent Brady was a black insurance agent in National City. Finally he tricked a bank employee into inadvertently revealing the address of the Vincent Brady property he was after, in La Jolla. He drove there, parked a block away, and walked past. The place was dark and shuttered; nobody had been here in days. Across the street in a car were two men eating ice cream. They had not noticed him. Good. He went back to his car.

Eating dinner at a restaurant, he read the newspaper, and an article caught his eye:

SAN DIEGO (AP) —Police are still puzzled by the stabbing and bludgeoning of a well-dressed woman at an expensive condominium complex. A large amount of cocaine was found at the scene, leading police to suspect she may have been part of a drug deal gone sour. The as yet unidentified woman remains in critical condition at University Hospital. Police are looking for a middle-aged man who rented the condo for the weekend and then disappeared without a trace. Witnesses at the condo complex described the man as charming, gregarious, and attractive. An informed source indicated the man is wanted in connection with a Drug Enforcement Administration (DEA) investigation... Hugh read on, and as he did so, a picture of Vincent sprang to his mind. The woman sounded like someone he knew. After some puzzling, he remembered meeting a woman like that. But where? His birthday party! Jane...Jana... what was it? Andrews! And Vincent had been proud of getting her phone number. And all this in San Diego. Perhaps, Hugh thought, my quarry is closer than I think.

42 . San Diego

San Diego's warmth wrapped itself around Blue as she stepped from the plane. The palm trees, the harbor, the sails leaning in a noonday wind greeted her. First thing, she showered in her room at the Hilton. The cold, the grime, the sadness of her East slipped away. Eddie's death remained like a cold hand, but the funeral was behind her, and she could get on with her life.

She stopped in at the office. Barnes was out. Her notes and clippings were strewn about as she'd left them. She felt a pressing urgency to do something, to somehow make good the loss of Eddie. Just then, the phone rang.

Hugh called SDPD, which directed the call, and she answered on the second ring: "This is Laurel Humboldt."

"Oh hi," Hugh said, "this is Father Jenkins from Hamilton."

"Have we met?"

Another bulldog like Stosik, he thought. "I was referred to you by Father Binder."

A pause. Just like damn Stosik. "Yes?"

"We're after Vincent Gordon, Miss Humboldt. He stole a lot of money. I'm just wondering what progress you're making."

A pause. "I'm sorry, Father. That's sensitive information. I can't just talk about it like this. Maybe if I met you first."

"I'm going to be in San Diego shortly."

"Why don't you give me a call then?" she said.

"I will," Hugh said, brightly. They thanked each other, said goodbye, and hung up. They had no clue, the poor fools. Yet he was at a disadvantage too. He must find out what she knew.

"Blue!" Martha Yee stepped in, wearing a beige skirt suit with white blouse and chocolate droopy bow tie that went well with her custard skin and rich black hair. "Welcome back."

"You okay, Martha?"

"I'm okay." They both laughed nervously.

"How's the patient?" Blue asked.

"She'll pull through, is the word."

"Still no talk? No revelations?"

"No, but we're watching her around the clock."

"Anything on the lady with blue neon glasses?"

"Hasn't showed at her house in days. We're watching."

People were not returning her calls and she was getting nowhere today. Tired from traveling all night, she went to the hotel and slept. Late that evening, John Connor called. "You need a nice midnight dip in the pool."

"Nice to hear your voice. I'm very tired, John."

"The pool is heated, Blue."

It took her twenty minutes. Her system demanded a cigarette, but she resisted because he would smell it. Instead, she ate an orange. He kissed her as she stepped across his doorway, but she dodged aside. "Where is that heated pool?"

"Orange breath," he kidded and removed his bathrobe. He wore a baggy purple bathing suit. She went into the bathroom and put on her bikini. The pool was divine. John dove in with a rattle of the board and a neat slicing sound of water. The night air was cold if you exposed your shoulders, so she kept down low in the water. The interior of the pool was illumined. She kept diving down and slowly floating up. He performed a mating dance around her.

Stars twinkled high up in the black sky.

The city skyline shone like toy blocks.

He cornered her and she let him kiss her. His tongue hungrily pressed against hers, his arms encircled her, and his hands played along the firm curves of her body. What am I feeling? she asked herself. Her fingers half-heartedly explored his abdominal muscles, his puckered brown nipples, his muscular upper arms. Her hands clasped his head, his neck, his face.

"It's late," she said. He pulled her top off, and she let him; it would be one less piece of work she'd have to do. She pulled the top with its trailing straps close to her pointed, hard breasts and turned to heave herself out of the pool. "John," she whispered, "please be patient with me just a teeny bit. I'm—out of practice."

He ruffled her hair. "Romance, remember? No rush."

They showered and, chattering, wrapped in towels, hurried inside. "Can I brush my teeth?"

"Sure. Use my brush."

She brushed slowly, letting the minty taste assault her taste buds. She felt safe with him, and she hoped he would have patience with her. The less he pushed, the more she liked him.

When she stepped out of the bathroom, he was asleep on his back, mouth slightly open, breath escaping in slow, measured exhalations. Turning the light off, she gingerly got into bed so as not to wake him. She lay awake for awhile, smelling the place. It smelled of wood and paint and linen and not-very-often-cleaned carpets. It smelled of him, and she let that soak into her tired being. Pretty soon, as the moonlight washed over her, she fell asleep.

She awoke later. Fontainebleau was meowling outside the sliding glass door. She slipped out of bed and let him in. "Prrr!" he said, thanks, and jumped up on the bed. She shivered and closed the door, locking it. Her upper arms and shoulder blades and bare breasts had goose bumps. She found his shirt and slipped it on, along with her panties. Then she got back in bed, lightly, like a feather falling to earth. He was snoring softly. She nuzzled under the sheet and sighed deeply. The cat made circles and then settled near their ankles, purring. She snuggled close to John. He put his arm around her back without waking. She fell deliciously asleep with shivers running up and down her spine where her back was spooned against his belly.

Sometime during the night, they both woke. She felt a stray fingertip, not hers, on her sheer panties. She squirmed, feeling aroused, wet. They stroked. Moaned together.

"John, do you really like the women you sleep with?"

"What's this, a quiz show?"

"Okay, I'll rephrase it—"

"Your chin digs into my nipple when you talk."

"—Sorry." She kissed his nipple and blew on it. He rolled his eyes up, stirred sensually. "Do men like women they sleep with?" He ran his hand down her back, and she knew her skin had a smooth, heavy feel. "Do they?"

"Laurel, yes. Ohh.."

"You like me, don't you?"

"A lot, Laurel." He pulled her close. "A lot."

When she felt his breath on her face she parted her lips and met his mouth hungrily. Their tongues thrust together. Her fear and stiffness evaporated in a flood of longing. His hands explored her body. A tingly feeling of powerful pleasure rose along her spine in waves. She felt a deep longing, a forgotten hunger that she had not felt in a long time.

If it was just a brief affair, or even a one-night stand, she did not care anymore. She tenderly held his head between her hands and devoured his mouth. She slid down a bit and kissed his chest, catching his nipples with her teeth. She grasped his genitals, rocking them violently, wanting to suck.

He jack-knifed in bed, holding himself.

She kissed his shoulder, afraid of what she had done. It had been a long time, and she'd forgotten..."John, Johnny, did I hurt you?"

He lay back laughing. "Blue, you'll have me singing alto." Seeing her hurt, embarrassed look, he put his arms around her. "You've got a lotta woman bottled up in you, baby."

"I'm such a klutz."

"No, you are perfect."

He meant it. Passion walloped him. Romance. Her body was perfect for him: Full-bodied, just right; curvy and athletic, small-breasted, round in the butt without overstatement. They nuzzled for a long time, growing ardent, hands exploring, touching, caressing. Blue pulled him on top of her. Eyes closed, mouth open and upraised as if to catch some invisible rainwater, she cried out softly. With a force that seemed to not his own entirely, he thrust into her tight body. She orgasmed sobbing, biting her wrist. When he tightened his hands around her firm butt, she shoved her heels against his shoulders and tossed her head from side to side. It was Lollie redux, but with a deeper passion by far. Sweat flew from his hair, dripped down his nose. He blew beads of sweat off his upper lip. Her legs were spread open, held apart for him. Her face was upturned in a delicious agony and she gasped with each pounding arrival. He felt a wildfire flashing up his spine as the tremendous pleasure overwhelmed him.

She, sensing that he was approaching climax, cried out for him, reached for him, shook him by the arms. She let herself go, twitching as waves ran up and down her body. They wailed together. He shuddered as orgasm flooded him. She felt the change in his rhythm. She hugged him and kissed the shell of his ear. She turned him to the side and wrapped her arms and legs around him like a reward. They were both soaking wet with sweat and her secretions and his cream. He let her stroke him and whisper how good she felt. He pinned her wrists back and kissed her and told her how good he felt. She had a golden warmth inside and forgot her fears.

५३ · Palm Springs

Hugh flew to Palm Springs to wrap things up.

Astrid was in a froth, pacing the halls in high-heeled boots and tight black pants. She wore too much make-up, as usual, and in one hand she was waving a tattered piece of sheet music. "Dammit, Father! Dr. Johnston came by in his own car, followed by an ambulance. They took mother down to Bayside. Where were you? Gone, as usual. I ache when I see how you treat mother."

"Sit down," he told her, pointing to the sofa near the piano. She did as she was told. He went about closing doors—not necessary, because the servants had all left. "Astrid, you need to get out. You need your own apartment in, let's say New York City. How would you like that? Chicago? No, Frisco."

Sensing a weakness, an opening, something she was an expert at, Astrid rolled her eyes up and exclaimed: "Oh, so now you want to buy me off."

Hugh said: "I have loved your mother and I still do. This is what is right for her. She is going to die if she doesn't get the help she needs."

"Bullshit," Astrid said, forcing the perceived opening.

Hugh held his finger up, and when she saw the look on his face, she knew to shut up. "Astrid, you are the one who does not love anyone. The reason is because all your life you have been given things. Maybe your mother and I were not always the best parents. Between her drinking and my preoccupation with business, we neglected your upbringing. We both have to pay the price for that now, because I don't think you are able to stand on your own feet. You have learned to survive by using people. If there is one mistake I made with you the last few years, it's been in always pulling you out of the holes you dug for yourself. I'm not going to do that anymore. I'll give you an allowance, and that's it."

Astrid looked shocked. "You bastard."

"There is no love for me in you, is there?"

"You are not throwing me out."

"Oh?" He was surprised. He'd half expected her to burst into tears. If precedent held true, he would comfort her, beg her not to cry, and offer some new enticement to live sensibly. Instead, Astrid sat back coolly. "Listen, Father. I know you have been involved in drug dealing. Pierre LeSable. Does that name register?"

"You are too clever for your own good."

Astrid lit a cigarette. "Mother rants and raves when she's drunk. I found it out from her." The lighter clicked shut, and she was enveloped in fragrant smoke.

"So she knows."

"Of course she knows. She may be sick, but she keeps tabs on you. Without her, you'd have gone to jail years ago.'

"Without me, you'd have been in the street years ago."

"I loathe you," she said.

He loved her, and this hurt. "After this, I must be firm. You have to go, Astrid. You have no love for me, and under those circumstances I see no reason for wasting my time on you."

"Oh but I do," she said.

"Reason with me."

"I have records hidden away in a bank vault. I could have you sent to jail."

He grinned. "Do you realize that if I were convicted, this whole estate would be turned over to the courts and you'd get nothing? Are you so dumb, despite all of your cunning?"

She bit her lip.

He laughed out loud. He had her now. "No, my dear, we have a stand-off. You have to sacrifice your loathing for me in the interest of the money you will inherit. In turn, I have to be careful not to turn you out. Does that suit you?"

"What are your terms?"

"That you get out of here and stay out. I'll pay whatever you want. You keep your mouth shut and stay out of my house."

"You have to certify your will, leaving me everything."

"That's no problem."

"All right. I'll be out of here by this evening. I have a lawyer. Our lawyers can write up something."

He nodded. "You may yet make it on your own as a pianist. In the meantime, don't shit in your nest."

She turned and stormed out of the room.

He felt a vile taste in his throat. It had turned out badly. He poured himself a large glass of scotch. He had never wanted it to be like this. He dialed the hospital to ask after Margaret. Maybe, in time, Astrid would acquire some humanity. Hugh toyed with the razor in his pocket idly while waiting for the hospital to answer.

Next morning, Hugh called the bank. He was told the papers were being drawn up, but it would be a week because contractors were examining the buildings minutely for structural soundness.

Hugh called LeSable. "I will have the money in one week."

"Sorry, *mon ami*. The management is firm. No deals. They don't like the way you handled the Connecticut mess."

"Get me another week," Hugh begged. "I'm selling my home, for chrissake."

"I'll see what I can do." LeSable's voice sounded unsure. "I'd be careful if I were you. They don't trust you."

"Thank you. I'll be careful." In reality, he planned to disappear before LeSable's handlers could get to him.

At nine a.m., the real estate people came. Hugh stood on his front portico with his hands behind his back and regarded the eerily deserted estate. Astrid had moved out the night before without a word of goodbye, the ungrateful bitch. With Marga gone, dying in the hospital, the place was unbearably empty. I am finished here, Hugh thought. He had arranged for the money to be wired to him in Toronto. If the authorities did not track him down and freeze his assets, or the Colombians did not kill him.

Within hours, Hugh was on the 757 shuttle from Los Angeles to San Diego. A stewardess—pretty young thing, he was beginning to notice these things more now that he was finished with Marga—leaned over to ask if he wanted a drink. He shook his head and she walked on down the aisle. He pulled out the Rasurex shaving kit and held it on his lap. He expected it would be Garth who would come for him. He and LeSable would be shipped in boxes. It would be a statement. The mob would figure out that it was the same gun that had killed Guzman. It would be the Colombians' admission of defeat, a gesture of appeasement to the Mafia. But you gotta catch me first. He snapped the Rasurex box shut. The other thing: How could he let Vincent get away with 3.5 million dollars? No way. He would die first.

44 . San Diego

Soft rock music and the aromas of bacon and coffee awakened Blue. She groaned and rolled over in bed, remembering where she was. The curtain was open, but the sliding glass door was closed. The patio was enveloped in a thick fog, and the wood floor was steeped in colorless solemnity. "I hear you," John Connor said offering a glass of orange juice. "Breakfast in bed, coming up."

She sat up. "That's nice." He kissed her, and she sipped. "Last night was wonderful."

"Yeah. Hold on, I'll bring breakfast." He did, and she chewed salty, crispy bacon. He ate from a plate in his lap. She sat with her feet on his knee and felt very comfortable.

"If you came to San Diego to live, you could stay here."

She nearly choked on her coffee. "You think you could tolerate me for a few weeks?"

"I could always send you to the Hilton."

"I'd be fifty before DEA transfers me here."

He was about to open his mouth to say something, when the phone rang. It was Barnes, for her. "Humboldt?"

"Yes. How did you know I'd be here?"

"A wild guess," he said dryly. "I need you right away, you and Yee. It seems our bird has flown the coop."

"Who?"

"The woman in the hospital."

"No. I thought she was on IV's and all."

"The IV's came out yesterday. She ate a pudding about six a.m. The officer outside the room says everything was okay until the nurse went in with medication at seven. The bed was empty."

"She walked right past her guard?"

"U-huh. The man looked up and even said hello to her. Beautiful tall dark-haired woman, he said, dressed to kill. He never made the connection. There was a man with her, dressed in a dark gray business suit, very conservative."

"Got a description?"

"Yes. We'll start at the hospital and work from there."

Blue handed Connor the phone. "Gotta run." She found her clothes and changed in the bathroom. He saw her to the door. She wrapped herself tightly around him. "Don't you go away, okay? Or what is it they say? Hang on to that thought."

It was a five minute drive to UCSD Medical Center in Hillcrest. Barnes wasn't there yet, but Martha Yee was, dressed in a white summer skirt and pastel blouse. The fog thinned, and sunshine began to slash the haze. Barnes's car pulled to a screeching halt at a forbidden red curb. Out of the car, jacket flapping, he waved them along with him. "The lobby is full of reporters, I'm told. Pretend we're visitors for some patient."

"Was the man with her the Slasher?" Blue ventured.

"First thing I wondered," Barnes said over his shoulder. "Not if the Slasher and Silverstone are the same person. Silverstone is in his late fifties. This guy was a tall, good-looking guy in his late thirties. Pampered. Ivy League, certainly had breeding. Money. That fits with the lady."

They entered the University of California, San Diego Medical Center, a cluster of buildings located against a deep leafy canyon. A Life Flight helicopter was just taking off from the helipad on some errand of mercy. The corridors were austere and labyrinthine. Barnes seemed to know his way around. They emerged on 5 West, the General Surgery Ward, and bypassed the nurses' station. Uniformed officers kept reporters away. The three detectives had to show badges. There was still an empty chair in front of the single room where Madame X's guard had sat. The bed had a slept-in look, nothing out of the ordinary. "No signs of struggle, nothing," the uniformed officer told them. "Some guy, somebody she knew and trusted, came and got her. She dressed in clothes he must have brought, and off they went."

"Must have been a man who knew her well enough to know her clothing sizes," Barnes said.

"Yes," Martha said. "Maybe her husband? Boyfriend?"

They took the elevator down and stood looking on the ER platform. "That sure is a big wide world out there," Barnes remarked with a forlorn look.

45. San Diego

Blue stopped at her office and found several messages there. One was from Mr. Andreas Gump of the Akron, Ohio newspaper morgue. Another was from Mr. Denton Horowitz of the Dolly Agency in New York City.

Blue called Gump first.

"Oh, Miss Humboldt. How nice to hear from you. Say, I checked every lead I could think of. A Jana Andrews graduated from Kennedy High School in Akron. Lovely girl, really."

"What color was her hair?"

"I checked into that like you asked me to. She was a red- head, Miss Humboldt."

"That's what I thought." LAPD had said the girl in the car crash had red hair. "Mr. Gump, could she have had a dark-haired girlfriend in high school? A tall, very attractive girl with a name like, let's say, Jane Willoughby?"

"There was no female student with that name in any of the graduating classes in Akron the years I checked. A Bill Willoughby graduated from Kennedy High, is as far as I got."

"Brilliant, Mr. Gump. Can you find out where this guy Willoughby is today? I'd like to talk with him."

"Sure, Miss Humboldt. I'll be glad to."

"You won't get in trouble with your boss?"

"No, on the contrary. My city editor told me to pursue the story and I might get a job as a reporter."

"I'll put in a good word for you, Mr. Gump."

"I'll do all I can. Am I really helping your police work?"

"You are providing a vital service. I intend to have a letter of commendation sent to your city editor. Could you hop on it, Mr. Gump? I love you, I really do."

"You have a sexy voice, Miss Humboldt."

"So do you. Next time I'm in Akron, let's do lunch."

"I'd like that."

Next, she called Horowitz.

"Oh yes, Miss Humboldt," the dry little old man voice said. "How have you been?"

"Fine, Mr. Horowitz. You have something more for me?"

"Well, it's not much. On the first thing, I was not able to locate a fingerprint. We don't deal in that sort of thing. I checked the file on the off-chance, but there wasn't a fingerprint on record. Rarely need 'em, unless there's a lot of jewelry involved on a job."

"And the other thing?"

"I was able to contact a woman named Lila Murdoch who is now a high school principal in the Bronx. She was a model for the Dolly Agency. Very reserved, very proper, very, very, you know what I mean. That tall English look, you know? Well, Miss Murdoch is now Mrs. Cannon. The important thing is, she did some jobs for us and she remembers a girl named Jane Willoughby. Tall, dark-haired, with deep blue eyes. That's what Mrs. Cannon remembered most, the deep blue eyes. And there was some red-head the Willoughby girl was hanging around with a lot."

"Name?"

"Mrs. Cannon could not remember, but it sounds like Jana Andrews. That's all I got, Miss Humboldt, have I been of help?"

"You most certainly have, Mr. Horowitz. The woman we want matches the description you just gave of Jane Willoughby. When I get back to New York, I'm going to give you a big hug."

"My wife might not like that."

"She doesn't have to find out."

"We could start some awful rumors about you and me."

"I'd enjoy every minute of it. Will you keep checking?"

"I will, young lady."

46 · San Diego

Blue and John sat by the pool in the evening breeze, dressed in terrycloth bathrobes. They had made love, gone for a swim, showered, and were eating left-over enchiladas with rice and beans. Balmy wind in the canyon sent smells of jasmine and lilac. The night sky hung around them like a canvas spattered with stars. A distant freeway whispered like a seashell.

"I wanted to talk," she said. "Are we going to see each other again after I go back to New York?"

"I've been wondering."

"Do you want to?"

"Yes. I want to."

She took a deep breath, held it, and exhaled slowly. "It's so far. Are we serious? Or is this just a little you know..."

He took her hands. "I dream about you, Blue."

"Oh, you're full of it."

"We make love in my dreams. I was married once, and it was a bummer, and maybe—no, not maybe, for sure—I'm leery. But you are special. You are always happy, Laurel."

"Not always. Only an idiot would be always happy."

"I wish you lived here. Or I lived there. We would have time to get to know each other. It might work out, you know."

She felt her heart skip. She grabbed his face. "Did you really say that?"

He nodded. "Yes."

She kissed him on the lips. "I was hoping you'd say something like that just one time so I could remember it."

"My luck. Somebody comes into my life and she has to leave."

"You could write to me," she suggested. "You could come visit me in New York. I have a nice apartment. Well, nice inside when nobody's throwing beer bottles off the twentieth floor. It's warm, and I've got a big cozy bed."

"Is that an invitation?"

"Sure."

"You don't have a dozen boyfriends back there?"

"Not a one. The closest thing—" she thought of Vito, and laughed. And Maggie—and frowned.

The air got fresh. John put his arm around her and they went inside. He put a log on the fire. She brought two glasses of wine. They cuddled on the couch and ignored the game. Blue felt happy, but unhappy too; she wanted to blurt out the truth. Was she a fraud? Would he be hurt like poor Martha? Sipping wine, she said: "I think you'd have to be an actor to pull this off if it's not real. No offense."

He sipped his. "No offense taken. I can't believe it myself. But Laurel, I don't know everything about you either."

That hit. She lowered her eyes.

"Are you okay, Blue?"

"You're right. I haven't been totally honest with you."

"Now would be a good time."

"I've been wondering if I should tell you."

"Go on, tell me."

"I've been agonizing about it."

"Tell me, Laurel."

"All right."

"Silence fills the room."

"I have to gather my thoughts."

"A guy."

"No."

"A disease."

"No."

"Speak, for crying out loud."

She felt tears welling up. "I wish...there were more time...because I don't want to tell you...maybe I'm a fool to tell you...because I don't know how you're going to feel about me after I tell you." She began to cry, big alligator tears that rolled down over her fingers and fell like rain from her lips.

"You're drenching my couch."

She went into the kitchen. Returned with tissues and wiped her face. Sat down feeling like a kid confessing that she had broken the window with her ball. "John, I'm not really sure about myself." She gulped twice, and he wondered if she were going to cry again, but it appeared that she had cried herself out. "I've had boyfriends here and there. I went with one guy all through high school and he dumped me for a big blonde. I had a couple of boyfriends in college, but no offers of marriage or anything, and I was too shy to really go out of my way to meet guys. Funny thing was, I was always athletic, and I knew a ton of guys. Everyone at my karate studio liked me, I think, and they were a bunch of really neat guys. They used to pull tricks on me like putting shaving cream in my bra while it was in my locker during practice, or turning my wristwatch forward an hour so I'd be all screwed up the next morning. But they always treated me, well, they almost spoiled me. Other girls used to be jealous because I seemed to have boyfriends coming out of my ears."

"My sweet little angel, what is the point of this Iliad?"

She embraced him hard. "Kiss me."

"Am I going to lose you?" He kissed her passionately for long minutes. Then when she lay on her back looking up into his face, she told him. "I am sometimes attracted to women. I want you to know that, because I'm trying to be fair with you, and I hope you'll be fair with me. I've made love to women. I don't think of myself as a Lesbian or anything, because I do love men, and John, I am just crazy about you."

He was silent, and she thought He's gone.

"I'll leave if you want."

"I'm falling in love with you. I can feel it in my heart, and my heart never lies."

"Even after what I just told you?"

"Falling in love and being rational are two different things." He agonized. "We need to look at this rationally. If you said you are attracted to me, would I have this lovesick, hurty, wonderful, deep feeling like my heart fell into my stomach? No. Am I nuts about you? Yes. Then the only other question is, if we're in love, will you be seeing women?"

She said simply: "No. Will you?"

"No." He dabbed her eyes tenderly with a tissue. "Blue, I think I knew sort of. The way you and Martha Yee seemed to hit it off, and I knew about Martha Yee in any case, from a friend."

She blew her nose. "I walked into something here in San Diego. I didn't mean for it to happen, and I killed it. Poor Martha. It's over. Can you trust me and believe me?"

"Yes."

"I want you to know something about me. I'm very loyal. I never cheat. When I'm in love with a guy, I'm in love. That's how I got hurt so bad. That's why I'm so afraid to fall in love with a man again. Can you understand that?"

"That's an awesome responsibility you thrust on me, Blue."

"All I ask is that you be honest with me. The two guys I was in love with didn't do that for me. Will you promise?"

"I promise. In fact, Fontainebleau raves about you when he comes out of the canyon for his milk. He's a smart cat. I listen when he talks."

"You're a pretty smart cat yourself." He was taking her clothes off. I'm 3000 miles from home, alone, a cat up a tree. Now I've done it. I'm in freefall without a parachute. And as he touched her she cried: "Yes!"

47 · San Diego

Martha Yee and Blue had lunch at a La Jolla gourmet French- style restaurant (with Mexican and Southern California undertones). It was Martha's day off, and she had asked Blue to go shopping with her. Their bright parcels were stacked in the trunk of Martha's car.

"Cold vichyssoise," Martha said. "Mm-mM." She spooned enthusiastically.

Blue munched on a chef salad with walnuts, chicken bits, and creamy Italian dressing. "I'm not so crazy about onions," she said.

"You're the fast food type, I take it."

"Only in emergencies. I've been back on my workout schedule. Jog five miles a day, work out on the beach, practice my katas."

"How is Mr. Wonderful?"

Blue reddened. "Pretty wonderful."

"That's nice," Martha said pleasantly, enigmatically, spooning soup.

"I suppose you think I'm a fool."

"If it itches, scratch it."

"Oh Martha."

"No, I mean it, he's a doll. Most women probably don't get to base one with him." Blue shrugged and took a long sip of her lemon-lime fizz. Martha added, "If it ends, it ends. Enjoy it while it lasts. Make sure he's not using you. You know men."

"I had forgotten."

"You are the girl next door, when you dress nice and aren't punk. I kind of envy Mr. Connor. You make a lovely couple."

Blue felt her cheeks burning. "Martha, it's not that hot and heavy yet."

Martha made a wry face. "I think I know you by now, maybe better than you know yourself. You wonder about yourself. I don't think you belong in my world. Go for it, if it isn't him it's some guy like him you're meant to fall in love with."

48 . Chicago

Vincent Brady sat in the dining room of the Park Plaza Hotel, eating one egg poached, three strips of bacon, and a sliced banana in light cream, when the waiter brought him the morning paper. "Mystery Woman in Murder Case Disappears!" the headline screamed. Chewing more slowly, soon not chewing at all, Vincent read the newspaper story several times. He left the paper on the seat, paid, and quickly left.

Collar up against the cold, Vincent cursed his bad judgment in getting involved with Jana Andrews. Something about her haunted him, and he could not say what. Now the game was nearly up. Vincent would have to move quickly. Because if Jana was alive, she would surely be coming back to Chicago. No matter how big the city, he would always have to look over his shoulder to see if the Angel of Death were coming after him with a knife again. Besides, Vincent had no doubt Hugh was after him, not just for the three million, but for his throat.

He stopped by to see Mr. Graham, who bounced up from his chair and pumped his hand. "Mr. Ulric. How nice to see you!"

"You are looking well," Vincent said. "I need to immediately cancel all my accounts here."

He thought for a second Graham was about to faint.

४९. Uruamac, Colombia

The time was up, and Pierre LeSable was called to Uruamac. Alvaro was ready to ship, and he wanted his money. First Pierre had thought of running, but he knew Alvaro's people would find him somehow. So he returned to face his master. How charming Sr. Alvaro was! The silvery fuselage of a DC-3 glinted in the running lights of a jungle airstrip near the great mansion. Odors from the workers' camp—cooking, urine, engine oil, cigarette smoke—drifted in the air under the fuselage.

"It is nothing," Sr. Alvaro told Pierre in his modulated Castilian Spanish, "you tried hard. A temporary setback."

"Bless you," LeSable said. In his nervousness, he was eating chocolates. He offered them to Sr. Alvaro, who accepted a hazelnut truffle with fondant flourishes, and to Bill Garth, who was smoking a cigarette and dourly refused.

The plane was fueled, checked out, and ready for take-off. It would fly north to the Mexican state of Chiapas on the Honduran border, refuel after a flight of about 1100 miles in the state of Sinaloa on the Gulf of

California, and then, hugging water most of the way, fly out to sea over Baja California, angle to the northeast, and, flying low under coastal radars, land in the Arizona desert. Arrangements would be made to deliver the cargo on the U. S. east coast. This was that first shipment Pierre had worked so hard to arrange. Office equipment. Copiers, computers, and the like. Only one of the copiers contained the drugs, worth millions on the street.

The DC-3 took off smoothly on twin engines. Sr. Alvaro made small talk, and Pierre felt relieved. He outlined his plans for a new attack on the New England market, and Sr. Alvaro smiled with his narrow face and cupid-bow lips, nodding often. The jungle was pitch black as a vast ink blotter. The night sky shone clear. Sr. Alvaro went to sit with the pilot. Bill Garth excused himself with a copy of the San Diego newspaper, a week old, and headed for the bathroom. Pierre moved to a window. He tried to count the stars and identify the constellations. This would all work out all right.

In the bathroom, Bill Garth screwed the silencer onto his .357 magnum. He would have preferred to use a .45, whose slug would not go through but would whiz around tearing the victim apart inside. But it had to be this exact gun, which had wasted Guzman. As Bill left the bathroom, the old frog turned. A grimace, a scream, grew in his face. The whites of his eyes, the pink of his tongue flecked with spittle, looked terrified. "You have chocolate on your face," Garth said and shot him three times. Pop pop pop. LeSable's body slumped.

"Good work," Sr. Alvaro said, emerging from the cockpit. "It was good of you to reconsider your alliances."

"His choice of partners was terrible," Alvaro said minutes later as they packed LeSable's body into a coffin, surrounded by dry ice. "You can never trust a man like this."

Alvaro, cutting Pierre's stomach open with a gutting knife, said: "We send a clear message to our friends." Bill Garth carefully wiped the revolver down to remove fingerprints. Then he wrapped the weapon in tissue paper and stuffed it into the body. "Yes, Mr. Alvaro."

In Sinaloa, as dawn broke, the plane landed. A Mercedes picked up Bill Garth and Sr. Alvaro. The DC-3 flew on.

Alvaro was content things were back under control, almost. At the airport in Mazatlan, he ordered Beel into his car. He lit a cigarillo and filled the car with acrid smoke which he found comforting but which obviously irritated the Norteamericano's eyes. "Beel, you must eliminate Mister Stone to wipe out the last traces of this mistake."

Garth nodded. "I understand. I'll be in Palm Springs by tomorrow, and I'll settle the score."

"This may be of some help to you," Alvaro said handing Garth a folded piece of paper.

A name, an address, a phone number. Bill Garth frowned.

Alvaro had a weary, crafty grin. "It always amaze me. His own daughter. She found out about the deal and called me. I think she hates him. She may do business with you."

50 . Chicago

"So I want to move back into the mansion," Astrid told Sonya Braxton, her father's realtor.

Braxton laughed nervously, off-guard. "Why, Miss Stone?"

"I have reasons. It's just temporary, you understand. I'll stay in my personal apartment, and I won't bother you and your associates. I could even show the house for you."

Mrs. Braxton dubiously said, "that might work." She regained a bit of composure. "There is nothing in your father's stipulations that prevents you from being in the house before it is sold."

"The will," Astrid said.

"What do you mean?"

"Have you seen his will?"

"Really, I had no idea this was going to be so complicated."

"It's simple, really. My father promised mother and I will inherit everything, but I don't believe a word. He never loved us, you know. He plans to sell the estate and not provide for my mother and myself. Rest assured the sale will be highly contested. I have some money, Mrs. Braxton, and damn good lawyers. I just want you to be clear on that."

"What do you want me to do?" Mrs. Braxton said, slumping.

"I want you to keep me informed about the details if any offers are made. We can then negotiate."

Mrs. Braxton said, "I'll keep you informed. I hope lawyers will be unnecessary."

"That's the idea." Astrid slammed the door as she left.

"Hello, Mother," Astrid said on the rolling green lawn of the Hollycrest Institute.

"Baby," the trembling old woman said and raised bony purple arms. She sat in a wheelchair on the concrete walk. The nursing assistant, a Mexican girl, curtseyed and left them alone. Astrid hugged Marga reluctantly, relieved that they had cleaned her up so she didn't smell. "Mother, how are they treating you?"

Marga managed a grin. "They're trying to reform me, and I'm afraid they're having a helluva time. You look splendid, darling. Are you eating right? You look a little thin."

"Father has put the house up for sale."

Marga registered shock. "So." She folded her hands and stared off into space, into the past. "Where is he now?"

"I don't know. He threw me out of the house."

"Oh darling." Marga reached for Astrid. Astrid chose that moment to allow herself to be hugged again. She would take good care of her mother. "I always knew that one day he would walk away. I know I haven't been a good mother—"

"Mother!"

"No, it's true. I wasn't a good wife. I drank and I smoked and look where I am now."

"It doesn't have to end this way," Astrid said. "You don't have to stay in this place."

Marga raised her chin. "My darling. I can't cope, you know that. Here at least they keep me out of trouble."

Astrid knelt down and gripped Marga's hands. "Mother, I can get you out of here. We can get a house together. You'll have nursing care. You'll be near me."

Marga shook her head. "He has everything in his name. I don't blame him. I was—out—most of the time." She held her hands up to her face and looked away. "Forty years we were married...we loved each other very much...and this terrible drinking...do you know, right now I can't even picture his face...we haven't had a sober conversation in twenty years...but just think, I don't remember his face!"

Astrid shook her gently. "Mother, he put you here and threw me out so that he can take off with all the money."

Marga touched her daughter's face with trembling bony fingertips. "He can't do that to you, darling."

"He is doing it!"

Marga shook her head gently.

Astrid had her purse handy. "Mother, I have some papers here. My lawyer drew them up. I can get you out of here."

"Oh?"

"Dr. Johnston will go along with it. Legally, he has to."

Marga looked at the crisp new documents typed on heavy bond.

"If you sign there, Mother, you'll become my ward. I know it sounds terrible, but I'll take good care of you."

Marga laughed. "Is this a step up or down for me?"

"It's a step out," Astrid said. "You don't have to sign. If it's about your dignity, I understand."

Marga shook her head. "I'm nothing but trouble, darling. I'll start drinking again. You'll see how much trouble I can be."

Astrid shook her head. "I'll have nurses to take care of you. Take you shopping. Do your hair. You don't have to be in a prison like this."

Marga chuckled. "Well, I've always been one to try anything." With that, she signed the papers.

Astrid hugged her. "I'll have you out of here in a week or so."

Marga folded her hands. "Send the nurse to me on your way out, darling. Listen, I know you better than you know yourself."

"Oh, mother."

"Don't oh mother me, Astrid. I can see gears and wheels turning in that pretty head. Just don't outsmart yourself."

Astrid dropped the papers at her lawyer's (laughing to herself picturing the expression on Dr. Johnston's face when he learned he was losing his lucrative patient).

Wearing sunglasses, she drove her convertible Jaguar across town. Stray wisps of blonde hair blew around her high forehead, and her pampered skin looked tanned and lovely. The Carleton Lodge, a three hundred room hotel, loomed on the desert horizon like a sugar cube. She parked in the shade of some big palms overgrown with ivy near the hotel's golf course.

She walked in a side entrance, avoiding the front desk, bypassing the elevators, and climbed up an outside stairwell to the third floor. She sauntered down a dusky, air-conditioned corridor smelling of carpet cleaning fluid. Twirling her sun glasses amiably, she let her eyes adjust to the dim light. She inspected the room numbers one by one until she found the one she wanted, and knocked.

William Garth opened the door. He looked tanned, refreshed, and ready. He looked her up and down.

"Hi there," she said.

He glanced up and down the corridor. Old habit, she supposed, repressing a giggle at his ridiculousness. "Come in," he said. He had a deep burring voice. As she stepped in, she noted he was very muscular. Hair billowed in clouds around his limbs. He wore a bright Hawaiian shirt, short white corduroy shorts, and one white cotton sock. He held the other sock in his hand. "I was just about to go for a swim."

She closed the door, walked to the patio door, and looked down on the edge of the desert. The pool was a kidney-shape of greenish light. Tanned bodies in bikinis and shorts lounged under Cinzano umbrellas. She let him stare through her thin dress. "Well, Mr. Garth—or do I call you Bill?"

"Bill will be fine." He had a long, youthful face, marred only by a slight scar on one cheek. He had a masculine beard shadow. He sat on the bed and took off his other sock. "Miss Stone, I understand you contacted my employers."

"I'm sure you were surprised, Bill. You're such a good-looking man. I had expected—"

He laughed. "What? A little greasy guy in a gray suit and a big hat?"

"I understand why you are here."

"You do?"

"Yes. You are to kill my father, and I want to help you."

He threw the sock down. "Miss Stone, not much amazes me anymore."

"Would it help if I told you that my father ignored and abused me all my life? That he drove my poor mother to drink and that she's now dying in a sanitarium where he stuck her? That he has disowned me and is selling everything and planning to skip town like a thief in the night?"

"You have your problems," Garth said.

"I thought it would make your job easier to know that."

"I don't really care. I met him once or twice and he seemed like a jerk, but that's just a personal opinion."

"I'm glad your mind is made up."

"I can do what I have to without any help."

"Sure," she told him, "but I can make it so much easier."

"What can you do for me, Miss Stone. Or should I say, what do you think you can do for me?"

"I can set it up for you."

He lay back. "Okay, you have my attention. Talk."

"He's skipped town already. On your own, you're too late. But I've thrown a monkey wrench into the works. I'm moving back into the house, and I've let the real estate people know it. If they get an offer, and they will at the low price he's asking, they'll have to negotiate with my lawyers. That's going to bring him back here, I promise you, because my father never forgets a grudge. He never leaves anything undone. It would be so much more convenient for mother and me if you would eliminate him."

"So?"

"I'd like you to be in the house when he comes."

"The house must be under surveillance."

"I'll smuggle you in the trunk of my car."

"I'd be a sitting duck."

She let the light X-ray her skirt, displaying her slender tanned limbs and black briefest of briefs. "You'd have me right there, as a hostage. Piece of cake." She stepped closer, keeping between him and the sun. "You will not be bored."

He hardly let her step out of her skirt. This was a hungry man. Ravenous. He threw her on the bed, half in half out of her skirt, tearing at his belt. She would not be bored either, for a change.

51 · San Diego

In the morning, Blue sat in her office and noticed that both Jana Andrews and Jane Willoughby had given Ohio homes of record while employed at the Dolly Agency. Bless Denton Horowitz!

The phone rang. "Miss Humboldt? This is Andreas Gump in Akron. I hope I didn't catch you at a bad moment."

"There have been worse."

"I located Bill Willoughby. Remember, he was a football hero at Kennedy High. Turns out Bill Willoughby is now employed by an insurance firm and he's out of town. But I talked to his wife, a gal with a French accent, and she seemed to remember that he was going steady with a beautiful tall dark-haired girl in his senior year in high school. She said the girl's name was Joanna. No last name, but Bill might remember."

"What's the connection, Mr. Gump? Lots of beautiful dark-haired tall girls latch onto football heroes."

"Well I thought you understood," Andreas Gump said. "This girl Joanna had startling blue eyes, like a top fashion model's. Which is what Mrs. Willoughby seems to remember Bill saying that Joanna went on to be, in New York City."

Blue grabbed the oyster ad. "Yes! I think that's her! Please, Mr. Gump, call me the minute you find out her last name."

"I will, Miss Humboldt. I'm really doing fine, am I?"

"You are an ace up the sleeve, Mr. Gump."

"You have a sexy—"

Blue hastily said thanks and hung up.

It was bedlam outside. Phones rang constantly, and clerks kept getting tips about the mystery woman in the paper. Blue saw Barnes briefly; his tie was loosened, and he looked harried. He waved to her from a meeting inside a fishbowl office.

Late in the morning, Martha Yee stopped by with a secretive look. "Blue, remember the lead I was checking? The lady in the sexy hat and glasses, Virgie DeSanto? I nosed around the Sapphic grapevine, you know what I mean, and I found her."

"No."

"Yes. She knew about the ruckus in La Jolla. That's why we haven't seen her at her house. She's been laying low with her girlfriend, the Amazon we saw in the bar that night. Virgie is sorry about Jana Andrews. She wants to help. She admits she planted the package of news clippings at Connor's house."

They met Rae Donovan in a bar on Adams Avenue. The air was tranquil, sunny, innocent. A hawk hovered in the wind over the canyons. Wind rustled in eucalyptus trees. Rae Donovan was, as Blue remembered her from the dance bar, a knockout. Tall, with curly blond hair, and a freckled complexion. Wide shoulders, slim waist, wiry arms. She had an Irish look that reminded Blue with a pang of Tessie O'Brien, the girl who had stolen Donnie away from her. Lush lips, gray self- assured eyes, a small nose in a square face, a tall forehead. She had a nasal, husky voice. Her demeanor was direct and without apology. "Virgie told me you were asking. I talked it over with my sister and she thought you ought to see her."

"Rae," Blue asked, "why do you think you know the woman in the police sketch?"

Rae Donovan regarded her with a directness that made Blue flinch. "Baby, you don't know the half of it. But Louise is the one to fill you in. You're a cop, huh?"

Blue sensed an uneasy dynamic at the wind-blown picnic table outside the bar. Martha was telegraphing her awe of Rae, and at the same time seemed to be staking a claim on Blue. Rae in turn was like thunder awakened. Her lips glistened greasily as she devoured a chicken sandwich, and she took a direct interest in Blue. It appeared that Rae Donovan was top of the pecking order. She could have most any woman (or man?). Rae ripped at her sandwich while her eyes tore into Blue with hunger.

"Yes, I'm a cop. Drug Enforcement Administration." While answering, Blue watched the hard female muscles in Rae's arms. This woman could be on the cover of any magazine. Surf, sun, and sand. The American ideal.

Rae nodded. "I thought about applying for the police department. But I've been too involved with body building. I won Miss Southern California last year, not that I'm bragging, and I'd rather spend my time building up to the state championship. When Virgie showed me the pictures, I had to take a stand. I've seen that woman before, and I thought your friend here ought to be the one I contacted."

"We appreciate that," Blue said.

Rae laughed. It was a hard, uncouth laugh. She belched. "My sister Louise..." She swallowed a mouthful of chicken and washed it down with beer. "My sister Louise knew that woman. I called Louise this morning, and she agreed to talk to the police."

"Why didn't Louise call us directly?"

"Because," Rae said, "Louise is shy. Well, that's half of it. We're from an athletic family. Dad was head coach at San Diego Union High School. I earned letters in every sport women could compete in. Louise is two years older than me, she also earned a lot of letters. She broke her spine in a skiing accident at Vail a couple of years ago, and she's paraplegic." Rae wiped her mouth with a paper napkin. "She won't see many people, especially after what this Brady asshole did to her."

"Oh no," Blue said.

"Yeah," Rae said, "if I catch him, I'll kill the fat blob."

"It's good you turned to us," Blue said.

Rae nodded. "I have to get back to the gym. I teach an aerobics class. Call me if you need anything more." The remark was aimed directly at Blue. "I mean it," Rae commanded. She rose, her wide shoulders flaring in her tank top shirt. Her gray eyes raked Blue's like a poker going over coals. "I'd like to hear from you. Bods Gym, OK?"

"Holy Smoke," Martha said on the way to La Jolla. "I think she was asking you for a date."

"In a roundabout sort of way," Blue said.

"What a goddess," Martha said.

"A messy eater," Blue said. Fog moved in gray and dismal sky. Scudding wind sent bits of morose clouds belting against twisted junipers and pepper trees, whose long dangling branches rustled uneasily. Wealthy people had high properties overlooking the ocean. The courtyard was haunted by stray leaves. Blue wished she were elsewhere. Martha rang a doorbell. A wind chime made Zen noise. The two women waited.

A light drizzle, fine as feathers, blew gritty against their faces. The Donovan estate loomed with marine pylon decor. Windows looking black reflected light. After a few moments, a door opened automatically. "Come in," a voice called.

They stepped into a sterile floor wax atmosphere. The woman in the wheelchair looked handsome, like her sister, but there was something missing. Maybe the arrogance. Maybe the spark of liveliness. Same rich lips and freckled complexion, but she appeared matter of fact and humble. Pale. Her hair was styled severely, in a mousy page boy. Her eyes were gray, but it was a duller, resigned color like the sky outside. "My name is Louise Donovan," the young woman said as though she were in court. "I know who your mystery woman is."

"I'd like to hear about it," Blue said carefully.

"Last year a pleasant man approached me. His name was Vincent Brady. We met through Sunday services at St. John's by the Sea. That's an Episcopalian church I go to. He was so nice. He didn't seem to mind my invalid state. I was grateful. He breathed life into me, where I'd been depressed. One thing led to another, and he seemed to be courting me. I was so happy. I was used to having men at my beck and call, and after the accident that stopped. Vincent was the first man who brought me back. He'd take me for long walks. How innocent, how naive I was. Well, to make a long story short, he told me he was starting a burn institute. I felt sorry for him and his burn victims. I gave him twenty thousand dollars. And then he stopped coming around. But this woman came to see me; Jana Andrews. She told me what a bastard he was. At first I didn't believe her. But I have common sense, and I began to see the truth. I was so sad. She told me all about this guy. Vincent Brady. I'll never let anyone like Vincent Brady take advantage of me again."

"Amen," Blue and Martha said in unison.

"She is a sweetheart, this Jana Andrews. I'm just sorry she ended up in the hospital. Probably because of Vincent Brady. Seeing her name in the paper I asked Rae to call someone."

"Do you know her real name?" Blue asked.

Louise's face clouded. "She swore me to secrecy."

"This is life and death," Blue gently urged.

Louise nodded, swallowed. "All right." The silence was total except for a clock ticking and a distant roar of surf. "Her name is Joanna MacIvory. Her husband is running for governor in Ohio."

52 · San Diego

"It's one o'clock in the morning," John protested, answering his phone.

"I have to talk to you," Blue said.

He sat up rubbing his eyes. "It's dark out. Where the hell are you? I thought you were sleeping here."

"I'm at my hotel packing and I could use your help."

He stumbled to the bathroom and whizzed while cradling the portable phone under his chin. "Are you running out on me?"

"No, silly. Say, are you by the pool?"

"No, I'm in a canoe. Can you hear the surf?" He flushed.

"My, we do have our sense of humor at one a.m. Do you want to help me find Madame X?"

He washed his hands. "Now?"

"Yes, now. We have to catch a plane to Ohio."

"Ohio," he said. He looked in the refrigerator. The cat rubbed against his ankles. He listened to Blue's story, pouring milk in the cat's little dish. Then he rolled himself a burrito using a flour tortilla, a slice of cheese, and a dab of refried beans. Microwave, one minute. "No kidding?"

"We're not telling the Akron police yet. In fact, we're not telling anyone. Only Martha Yee knows, and she can't leave her jurisdiction without written orders and so on. I thought you'd be the perfect person to tag along with me."

"Let me guess. You need me as bodyguard."

"Oh stop being difficult. I just want you. With me."

"Okay," he sighed. "Mmm."

"Sounds good. What is it?"

"A burrito," he said with his mouth full.

"Mexican food, huh? I'm not sure about that stuff. Spicy?"

"No. Are you hungry?"

"Could you bring about a dozen along to the airport?"

Most of the passengers were asleep. The night sky was turning indigo, but stars were still visible. Blue was glad he'd come along. "Yesterday evening I called a guy I sorta know in Akron. Andreas Gump, don't laugh or I'll slug you. He works for the newspaper there. I woke him up—I'd forgotten it's three hours later on Eastern Standard Time—and asked him if he knew anyone called MacIvory. He nearly jumped out of his shorts. MacIvory, he told me, is a State Congressman who wants to run for governor in the next race. I said thank you, than-kyoo!"

John whistled.

Blue said: "We may meet your Lady with Blue Neon Eyes."

"Oh GGGG," Blue said as they stood side by side on a street corner near the airport in Akron, Ohio.

"GGGG," John said. The temperature at 2 p.m. was twenty. As they watched, the display over a bank changed: "2:05...20 F...2:05...19 F..."

"Gawd," Blue said, "how soon we forget."

"No bull," he said. "Let's get our bags into a hotel room. I want to take a hot shower." Traffic roared around them. It was Middle America in February—gray, subarctic, closed in, allowing strangers to visit, charging dearly for hospitality.

"How about a nap?" John said in their Crazy Eight Motel room.

"No time." She was on the phone, first, to let Tomasi know she had arrived safely, then: "Hi, Mr. Gump."

"Hello, how is the weather out there in sunny San Diego?"

"Warm," she said. "Real warm. I'm sitting on the balcony of my hotel room in my bikini, and it's pretty darn warm. You can almost hear the sun oil sizzling."

"Ooo. That sounds divine. The sun oil, too. I was able to roust up Bill Willoughby for you. Want his number?"

"Shoot."

He did. "On MacIvory, is there a local story in it for us?"

"Not quite yet, Mr. Gump. One of these days I'll make it to your fair city and we'll have lunch."

"You have a very—"

"Thank you, Mr. Gump. I hope you like large women."

"Well, I, uh..."

"Because I weigh three hundred pounds and you sound like my kinda guy. Are you going to be there for me?"

He hung up.

"What was that?" John Connor asked. He toweled his hair. He wore tight jeans and was bare from the waist up. A lot of dark curly hair was matted damply on him. He sat on the edge of the bed and poked a finger into one ear. "An admirer," Blue told him. "Wants me to come to Ohio and marry him."

"Oh. That's okay. I have a return ticket."

She threw a pillow, then dialed Bill Willoughby's number. A child answered the phone.

"Is Mr. Bill Willoughby home?" she asked. There was a lot of background noise. Children playing. "Yes," the little voice said timidly. The receiver bobbled on a table. John jumped on the bed and made gorilla arms. Blue shushed him. "Hello?" a man's deep voice said. It was a responsible, tired voice.

"Mr. Willoughby?"

"Yes?"

"This is Laurel Humboldt. I..."

"You're the woman that Gump guy has been calling me about."

There was a nasty, suspicious edge to his voice.

"Yes, Mr. Willoughby. I just wondered if you would answer a few questions."

"You're with the federal government?"

"Yes."

He was silent a moment. "Hold on. Let me take this into my office." John was blow-drying his hair. Blue made a furious face and waved him away. John closed the bathroom door.

"All right, Miss Humboldt. What do you want?"

"Just some information."

"Where are you?"

She told him.

"You're lucky you didn't call ten days later."

"Why is that?"

"Because my parole ends in ten days and I'd be hanging up in your face. Look, I don't want my family involved in anything more. I'll drive over to see you, okay?"

"That'll be fine, Mr. Willoughby—" He had hung up.

Twenty minutes later, there was a knock on the door. Blue had quickly showered and dressed. She knew the time was too short to call Tomasi for a crime check, and she figured it best to have Johnno out of the way, so she sent him out for food.

Bill Willoughy had shoulders like a Mac truck. He was a big, graying man with a troubled face. Blue put him at 40, but he looked far older. "You got a badge?"

She showed him. "Look Bill, just call me Blue. I'm with the DEA, and I had no idea you had a sheet."

"I embezzled twenty thousand dollars from the bank I was working with. That was seven years ago, minus ten days. I paid the money back, and they gave me two years in, five out. Now what can I do for you, Miss?"

"Did you ever date a girl named..."

"Joanna?" He made a bitter face. "Yes. There was a girl like that. A tall, dark, beautiful girl. I was young and dumb. I gave her the razz. She was madly in love with me, the dumb bastard who later embezzled twenty grand and thought he could get away with it. What a fool I was. A couple of newspaper people have tried to get my story over the years. I've always turned them down. But you're flashing metal, so I'll cooperate."

"Mr. Willoughby, please relax. I just want you to tell me what your relationship with this woman was."

"We were sweethearts, until I got drafted and went to Nam, and Joanna ran off to the big city. She came home a few years later and married MacIvory, Mr. Big on the rise. I was headed for prison by then."

"So," Blue said, "I'm trying to locate a woman who was a model in New York City going by the name of Jane Willoughby, which we know was an alias."

He nodded. "That was Joanna. I came home from Vietnam and raised hell for a while. I went to New York City a few times to see her. We laughed about the fact that she used my name as her alias. She didn't want to reflect badly on her parents, you see. They're in some staunch church and all."

Blue injected: "Same church as Jana Andrews?"

"Yes. They were pals, those girls, growing up. But it wasn't going to work out between me and Joanna. And it's just as well. She gave it up and returned home. I headed for jail, and she met this guy MacIvory, just out of college, a hot shot lawyer, and the rest as they say is history. They're on their way to becoming Mr. and Mrs. Governor. And, Miss Humboldt, I hope you understand this, it's the only thing I have left to give the girl. I don't want her name associated with me. I don't want them to have to go through any of that press bullshit that ruins good people. I'm just a stiff out of her past. I've made a new life for myself in insurance. I'm a successful underwriter and I have a really nice practice. I'm about done with parole, and I don't want any more trouble."

"I understand," Blue said. "I won't make any for you. Just one more thing. What was her maiden name?"

He looked at her long and hard. "You really don't know?"

"I wish you'd tell me."

"Her maiden name was Joanna Travignan."

"Oh God," Blue said. "Oh my God, my God."

"A tragic family," he said.

"When I checked Joe Travignan's background, there was no mention of a sister."

"Half-sister," Willoughby ironically. "There's been a lot of covering up for the MacIvorys. She and Joe had different mothers. Their dad, old man Travignan, married a widow with a little daughter many years ago. With Joe's activities, they probably felt it was best to keep the connection secret. To spare Doug MacIvory. Governor MacIvory, soon, I'll bet."

Blue said: "Her brother just got murdered a few weeks ago. The press carried it locally, but I bet it was hushed up."

He said: "I knew Joe, too. Nice guy. Went on to be a priest. Got involved in drugs, who knows, I'm nobody to be casting stones. The MacIvorys are good people, Miss Humboldt. They deserve a shot at governor."

"What's past is past," Blue said. "Go on, get out of here." She offered her hand. "Congratulations on the parole."

He shook her hand. "Thanks."

Blue rented a car on her VISA card, and they drove to the MacIvory house. The house was a large, maybe six bedroom, two story building with 1860ish overtones: Twin white pillars on a small porch, ornamental window frames, woodwork in the eaves.

They circled the block twice, absorbing the flavor of upper class wealth: Each property one or more acres, trees among the white-daubed lawns, Jaguars and other sports cars mixed with the occasional Rolls, Lincoln, or Cadillac. They knocked, and a tall, handsome man wearing a long red house robe and slippers stepped into the doorway. "How may I help you?"

She showed her badge. "Laurel Humboldt, Drug Enforcement Administration. This is my associate, Mr. Connor. It's about Joe Travignan. And Vincent Brady. And Mrs. MacIvory."

"Oh? DEA, huh? What could you possibly want with my wife?"

"Could we step inside?"

"Of course. It's cold." He stepped aside, and John and Blue hastily entered a carpeted, cozy world of warmth, dim lights, and soft music. Blue put her badge away and pulled out a pair of sketches. "This is the sketch of the man who came and got our lady out of UCSD Medical Center in San Diego. And here is a picture of the lady. This is you and your wife, I believe."

He swallowed, rocking on the balls of his feet. His eyes flicked to his right, and a harsh voice spoke: "Don't talk to them, Doug." The owner of the voice, a tough-looking man in his sixties with a gray suit and white wavy hair and a red face stepped into the foyer and took MacIvory's arm. "Doug, think about your career. At this point the slightest thing..."

MacIvory shrugged the hand away with stoic nonchalance. "It won't be the first time, and unless we clear this up it won't be the last. Come on into the living room, you two, and get warm."

"Thank you," they said in unison.

"Drink?" MacIvory indicated a bar. Bottles glinted under crystal window panes. The bar was interior lit and had a sink built in, and an ice machine. Everything in the living room, from the cathedral ceiling to the marble floors, the shag rugs, and the leather furniture, was quietly posh and smelled of booze and leather and ashes, for there was a fire crackling behind a grating. "No thanks," they both said about drinks.

"Have a seat then. How about hot chocolate." MacIvory signaled to his companion, who shook his head and stormed out, presumably in search of a maid. "That was my lawyer, Ed Schwartz," MacIvory said dryly. "First, let me assure you my wife has no part in any drug dealings. I am frankly surprised you found us so quickly. And I would have expected FBI maybe."

"Why, Mr. MacIvory?" Blue asked. She wanted to draw him out, let him do the talking.

He seemed to deliberate how much to volunteer.

"Let me explain something," Blue said. "There is a man out there who is slashing people's throats with a razor. He has already killed at least four people."

"Is Vincent Brady one of them?" He showed sudden venom.

"No," she said.

"Can we wait until he nails Brady?"

"Until who has gotten to Brady, Sir?"

"I don't know. Whoever the Slasher is. I read the papers."

"You ought to help me to the fullest extent."

"Who is your friend here? He hasn't said a thing."

"This is Mr. Connor. He is a material witness. If I'm correct, your wife bought a ring from him later found with her brother's body."

MacIvory's composure was visibly deteriorating. Sweat stood on his forehead. "Miss Humboldt, can we spare my wife this? She is recuperating from a head injury and stab wounds."

"It would be best if I could interview her. Even if it's only briefly. You understand that the game, whatever it was, is up and we're now just interested in getting answers."

A maid in black dress and white apron brought a silver service smelling of cocoa. She set china cups on the coffee table for Blue and John and poured. MacIvory waited until the maid was done. He signaled for Ed Schwartz to close the door. "The jig is up, so to speak. Where do I start?"

"How about with your wife's modeling background." Blue produced a small notebook and pen. "Her maiden name is Joanna Travignan?"

"Very astute. I may not have much to tell you."

"She grew up in Akron and attended Kennedy High, where she dated a Bill Willoughby, later jailed for embezzlement. Am I correct so far?" Drained of all color, he sat down. "Her brother Joe became a priest a few years ago. He went to San Francisco, got mixed up in drugs, the Church offered rehabilitation. He was in and out of drug programs like Episcopal Winners in Hamilton.

"Bill Willoughby had gone to Vietnam. Joanna ran away to New York City as a model under the alias Jane Willoughby." She looked up. MacIvory nodded. She continued: "After several years she returned home to meet and marry you." She skipped the rest about Willoughby. "Joe became involved in drugs again in Hamilton. He also got in with Vincent Brady. Here is where my understanding gets hazy."

"I'll tell you what I can," MacIvory said.

"Vincent Brady used the alias Vincent Gordon, a monsignor in Hamilton. I suspect Vincent Brady was skimming church money for years. Somehow, he got Joe involved. Any idea how?"

MacIvory said: "Joe was skimming the poor box when he got back on junk. Brady was also paying for Joe's drugs from the outfit your people busted in Hamilton. In turn, Joe introduced Brady to elderly widows ready to donate funds to the Church. Brady got the money, Joe the drugs."

"Who killed Joe and why?"

"I don't know. Ed checked into it for me. Looks like Joe was in the wrong place at the wrong time." He poked the embers with a poker. "My wife and I have had our differences over the years, but we love each other. We have a common interest in politics. The upcoming run for governor means everything to us. Joanna needed to expose Brady without getting his dirt on us. When she learned Joe was dead, it made her mad with grief. I lost track of her for a week until she called from the hospital."

"What day was that?"

"Wednesday. She called from San Diego. Naturally, I brought her home."

"Secretly," Blue added. He licked his lips and glanced at his lawyer, who poured himself a large glass of booze. Blue said: "Joanna had a girlfriend from Akron who was a model in New York City. Jana Andrews. Jana and she kept in touch a little bit over the years, I suppose?"

"I think I can help you out," Joanna MacIvory said. She had opened the door quietly, and leaned against the frame. A heavy bandage was around her head. One arm was in a sling, and she had draped a robe over her shoulders, flannel nightgown underneath. Her face was not swollen anymore, and her beauty shone through the fading bruises. MacIvory jumped to his feet. "Darling, you shouldn't—"

John Connor rose too. "That's her, Blue."

Ed Schwartz rushed to assist Joanna, but she brushed him aside. "Come in here, please, I have to lie down again soon."

With Doug MacIvory in the lead, they trooped into the adjoining large room with hospital bed and wheelchair, walls covered with blown-up photo posters. "The history of my modeling career. Call it a woman's ego. You can see, I was in quite a few prominent ads. Including, Mr. Connor, our Rolex ad."

"There it is, Blue," Johnno said, pointing to posters with Joanna as Lady with Blue Neon Eyes, mystically opening wonderful cars while her eyes poured forth cool blue light.

"Hello, John Connor," Joanna MacIvory said.

"Nice to see you again, Joanna Travignan," he said. He remembered the scratchy touch of her fingernails on his cheek that night at Ajanian's when she'd bought the ring. "I thought we'd meet again somehow, but not to compare covers, after all."

"Jana Andrews had quite a crush on you," Joanna said. "She used to talk to me about you. And I liked you too." She looked pale, and thin, and had circles under her eyes.

"Thanks. I guess you know about Jana..."

"Poor girl. It was downhill for years. In a way, she's better off. I do miss her."

Blue asked: "Why did you impersonate Jana Andrews?"

"Impersonate? Funny, I never thought of it that way. Sounds criminal, and maybe it is. Poor Joe told me he was in a racket with this phony monsignor. I was afraid of exposing Doug to any sort of smut. How innocent that all seems now. I wanted to ruin Brady, and I wasn't sure how. I couldn't harm him physically; look what he did to me when I finally tried. I hated him for the way he was using my brother and the church and various people. I took on Jana's identity..."

"Let me guess," Blue said. "You tracked Brady to Louise. Or to Virgie DeSanto. You were going to set Brady up."

"Yes. I'm the one who turned Father Binder onto him. I was going to ruin him. Expose him in a scam with fast cars and women and drugs and stolen money..."

"Do you use cocaine?"

"No. That was part of the setup."

"There was cocaine found on you the night you were stabbed."

"I brought that along to plant it on Brady."

"Where did you get the cocaine?"

The MacIvorys exchanged startled looks. He looked startled, to be precise, and she looked guilty. "Well, I have a, a connection. Someone in the police department. I misappropriated some cocaine that was intended for destruction. It had been used as evidence in a trial, and the trial was concluded."

"Fair enough. I'll bargain with you. I may be able to ignore that if you just help me along further."

"Whatever you say!"

"Virgie dropped off the clippings outside John Connor's house. Why involve John?"

"I never had any intention. It's only because Joe died, and they found the ring. I just went there from nostalgia; to see his oyster once more. It sort of turned into an opportunity."

Blue said: "Now about this Slasher."

Joanna's eyes slitted. "That sounds like Hugh Stone."

"Who?" several people blurted at once.

"One of the drug people running Brady. I went to his mansion in Palm Springs. That's where I first met Brady. Hugh Stone! He has the most chilling eyes. I believe he would be capable of slashing."

"I need a phone, Mrs. MacIvory." Doug MacIvory's face was in his hands. Schwartz looked as though all the blood had been drained out of him. Joanna offered a cordless phone, and Blue dialed Tomasi's number. While the phone rang in Manhattan, she asked Joanna: "Give me Stone's address."

"Tomasi," her boss said.

"This is Humboldt. I'm interviewing our missing lady, and I think I have a lead on our slasher."

"Jesus Christ, Humboldt, let me have it."

Blue relayed the information as Joanna fed it to her. The location of the mansion. Palm Springs. The description of Hugh Stone. Seeing the weariness, the grief about her brother, on Joanna's face, she said: "Look, Joanna is about worn out and I don't have many more questions for now. Let's wrap it up."

Joanna said: "I want to apologize, Mr. Connor, for dragging you into this."

"I'm sorry about your brother."

The phone rang.

"For you, Miss Humboldt," Doug MacIvory said.

Tomasi. "Yes, Chief?"

"I've got word out to the FBI and the Palm Springs PD. They know the mansion, and they're putting people on it right now. They say the place is up for sale, and only a young woman is there. Hugh Stone's daughter. What's going on in Akron? Are we busting the MacIvorys for the cocaine she was found with?"

"Please, no. I'm making a deal here."

"You'd better be careful, Humboldt."

"I can explain, Chief. We need the information more than we need a shaky charge."

"You're probably right. Well, the rest of it's up to the FBI and the several PD's involved. Want a few days off?"

"I'd like to take week's vacation in San Diego."

"That's reasonable. Got someone to enjoy it with?"

"Chief," she said, mortified.

"I assume, from what Barnes tells me, that it's Connor, and that's great. You need a little reverse PR. Go on, have a ball. Have a party. Take pictures."

Alone with Johnno at the Crazy 8: slow, intriguing rock music throbbed on MTV. The room flashed smoky red from the television while Johnno and Blue made love. Outside, a snowy icy grit blew against the windows. "Blue, I love you."

"That's nice to hear." They kissed slowly, languidly.

"I feel something I never felt before."

"Ladies' man."

"I'm talking straight with you. This is me here, on the line. Oh God, when you do that...Oh!"

"Oh, baby, oh, yes!" She climbed on top.

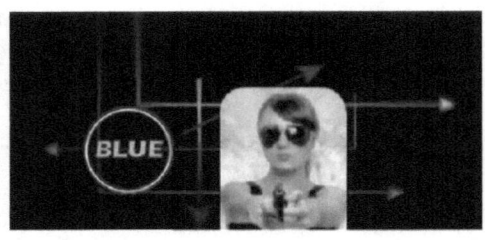

53 · Akron, Ohio

Tomasi called early in the morning.

Blue sat on the bed amid styro plates left over from their breakfast. John Connor lay behind her stroking her back gently, and she rubbed his leg.

Tomasi told her: "Once we fed the name Hugh Stone into the system, things got hot. INS worked all night. A German citizen named Hugo Stein, wife, and child were admitted into the USA in the 1990s. They became citizens. He anglicized his name to Hugh Stone. Made millions in electronics. Everything matches the occupants of the villa in Palm Springs. INS checked with Interpol in Paris. Wouldn't you know it, there was a Hugo Stein in Marseilles wanted in connection with a slashing murder in 1975. Seems he was working with the local equivalent of the Mob at the time. He was a German kid who lost his parents during the war and drifted into crime. His factory has gone belly-up. I'm afraid he's drifting again and we'd like to know where."

"Where does that leave us?"

"Never mind. I want you off this case. Go to San Diego and have yourself a vacation. Stay out of harm's way."

She and John stood in the airport in line for boarding passes to San Diego. She suddenly spotted a queue in the next line over headed for Palm Springs. "John," she said, "maybe I can apprehend the creature who murdered Eddie Stosik."

"No," John said. "Oh Blue, please, no..."

She kissed him and told him she loved him. "Right now, all I can see is Innie and those three little kids..."

54 • Chicago

Vincent Brady knew it was time to hit the road. He went to the bank and asked for Graham. The receptionist was bland. "I'll ring Mr. Graham, Sir."

Vincent waited, hoping Graham had the checks ready.

"Mr. Graham says he will come down to see you, Sir. If you'll have a seat over there..." She pointed to a circle of chairs in the lobby, where two young men in business suits were hunched over employment applications.

"Thank you." Vincent first sat down. Then he decided to wait close to an EXIT sign. Sure enough, Graham emerged. He had a security guard and two guys in gray suits with him.

Vincent took a cab to the hotel. He computed mentally that he had about a thousand dollars in his wallet, and maybe another thousand in traveler's checks in his suite. How ludicrous, considering that he had waited so long and worked so hard to put together a fortune of three million dollars.

Nobody waited for him in the hotel lobby. YET. Everything in his suite was as he had left it. Quickly he went to the bedroom, to the bottom dresser drawer, for the traveler's checks.

"Hello, Monsignor Gordon."

He whirled.

Binder. Gray hair, pinched lips, extremely unhappy eyes. "I thought I'd try to talk sense before the police get to you."

"I have nothing to say," Vincent said, getting the checks out and stuffing them in his inner jacket pocket.

"Turn yourself in. It's all over."

Vincent went toward the door, but Binder stood in his way. "We are priests, Vincent. We have a sacred duty."

"Get out of my way," Vincent said. He felt the Angel of Death and his mother and his father and the bible-reading congregation of Careyville at his back.

Binder, a far smaller and older man, stood his ground. "Don't leave now, Vincent. I talked with Mr. Graham. All the money is still there. You can give it back. Make amends."

"If you don't get out of my way —"

"Please reconsider."

Vincent slugged the old man. Binder staggered back, surprisingly resilient. Blood poured from his nose. "Jesus Christ is right here with us in this room," Binder said. "Remember your vows."

"Jesus understands," Vincent told him, "that we do what we have to do to survive." Vincent hit him again, and this time the old man went down hard. Vincent bent over him and felt for a pulse. It was there, beating faintly. Vincent gathered the few possessions that mattered and hurried downstairs. From a phone booth, he called the lobby and told them of a sick man in his room who needed medical attention. Then he drove north toward the Canadian border.

55. Chicago

At Ajanian's, John Connor could hardly keep his mind on his work. He longed for Blue, worried about her.

"You've been daydreaming," Gregor Ajanian teased. Ajanian's wrinkled hand patted John's shoulder. It was nine o'clock, and most of the sales staff had already gone. Ajanian had his tailored buff linen jacket on. It hung deceptively, padded in the shoulders, disguising his arthritis-racked frame. "I see symptoms," he told John, "and I hope it is love requited."

Johnno grinned. "I feel like a teenager." He locked display cases and damp-toweled fingerprints as he went.

Ajanian's gray eyes looked bright. "I was beginning to think you would never fall in love."

"Don't tell me it shows."

"Oh, it shows," Ajanian said with a wink. The gesture had a kind, smug delight, like a cat's pounce without the claws.

After Ajanian left, Johnno let the last of the sales staff out. He took his time, puttering about. He swept up little messes here and there, dabbed at fingerprints. Where was she? Was she okay? What was she doing? Was she thinking of him?

Toward nine-thirty, he put on his coat. Turned off the store lights and switched on the night lights. Made sure the emergency lights were functioning. Turned on the alarm system. Each store in the mall had its own alarm system tied to the police department, the fire department, various alarm companies, and the mall's own security agency. Satisfied that everything was in order, he stepped into the dark alley and locked the steel door. Startled by a sound, he whirled.

A cat had jumped from a high wall and landed on a dumpster it intended to scavenge. A clear, chilly night. Stars shone in a sky as black and mysterious as a velour display case. The silence was unnerving, now that the elevator music was off. He stepped into the deserted main part of the mall.

"Mr. Connor."

He jerked around. A pleasant looking man with white hair and a chilly smile walked toward him. A hand was extended. The other hand remained in the pocket of the stranger's raincoat. "I'm Father Jenkins. Father Binder referred me to you."

56 · Palm Springs

If Tomasi knew, he'd kill me. Blue rented a car at the airport. Desert heat hit like a fist, and she was glad to be inside the car with the air conditioner on. The California landscape of sandy hills, chaparral vegetation, and palm trees drifted past as she followed the map. She longed for John Connor. Blue, she told herself, he's a ladies' man. With your luck you are preparing to take another mud bath. Well, she replied, if it's another dunking, it feels good now.

At the Hugh Stone estate she whistled. Five acres of greenery, a veritable park, and a big white building with a pillared entrance. This man did live in style. A gardener on a tractor lawn mower was riding around on the front lawn. The roses were in profusion. As were the For Sale signs.

A slim, tanned blonde woman in a white terrycloth pool jacket and a pink bikini bottom answered the door. She held a tiny bottle of nail polish in one hand, the brush in the other.

"My name is Laurel Humboldt," Blue said.

"What do you want?"

"I want to look around the house."

"Are you with the real estate people?"

"Yes, of course. What a lovely property it is."

The thirtyish blonde had pampered skin, pinked lips, and arrogant brown eyes. "Why haven't I met you before?"

"Well, there are lots of us."

The woman waved her nails to dry. "I won't let you in."

"Honey, I thought you were eager to sell. So what's up?"

The blonde waved her polish. "That your dent-a-fender?"

Blue turned. "That? Oh no, I walked. Good for you."

"You're full of crap."

Blue stuck her foot in as the door closed. "Miss Stone?"

"Ouch," Astrid Stone said, stepping back and examining her violated fingernails. In her haste to close the door, she had left a zigzag of glossy pink polish on the dark wood.

"Not so hasty, Miss Stone. Please. I'm with a really big consortium. We can offer lots of money—if we decide to buy."

"I don't see your Jaguar out there."

Blue scratched her head. "I can have a Jaguar flown in, Federal Express, if that will make you happy. What if we all went around flashing Jaguars? Don't you get it? We're subtle."

Astrid stepped back. "All right, come on in. I'll give you a quick tour, but then you've got to leave."

Blue stepped into the spacious foyer and looked up. "Wow. Nice place." Twin staircases serpentine along the walls, leading to a mezzanine. Beneath, wide doors were half open, leading to what looked like an effing ball room. A pool glittered somewhere beyond—of course.

Astrid shook her head. The blonde wisps flew. My, Blue thought, but this lady probably has wealthy young eligible men falling all over themselves. Only she wasn't so young. Divorced? Probably, Blue assessed. Burned out probably.

"You want the dollar tour?" Astrid offered.

Blue nodded.

Astrid set her polish down and strode into the ballroom. "We used to throw parties here." She marched outside. "This is the pool. Come on, I'll show you my father's personal, private study." They looked into an abandoned room with empty book shelves. A desk was littered with papers. Blue had hoped for more than this. A frightened Hugh Stone hiding behind curtains, perhaps. It would take an army to go through this place inch by inch. She wanted to leave and forget the whole thing.

There was something spooky, cold, frightening, heartless about Miss Stone. "Very luxurious," Blue said as they walked through room after room. "Thank you. Well, that's about it."

They were on the second floor. Blue looked: Corridors, rooms, doors, worn carpets. Plants in corners and under windows. Windows, needing a washing. "Miss Stone, sorry I bothered you. You were polishing your nails. Up here?"

"I was by the pool," Astrid said.

"I hear music."

"That's my stereo."

"You were by the pool, and your stereo was playing on the second floor. You can't hear it from here to the pool."

"You are sure a nosy bitch, aren't you? I could play stereos in every room of the house day and night. Who cares?"

"Just saying. Seems like a waste of energy. Is this the corridor to your apartment?" A long, dark corridor stood yawning ahead, waiting to suck her in, to kill her. The music had ceased. At the end of the corridor was a white door. Blue started walking that way.

"I said the tour is over. I thought you were leaving."

"Does your stereo have an automatic shutoff, Miss Stone?"

Astrid wrung her hands, and caught herself. "I think you should leave now. My apartment is my personal private business."

Blue shrugged. "We have to look at everything. Do you understand? With this kind of money involved and all."

"I'll show you out."

"Let me see the goddam apartment."

"I won't let you in there. It's private." Her pitch rose.

Blue stared down the long corridor. There was a spy-hole in the door. She heard a loud creak of wood. That would be a man's weight. "That's not your daddy in there, is it?"

"No, of course not." Astrid's hands rose to her chin. She stared with deathly fascination at that closed door.

"You seem nervous," Blue said and started toward the door.

"Garth!" Astrid yelled.

Blue felt a prickle on her scalp. Who? She half expected the door to open and a man with a straight razor to rush at her. At this distance, she'd have time to drop, pull her gun, and shoot. Nobody with a razor could cross this much distance quickly enough to stop her.

"Garth!" Astrid screamed. "Garth!"

The door opened, and it was not a man with a razor, but the jogger who had killed Olvera and Guzman. Blue recognized that long, scarred face. He held a gun, this time no silencer.

"Kill her!" Astrid screamed.

Blue dropped, rolling, and pulled out her automatic.

"This was a setup!" he bellowed at Astrid. "You bitch!"

He fired deafeningly. Out of the corner of her eye, in a fleeting second, Blue saw Astrid lying in a crumpled heap.

Blue rolled into the shelter of a doorway. The door was unlocked and she rolled into a room. It all went in slow motion. No way she would tangle with this turkey. She'd made a mistake, and now the only way out was OUT.

She heard his feet pounding on the wooden hallway floor as she dove through an open window. Lowered herself down an ivy trellis that collapsed cracking and popping under her weight. Caught a glimpse of him, of his gun, of his mean hard face framed in blond hair. The scar on his cheek.

Heard him crashing about, breathing hard, above.

Run!

She heard his feet thundering down the stairs.

Through the house, the only way.

He thundered down the stairs, and she ran as fast as she could, tossing folding chairs out of her way in the ball room.

Through the expansive foyer.

His feet on the stairs.

Caught a glimpse of him on the stairs.

He stopped to aim.

She crashed through the front door and kept running.

Across the lawn.

Pounding.

Breathless.

Grass, sweet and wet, under her feet.

Azure sky swaying around her as she ran and her lungs threatened to burst.

Roses.

She slipped, fell, rolled.

Looked back. Nothing.

Sirens, lights, squealing tires. Police cars rolled in.

"Jesus, lady, who the hell is IN there?" a Palm Springs cop asked. She lay back gasping and half-grinned up at him. "It's a man I can identify as a murderer. Go in and get him but be careful. There's a woman in there he shot. I witnessed that too. Better call for an ambulance real quick!"

First hints of darkness falling, and Blue left the Palm Springs PD. Her only concern now was to be with Johnno. Be with her man. She took the first flight out to San Diego.

57 • San Diego

On the flight back to San Diego, Blue reflected that Tomasi had been right. She should enjoy a little vacation with John Connor. Pursue the really important thing in her life.

The plane got into San Diego, and she took a taxi to John's house. No Porsche. Not home. Still at the store, of course. She paid the cabbie, tipping him two bucks. She let herself into John's house. Turned on the stereo. Fontainebleau came up out of the canyon and rubbed against her leg. She couldn't wait for Johnno to come home tonight. She fed the cat and debated calling the store, deciding against it. Didn't want to alarm John about what she'd been through at Hugh Stone's place. So she pulled a beer from the fridge and decided to go out and watch the lights from the back canyon. It was quiet on the canyon. Distant freeway noise barely reached her. She popped the beer and sat back.

Then Tomasi called. "I thought I'd catch you here, after all else failed. Father Binder says there is no Father Jenkins. Chief Murphy as his secretary identified the recorded voice as belonging to our slasher. You'd better watch yourself. He's probably after YOU, thinks you can tell him where Gordon is. Stay put where you are. Oh, by the way, you weren't in Palm—"

Blue hung up and dialed Ajanian's but there was no answer. Frantically, she dialed 911. "I'm sorry," the operator said, "we can't just send—" She dropped the phone, left it lying on the floor as she raced outside. Found a car, hot wired it, and ran every light on her way to the mall.

Father Jenkins told John: "I represent the Church. I was told Miss Humboldt would meet you here, and I thought I would bypass the police, the paperwork and the awkward questions, and speak with her off the record."

"Who told you she would meet me here at this hour?"

Jerkiness' eyes glittered like topaz as he kept pace with John. John stepped back, Jenkins stepped forward. "Mr. Connor, come now. I want to find Vincent and recover the stolen money."

Blue pressed her foot to the pedal. The stolen car flew along the night-time freeways. Wind whipped through her hair from the open window. Horns blared as weaved through traffic. Hoping to pick up a cop. TIP, anyone. Come on, where are you guys? Blare! Another slow car in her way. Holding the wheel with her forearms she checked the clip in her 9 mm automatic.

John, backing away, recognized the faint accent. This was no priest. "Miss Humboldt won't be coming here. You'll have to call in the morning."

"Nothing!" Hugh Stone raved. "No morning. Tonight!" He grasped John's lapels. His voice was smooth and cold. "I mean no harm. I need to speak with your girlfriend. You know who I am, don't you? Where is she?" John shoved him away, but Stone closed the gap just as quickly. "I need to speak with her," Stone insisted. "Brady has my money."

"Nobody knows where Brady is, Mr. Stone. The police are looking for him."

Hugh Stone had a black object in one hand. "I have something for you, Mr. Connor, if you choose not to talk." His smile glittered. "Tell me right now where your little Laurel is. You'd be very smart if you did that. Or else you'll be blind for life." He held up a black gun. "This water pistol has a powerful acid solution in it." He stepped closer, revealing the famed razor. "In my other hand, I have the means to make you into a most ugly man. Think about it. You're used to women swooning over you. Think how it would be if not only you were blind, but people went out of their way to avoid you because of the slashes on your face. What do you say, Mr. Connor?"

Still no cop. Blue screeched down the exit ramp, fishtailing the car, then righting it. A red light. Truck. She cut him off, accelerating. Blare...as he jammed on his air brakes and all thousand wheels smoked. She raced, sixty, seventy, eighty, down the long empty street. The parking lots were empty. The mall was closed. Johnno was in there ALONE with HIM. Frantically, she searched for an entrance. Drove through the parking lot. Under the building. Dead end.

John stared into the nozzle of a metallic-looking water pistol. Too late he caught on and raised a protecting hand.

"I thought of this little surprise especially for you," Hugh said, "as a thanks for all the trouble you and your friends have caused me." Once, twice, Hugh's finger squeezed. A searing, blinding fire splashed into John's eyes. He cried out and squeezed his eyes.

"Hydrochloric acid," Hugh Stone said calmly. "A dilute mixture, strong enough to blind you if you don't get water to wash it away. You'll be blind and disfigured when I am done with you. Where is Laurel Humboldt?"

"I don't know!" John cried. He was sightless in his left eye, and his right eye saw everything double. He saw Hugh Stone's eyes staring into his, four of them, blurry.

"Talk and you'll have water to wash your eyes out. No? I don't have time for this. I hope you appreciate that."

John felt a warmth along his neck. He touched it, then held his fingers near his remaining good eye. Thick saucy blood!

"That's right," Hugh Stone said. "I've just made a little nick. If I wanted to kill you, you'd be dead by now. But I don't want you dead—yet. I want information. Where is she?" The gun hissed again, and acid seared John's skin.

Lost! Blue backed out of the dark underground garage on squealing tires, knocking a fender off against a pylon. She'd only been in this mall once or twice before. Could not remember which end Ajanian's was at. Upstairs. Must get to the upper level! Seconds, precious seconds, were ticking by, lost forever.

There! Stairs! She leapt from the car and raced through the darkness, her soles slapping on echoing concrete. And came to a barred grill. Locked out! The stairs to the upper level glimmered in moonlight like ironic smiling teeth.

Before Hugh could get another word out, John stomped his right foot down on Hugh's foot. There was a crackle of broken bone. Through blurred vision, John saw Hugh bend over double.

John turned to run, and fell on his back rubbing his eyes.

"You'll pay for this," Stone gasped. "I think you broke my foot. I'll slice your eyes out one by one."

John sprawled in the garden strip down the mall's middle. His eyes burned badly.

Hugh Stone was right behind him, crawling. "I don't really care about you, Mr. Connor. Or about your girlfriend. I want Vincent Brady, and Laurel knows where he is. She has to."

John scrambled up, started to run, fell again.

"I'm right behind you," Hugh Stone said.

Through blurry eyes, John saw the razor outstretched in Hugh's hand, caught the glint of mall lights on the razor's shiny surface, saw thick droplets of his own blood in the hazy light.

Stone rose to his feet limping badly. So I've at least evened the score, John thought.

Stone waved the razor and laughed. "I've got you. You can't get away. You'll scream, and nobody can hear you here. I'll hang your balls up someplace. When they find you..."

Blue drove off with a roar, door closing as an afterthought. Only hope left was to bull it through, drive like hell trying to find a way in. The mall loomed around her, big, black, wicked, foreboding.

John could only see, blurry, out of one eye. He heard Stone scraping on the ground. "Your eyes are gone, and now I'm going to carve up your face."

John's hand encountered something solid. He made out the edge of a little planted island of tropical ferns and ivy.

"Try to hide in there," Stone shouted.

John's hand touched loose rocks. River rocks from the San Diego river, worn smooth, with a sandy texture. He pried one loose and threw it. Stone held up his hand and deflected the rock. John pulled himself up along a tree trunk. With his trailing hand, he pulled loose another rock. He threw it toward a store window. The rock lost momentum and bounced off the heavy plate glass. Stone grunted heavily, pulling himself along, razor in one hand, broken foot dragging behind. John could almost feel Stone breathing up his ankles. The shuffling, crawling noise drew steadily nearer. John pried loose another rock. This time he hoisted himself higher and wound up before throwing. The rock sailed through the air and shattered the window of a clothing store. An alarm bell began to shrill.

Hugh Stone's fingers brushed John's leg.

John pulled away and threw another rock. And another. Windows began to shatter. Glass rained down all around. He staggered away from Hugh Stone, rolling six or seven feet away to the other side of the little island.

Blue brushed away tears. It couldn't end like this. Nooo...!!" she wailed. She spun the wheel and raced out into the parking lot. Turned the car in a 180 and squealed up the access ramp. To a locked, blank door. Another dead end.

She heard crashing, breaking glass. Alarms were going off somewhere far away. Jumping from the car, she stepped on a trash can. It sagged under her weight. Her free hand caught hold of a metal railing. She hoisted herself. Heard sounds of struggle.

Over the railing.

She was at the wrong end of the mall!

It would take minutes to run, but run she did, fast as she could. As she ran, she heard more crashing glass. She sprinted.

Water began to spray and splash. The sprinklers. John buried his face in them. Held his eyes open. Let the water wash the acid out. The night filled with sirens. Alarm bells were ringing. Johnno pulled himself away, but Hugh had hold of his ankle. Johnno threw another rock. Penetrated the window of a jewelry store. Another alarm went off. Hugh Stone had a firm grasp of John's ankle and pulled himself along. John's pants tore. The razor glinted. Stone hauled himself erect and staggered forward. He landed on top of John. The razor flashed. "Now!" Stone cried. Connor raised a hand to defend himself. Stone slashed it, threw splatters of thick red blood everywhere.

Blue ran as fast as she could. There! Oh God, Stone was on top of Johnno. Had him pinned. Had the razor up in the air, ready to pull through the sinews of Connor's throat. She ran. Too far to shoot accurately. Her teeth were bared. She ran as fast as she could, short of breath already, air coursing through her neck like fire.

Stone saw her. Grinned at her. Madness flashed in his eyes.

The razor glittered, ripples of sadistic steel.

Connor had one hand upraised, eyes and mouth open in horror.

One more second and she would be close enough to kneel and aim. Dogs barked. Guards came running. Jeeps crashed through barriers. *Too late!* She tripped. Fell. Skidded on her belly, wind knocked out of her. Stone's grinning face turned toward Connor, and the razor descended. John's blood splashed up in a fountain.

Blue fired.

Once, twice.

58 . On Interstate Highways

Vincent Brady pulled over onto the shoulder of the long, empty highway leading into Canada. Let Mother think he had fled to Canada. He simply would never call her again. Done with the Angel of Death! He laughed. He was free, free, free!

The freezing cold sunny weather made Canada gleam as though it were made out of jewels. Vincent ate a sandwich and burped. Mayonnaise oozed between his fingers, and he took a healthy swig of ginger ale. The chameleon, he thought, survives because his markings blend with his surroundings. Not Canada. He took out one of his credit cards marked Vincent Gordon —the last of them—and hid it under the seat where they'd be sure to find it. He left the car where it was parked, suggesting he'd had second thoughts about crossing the border with those plates.

He walked along a country road lined with stunted trees, crowns beaten down but unvanquished by the Arctic winds of North Dakota. On either side the earth wrinkled and undulated in shades of purple and olive. At a drainage ditch, he dumped the big suitcase with all the fancy clothes he'd bought in Chicago. He buried the suitcase under rotting reeds and loaded rocks on top to be sure. Let them search Canada from end to end for a middle aged man with a big suitcase.

The border receded as he walked south, last thing they'd expect. Cars and trucks rushed by, insinuating icy cold through his clothing. He stopped in a gas station and washed up, letting hot water thaw his cold hands. Then he went into the restaurant filled with cigarette smoke and bustling waitresses in beehive doos and truckers loading up on flapjacks and chipped beef. He bought a cup of coffee and sidled among twangy drivers. He avoided the other people, the tired locals, the people who did not want to put miles and states behind them. He drifted from conversation to conversation, until he heard a familiar twang. "Howdy," he said.

The young man nodded. "Hiyuh." He was a tall guy with dungaree pants and jacket, cowboy boots and hat. He had a tattoo of a curled up dragon on one veiny forearm.

"I'm headin' south," Vincent said sipping his coffee.

"I got a load of wires and cables that's got to get to Natchez day after tomorrow. I could use another driver."

"I can drive a semi," Vincent said. "Been down on my luck lately. Spent a spell at Bible college, but didn't finish. Ran out of money. Done all sorts of work the last two year or so. I'm just plumb tired of eating Yankee bread. I'm just ready to head on back down south and maybe start a little Bible church."

"Ah know a town could use a preacher," the young man said.

"What's your name, son?"

"Tommy Ledbetter. I reckon there's room for you, Reverend."

Vincent his emptied his styro coffee cup across the frozen asphalt, where wind blew up little devils of snow, and as he held the door open, Tommy Ledbetter asked: "What's yore name, Reverend?"

"Call me Andrew," Vincent said with a cheerful little smile. "Andrew Vincent. Just call me Andy." They drove all day through blinding snow that swooped down from the roof of the Arctic and inundated highways in South Dakota. The big rig just purred along. Tommy Ledbetter, driving nonstop since Yellowknife, crawled into the cab for a snooze and Vincent had the road and the mighty truck all to himself.

In Nebraska the wind picked up, rocking the rig, shaking snow from its coiled tons of wire. By the time he passed Kansas City and Council Bluffs, the blizzard eased off, though the radio said roads behind him were being closed. He was getting sleepy as he passed into Missouri. There they stopped for a late lunch, and Tommy Ledbetter took over the driving while Vincent crawled back and slept several years' weariness away.

He awoke hours later to the shouting of a radio preacher. Lightning flashed, and rain pelted the cab. He poked his head in. "Where are we, Tommy?"

"We just crossed into Arkansas, Andy. 'Nother coupla hours, we'll be in Mississippi. Cain't you jest feel that rain wipin' down the sides?"

"I sure can," he said. "I'm going to start a little church of my own, dedicated to the Lord." Five years, he figured as they drove further south and the rain got gentle on dark green hills. Maybe it won't be three million, but I'll have enough to find Jana Andrews again.

They were almost home. Sunshine perked through rain clouds. Vincent dreamt of Jana Andrews when the big rig pulled slowly into a gasoline station in a mountain hamlet so isolated you could hear crickets chirping a mile away. While Tommy tanked up, Vincent stepped around the side of the gas station. The mountain air smelled wholesome. He found the men's room boarded up, weeds growing up around the broken door. Vincent walked away from the half-ruined building with its broken window panes and peeling paint. At the edge of the pavement, he unzipped his fly to relieve his full bladder. Whistling softly, he twiddled preparing to pee. The whistle died in his throat. There, behind a dusty cracked window pane, was She. The Angel of Death. Sour disapproving face, mouthing words he could not hear. Bile rose in Vincent's throat. He could not pee. She, the Angel of Death, stared and grinned hideously.

"I'm going to beat you now," he said, "I'm going to erase you, I'm going to be done with you."

She grinned a cold stinking skeletal smile. "I'm never going to let you go."

"You can't do this to me!" the boy cried. "No! My Daddy!"

"Straight into the hell fire of damnation!"

"No! No! No!"

Tommy Ledbetter got a cup of coffee while the meter clicked happily and gasoline gurgled into the big rig. Country music twanged among the pumps, and he smiled as a pretty girl crossed his path. She smiled back. He was about to ask her name, when he heard a weird shouting from the outbuildings. Sounded like that passenger of his. Warbling, or some shit. Odd fella, come to think on it. A man and a woman ran out pointing.

Tommy dropped his cup and said "Oh Jesus."

The passenger. There was a sound like curtains burning. Draped in flames, staggering, a scarecrow ball of fire, silent, mouthing words as fire belched around him, insulated by a blanket of black smoke, the man-like figure staggered effortfully toward Tommy Ledbetter's rig. Fell. Rose, reaching out. Tommy's passenger just made it to the pumps before collapsing in a consuming ball of fire. The fire flashed to the pumps and down into the underground tanks. Www—oooo—sshhh" went the whole pump island, exploding in a giant fireball. "Jesus!" Tommy mouthed and threw himself over the pretty blonde. Black billowing smoke could be seen for miles. And miraculously, nobody was hurt. Or killed. Except Tommy Ledbetter's passenger. It was a mystery Tommy Ledbetter would talk about for years, when the mood struck him. "Like something evil went up in smoke," Tommy would tell people. "I swear there was a scream as the pump burst into that fireball, but it wasn't his voice. It was more like a... a old woman's or something."

59 · Manhattan

Blue met Maggie at an old haunt, the Red Wagon near Cooper Square. Smoke filled the air. Hamburgers, french fries, the whole bit. Maggie looked thin and composed. She looked beautiful, with her long dark hair and mournful eyes. Smoke from her cigarette curled up into the air. "It was sweet of you to meet me here, Laurel," Maggie said.

Blue stubbed out her cigarette. "Maggie," she said, feeling a big tight thing curled up in her gut, "I want to somehow—"

Maggie put her hand over Blue's, dry and warm. "No, don't say anything." She had a wistful sort of beautiful smile. "I don't want to say goodbye. I've painted a thousand portraits of you in my mind, and somehow none of them got onto canvas. That's when I realized that I have to let you go." Tears streamed down her cheeks. "I won't be bothering you again. I just wanted to tell you just one more time." She reached out and touched Blue's cheek. Blue lowered her face. She felt devastated, but no tears came. "I just wanted to say one more time, how much I love you."

When Blue looked up, Maggie had gone.

60 · JFK International Airport

The big 747 whistled slowly to a landing.

Blue hopped from one foot to the other inside the icy cold tent. She, Tomasi, and Vito were dressed as baggage handlers, standing inside a room-sized tent alongside the runway. "This is the payoff," Tomasi told her.

Vito Caparelli sucked on a Camel. His nose looked big and his mouth small. His big dark eyes had a nervous, pleased look. Tomasi explained: "People migrate west but they ship their bodies back east to be buried where they grew up. It's a steady industry for the mortuary shipment firms, one or two of them Mob connected, according to Vito's intelligence."

A jet landed and taxied. Tomasi clapped Vito on the back. "Go to it."

"Right, Chief." Vito tossed his cigarette away and climbed onto a motor cart. Even in his bulky orange winter jumpsuit, head gear and all, he seemed to Blue elegantly Vito, even with his ear protectors. Blue could not help but laugh.

As Blue and Tomasi waited, the 747 was towed to a nose-in berth to discharge passengers. A snake of tow carts waited by the cargo doors to receive baggage, Vito's among them. The carts wound toward the processing point where their baggage was loaded onto conveyor belts to circle in the terminal until picked up.

"Our chain of command loves you, Miss Humboldt."

Blue lit another cigarette. "I wish Eddie were around to hear it."

Tomasi nodded grimly. "Alvaro probably sensed early that LeSable's scheme would not work, but he was willing to give it a shot. What did he have to lose, after all? Nothing. So he let Pierre LeSable blunder about, and when it became apparent that the Hugh Stone corporate approach wasn't going to work, he did a neat job of backing out, letting the Mafia know he was washing his hands of the whole thing. So here we are."

A single headlight loomed, growing larger and Tomasi shielded his eyes. Vito called out: "I've got it."

"Okay," Tomasi said. He lifted a flap, and Vito drove the cart into the borrowed Army tent. Tomasi and Vito broke the seals on the six foot six inch aluminum coffin and unscrewed the top. Probably, a mortuary company truck was already pulling up at the terminal to collect this cargo. The lid came off. A hint of decay met them under the bare light bulbs. "Ugh," Vito said.

"Yuk," Blue said.

Together, they unzipped the heavy black plastic bag. The odor of death and putrefaction, as well as embalming fluids, made them cringe. Inside the bag was a man's body packed in dry ice. "Pierre LeSable, aged 67," the manifest read.

Tomasi studied the blackened features. "Our man LeSable."

"Here," Vito said, pointing to a glitter of plastic peeking through curled tendons and sugary ribs. The body had been packed with tight plastic sacks of cocaine.

"Hey, look at this," Tomasi said. He lifted a gun wrapped tightly in plastic.

"Jesus," Vito said, studying the thing closely. "Why?"

"It's a .357 magnum Colt with a silencer." Tomasi undid the tape holding the plastic around the revolver.

"This guy's got three slugs in him," Vito said.

Tomasi removed the revolver from its covering, turned, and unloaded a single shot into a stack of storage blankets in a corner of the tent. "That's for the lab." He wrapped the gun up. Vito stuck it into the corpse. They screwed the coffin back together. Tomasi doused the lights. "Good work, Vito."

"Thanks, Chief."

Tomasi lifted the tarp and Vito backed the cart out. Vito whizzed along toward the terminal building to deliver the coffin as if nothing had happened.

"That's it, Humboldt," Tomasi said. He dug through the blankets for the bullet that would be matched to Guzman's. "Alvaro sends a message to the local mob. He tells them, sorry, a mistake, here's the guy at fault. From now on, we ship direct to you. Only thing Alvaro and the local mob don't know is, we've got their pipeline wired and now we can start going after them."

61 • Manhattan

Blue climbed the littered stairs from the subway up to the street, enjoying a rush of rubbery smelling warm air from below. Then she stepped into fresh, icy street air, the familiar traffic noises of her neighborhood: passing car, distant horn, slammed door. The wind pinpricked her cheeks with hints of new snow as she crossed the street and trudged past dark, silent doorsteps. In the brightly lit entrance of her apartment building, she checked her mail box. Nothing. She climbed the stairs, for the elevator was, as always, broken. A window slammed. A bag of trash sort of missed the dumpster in the central courtyard with shattering glass. Blue went two steps at a time on the last two landings. She extricated her apartment key, which she kept pinned inside her jacket.

Light shone under the door, and the Grundigs oozed out a symphony. Mozart? she wasn't sure, and it didn't matter; she always left the stereo on as a protection against burglars. She unlocked the door. The warmth of her apartment, her home, met her with a welcome glow. She kicked the door shut behind her. "Hello, kitchen. Hello, refrigerator." As if in answer, the refrigerator shook once, twice, and rumbled into life. Mozart rocked on in the bedroom, wave upon wave of violins, violas, and oboes over the bass-rich speakers. She piled clothes on a chair. Kicked shoes off. "Hello, music. Hello, old tea kettle." She touched the kettle. "Ouch!" Waved her finger, pulling a tea cup out of the cupboard. Tossed in a bag of Lipton's. Spoon of sugar. Poured from the kettle. Set the tea aside to steep. Felt something against her leg. "Hello, Fontainebleau." She bent down and rubbed his ear. As cats did, he winced away, but purred enthusiastically. "Hi, I'm home!" she called. In the bedroom, John looked up from a book. He turned down the stereo. She captured a mental snapshot of him as he had been the moment she entered: Unaware of her, absorbed in the book; stretched on her bed among the stuffed animals, a sheet pulled up over his otherwise nude lean body; concentrating; reading glasses (a secret only newly revealed) making him look older, bookish; hair tousled; foamed neck brace making his face look scrunched because his head was up on the Garfield pillow. "I didn't hear you come in," he said, putting the book aside. "It's about a million degrees in here." He stretched out his arms.

She sat on the edge of the bed, let him growl and bear hug her. "It's always a million degrees in here."

He pulled her close. Unbuttoned her shirt. She drew in a tight, delicious quick breath as he bit her earlobe. "MMMmmm..."

"You smell cold. Like fresh air." He kissed her pointing nipples. "Cold." He lifted the sheet, and she climbed underneath. "Fontainebleau seems happy."

"I think he misses his canyon, but I think he'll enjoy being a city house cat for a while." She kicked the jeans away and pressed closed to him, resting one hand on his shoulder while the other hand explored the stored warmth of his body. He wore, she quickly discovered, nothing at all.

He kissed her cheek, her nose, her lips. "I want to be part of your world, Blue. I want to stay in your life."

She cleared her throat. "Well, you can stay as long as you like." The boxes were still there, after all, because that was who she was, how she was, but the padlocks seemed to all be open and strewn about.

This Novel Made History

This novel made history as one of the two first true e-books ever published. The other was *This Shoal of Space*, also by John Argo. Both were bestsellers in the early days of the Internet, and were read around the world by avid readers (hence the Clocktower Books motto: Exciting books for avid readers since 1996). They were published in spring-summer 1996.

By calling these two novels the first of their kind in world history, we mean they are proprietary (not public domain), published online to be read in HTML format and for download as TXT (not on CD-ROM or other portable medium), and standard length (full novels by contemporary industry standards). They are not hypertext, but standard form and length.

Neon Blue and *This Shoal of Space* (original title until 1998: *Heartbreaker*) were published simultaneously, making history during the days before e-commerce, when the Web was still pure as virgin snow (no viruses, no gangsters, no trolls yet). Cullen & Callahan (*C&C*) published suspense stories on a website called *Neon Blue Fiction*, and SFFH on *The Haunted Village*. The umbrella publishing site was Clocktower Fiction, which was renamed Clocktower Books after 2000. John T. Cullen became sole proprietor of Clocktower Books and all its titles and properties in 2001. This included the acclaimed web magazine *Deep Outside SFFH*, renamed at that time *Far Sector SFFH*.

The SF novel *Pioneers*, by John Argo, followed in 1997 on *The Haunted Village*. All three novels were innovatively published in weekly serial chapters. Among other added fiction in the 1990s was John T. Cullen's political thriller *CON2: The Generals of October*. Clocktower Books restricted submissions in 2002 and has remained actively a boutique small press, member of International Thriller Writers, and acclaimed as early Internet pioneers and innovators. Visit the Clocktower Books website for more info including *Museum* pages, and info about other exciting titles:

clocktowerbooks.com

www.ingramcontent.com/pod-product-compliance
Lightning Source LLC
Chambersburg PA
CBHW030332180626
46810CB00003B/1327